JAMES AXLER

DEATH LANDS

Fury's Pilgrims

D1329954

A GOLD EAGLE BOOK FROM

WORLDWIDE.

TORONTO • NEW YORK • LONDON
AMSTERDAM • PARIS • SYDNEY • HAMBURG
STOCKHOLM • ATHENS • TOKYO • MILAN
MADRID • WARSAW • BUDAPEST • AUCKLAND

This is for all the members of the
Deathlands Dining Club, past, present and future,
who have had the best taste since Alferd Packer.
Seriously though, folks, this comes with my
genuine gratitude, respect and affection. Thanks.

First edition January 1993

ISBN 0-373-62517-7

FURY'S PILGRIMS

"Autodestruct in operation at ninety minutes and counting . . ."

"Goin' to blow us all with it," Abe shouted. "Let's go!"

Ryan still held the blue folder he'd taken from Krysty, and he glanced down at it. "We've got an hour and a half. No hurry. We could get back to the gateway and make the jump in a whole lot less than that."

The stylized black lettering on the file told him that it was the log for the previous six months. It was going to be interesting to find out about this top-secret establishment.

"Self-destruct mode operating at ninety. At eighty. At seven and seven and seventy minutes. One hour and counting. This is a practice drill. Not act . . . drill. Not. Fifty minutes."

"Fireblast! It's out of control. Let's go!"

Clutching the folder under his arm, Ryan turned on his heel and sprinted for the sec door, his friends close behind.

The alteration in the force of gravity threw their natural reflexes off kilter.

Ryan overcompensated and banged his shoulder into one of the consoles. His body slithered sideways, knocking into Dean, who took out J.B. and Mildred. Krysty might have made it, if Abe hadn't skittered into Doc. The old man dropped his swordstick, which somehow caught between Krysty's ankles. Her mane of hair splayed out like a dazzling burst of radiant fire as she fell toward the control panel of the sec door, clipping it with the heel of her boot.

There was the hiss of valves, and the slab of steel began to descend, trapping the companions.

"Destruct now forty and thirty and twenty minutes. Nineteen minutes and counting. Nineteen . . ."

**Also available in the
Deathlands saga:**

There is so much evidence that the future is totally shrouded from our vision. If you don't believe this then pick some odd moment from your present life. Imagine you have a video camera to film this moment and a time machine. Travel back to when you were, let's say eighteen, and show your young self the video. Five gets you five hundred that your past persona would be absolutely staggered at what you've become.

All Truth Is Perceived,
Therefore All Truth Is Fallible,
by Melissa Moore, 1991

Chapter One

Ryan could feel his brain starting to scramble. The last thing he heard was Krysty whispering gently to him, her breath soft against his cheek.

"Good time the last few weeks, lover. I envy Christina what she's got. Husband and baby. Nice home. Be good..." The words started to fragment. "One day ... you and ... real good ... us ... lover."

The rest vanished into the blackness.

RYAN OPENED HIS EYE, realizing that something had gone appallingly, hideously wrong.

The silver armaglass walls of the gateway chamber were gone. Now they were a rich, deep, glowing purple. The metal disks in the floor and the ceiling were fading quickly, and the mist that often filled the mat-trans chamber during a jump was almost gone.

Ryan's muddled mind was battling to try to come to terms with the odd color of the walls, seeking a hold on a memory that he'd seen something like that before.

"Where?" he croaked, his voice as dry as the sands of the Mohave Desert.

He shifted his position, closing his eye and opening it again, trying to work out just what was so terribly wrong.

Two things, he concluded.

Air and gravity.

And that also rang a feeble bell in the dusty west wing of his memory.

Ryan drew a long slow breath that somehow didn't seem to satisfy his need, then drew another and another. But still he felt a faint and disturbing echo of suffocation. His heart was pounding in his chest as if he'd just run a mile up a sand dune in combat boots, and the blood coursed through his ears like the tide along the gulf shore.

"Altitude," Ryan whispered.

That was the only possible explanation.

He remembered his hard-riding days with the Trader. They'd been moving westward across the rolling plains of what had once been Missouri and Kansas, making good time, driving at top speed for twenty-four hours solid.

They traveled past the haunted, hag-ridden ruins of Denver, straight up into the mountains, stopping at a trading post in a place called . . .

"Leadville?"

The Baby Doe Trading Post.

"Why am I . . ."

His mind was reeling out of control, staggering down side trails when he should be concentrating with all of his energy on what was happening right here and now.

But it *had* felt a bit like this, that first night in Leadville. The heart and the breath and the ears. Several of
the crews of the two war wags had suffered from
headaches, sickness and nosebleeds. And that had been
caused by altitude.

Ryan lifted a hand to brush a strand of black hair off
his forehead.

"Fireblast!"

This was something else, not like it had been in
Leadville.

Ryan's hand felt as though it were floating in soft
water. He moved it, experimentally, above his head,
then cautiously around in a slow circle.

"What the fuck is going on?" he asked.

But the others all seemed to be still locked away into
the dark coma that a jump often produced.

The six bodies were scattered around the chamber,
like the discarded toys of a petulant child.

Krysty lay on one side of him, her hair curled tightly
around her head protectively. Blood and watery mu-
cus trickled from the corner of her mouth.

Doc Tanner was sitting, oddly, bolt upright, his sil-
ver-headed sword stick gripped firmly between both
hands, his leonine head resting on the gnarled backs of
his wrists.

Abe lay one side, knees tucked up, hands thrust between his thighs like a sleeping child seeking security.

Mildred and J B. Dix were lying together, fingers
tangled. J.B. was bleeding from the nose, a steady

trickle of crimson that dripped across the floor of the chamber.

Ryan's young son, Dean Cawdor, was on his other side. The boy had been sick, with threads of golden vomit trailing onto his jacket. His eyes were squeezed shut, and he was gripping the turquoise hilt of his favorite knife in his right fist.

There definitely wasn't enough air.

Ryan knew from bitter experience that panic could be a very effective killer in its own right. With a positive effort of will he tried to take slower, shallower breaths, not allowing fear to control and overwhelm him.

He tried to stand, but when he pushed himself off the floor, the one-eyed man had the sickening feeling of swimming.

He dropped to a crouch, sighing.

Doc's voice startled him. "Perfectly simple, my dear chap. We are in a controlled environment with low gravity and a concomitant shortage of air."

"Concomitant? What's..."

"I'm so sorry, Ryan. Old habits die hard. Yes, Die Hard Two, Rambo Four. Close game that." The old man shook his head. "I do apologize. What on earth was I saying?"

"Gravity and air."

"Indeed, yes. It would indicate a return to that mysterious location that we've tripped upon before. Not an out-of-body experience but, perhaps, an off-planet one."

Ryan felt sick, his throat contracting to avoid actually throwing up. It seemed as though his brain were still in free-fall inside the whorled chamber of his skull.

"Off the planet?"

"We have suspected for some time that the gateways were being used by some other force. And that we had once ourselves been to some distant object in space. Do you not recall?"

"Yeah, yeah. Course. The air's so thin, Doc. How can anyone live with this?"

"Perhaps this mat-trans section is kept this way when not in use. To conserve energy." Doc scratched the stubble on his chin with the carved silver lion on his cane. "But I feel something is also awry with the Newtonian force of gravity. Do you not feel that, Ryan?"

"Sure. Like floating."

Doc Tanner was different, in a strange, subtle way that confused Ryan. He was much more concise, and sharper, somehow. There was a great deal less rambling than usual.

"Like floating, Ryan. Precisely." He steepled his fingers. "So, the thin air could be deliberate. But I do not believe that it would be feasible to maintain a part of a larger unit at a different level of gravity to other parts."

"You mean this has somehow broken away?"

"Perhaps."

J.B. was stirring, whistling softly between his teeth as he sat up and rubbed his bloodied nose on his sleeve. He picked up his battered fedora and settled it in place.

He looked at Ryan and Doc. "Something's wrong."

"Yes," Doc replied. "We believe that we are no longer on Earth, John, and that we may be the victims of some sort of malfunction."

"Thin air and strange gravity," Ryan added. Speaking was peculiarly difficult, as though someone had placed a layer of thick sponge over each one of his teeth.

The Armorer nodded slowly, his glasses reflecting the rich purple of the armored walls.

"Could be. We always wondered."

At his side, Mildred Wyeth was stirring. She rolled over, eyes closed tight, moaning.

"Feel rotten." She opened one eye, then the other. Mildred sighed, a puzzled expression creeping over her face. "Decompression or something. And... Gravity?"

"We could be off Earth," J.B. told her. "Take it real slow and easy."

Krysty was next to regain consciousness. She looked around, naked fear flashing for a moment in her green eyes. "Gaia! Where are we?" She turned to Ryan, her fingers touching his wrist. "Lover, I got such a bad feeling about this."

Abe hadn't moved, or given any clue that he was back with them. But he echoed her words. "Got a bad feeling, too, Krysty." He sniffed. "Thank God! I thought at the least I'd have shit myself after that lousy feeling. It always like this, is it?"

"This wasn't a bad one," Ryan replied.

"Well…hey, what's wrong with the…I can't breathe properly! Is it just me?"

Doc answered him. "It's all of us, Abraham. So I venture to suggest that we all move with great caution. In every way."

Dean was last to revive. He looked down at himself and blushed. "Oh, shit! I've puked all over. Sorry, Dad."

"Don't worry, son. Least of our worries, that is."

Slowly, with some staggering, the companions got to their feet.

It was amazing how the apparent change in gravity had made them all so clumsy. Doc dropped his cane and even the cat-footed J.B. stumbled and would have fallen if Mildred hadn't snatched at his arm to steady him.

Dean recovered with the infinite resilience of the very young.

He jumped against the wall, whooping as he found himself able to leap nearly three feet clear of the floor, almost high enough to touch the glittering disks in the ceiling.

"Cut it out, Dean," Ryan snapped. "Someone can get hurt here."

He hadn't heard any sound or sign of life beyond the ponderous door.

Krysty had closed her eyes again and was standing against the wall, shaking her head. "Can't feel anything, lover," she said finally. "Sort of general bad vibrations."

"No excitations?" Mildred asked, then shook her head. "Sorry. Doesn't make sense to you, does it?"

J.B. looked at Ryan. "Condition double red," he said.

"Yeah. Blasters out and ready, everyone." Ryan was conscious of the terrible shortage of breath, and hoped that he wasn't going to have to do anything to exert himself. He looked around to make sure everyone was prepared, then put his hand on the cold metal of the door-opening mechanism, releasing it.

Chapter Two

The door opened onto the usual small antechamber, with a view beyond it into the main control room. Both appeared empty.

There was no flaring burst of magnesium light to blind and no harsh amplified voice warning that they would be blasted dead.

Just a single body, lying sprawled outside the door.

It wasn't possible to tell its sex, as it lay facedown, with a strange goggled mask concealing the features. But it was wearing exactly the same uniform that Ryan had glimpsed, just once before, for the briefest fraction of a frozen, threatening nanosecond: a cream top, crumpled and stained yellow across the shoulders, maroon pants tucked into cracked leather combat boots, a broad black stripe zigzagging down the outside of each leg, a black belt with an unbuttoned holster on the right hip. The butt of a silvered handgun was just visible, and the hands were covered by gloves of some slick green material.

Ryan waited, watching, silent.

"Can't get any life response," Krysty whispered, her mouth so close that he could feel her soft breath against the hairs inside his ear.

He stood still, trying to taste the cold thin air. It had the long-dead flavor of an atmosphere that had been circulated and recirculated repeatedly.

"Nothing," he said.

He stepped out, over the corpse, into the totally bare room. Beyond it was the larger console area. Ryan squinted, his SIG-Sauer at the ready. The banks of comp displays were flickering and chattering, as they did in all of the other redoubt mat-trans units he'd ever found.

But there wasn't the least indication of any life. Not a scrap of paper. Very little dust, though the tip of his finger left a faint smear on the plastic desk nearest to him.

The main doors to the rest of the complex were firmly closed. While everyone else waited tensely behind him, Ryan walked to check them. They were locked from the inside.

The very act of stepping across the smooth floor made him feel vaguely nauseous. It was as though he'd lost about a third of his body weight.

"It's okay," he called.

Mildred kneeled and started to turn over the body, helped by J.B.

"Best if everyone moves away," she suggested.

"Why?" Dean asked. "Dead man can't hurt anyone, can he?"

She looked steadily at the boy. "Wrong, Dean. We don't know what killed him. Or her. Could be some unguessable disease. Best be careful until we're more sure."

"Oh." Chastened, he moved into the main room to stand quietly by his father.

Ryan laid a hand briefly on his shoulder. "All right?"

"Can't breathe properly."

"Yeah."

Mildred carefully eased the thick rubber-plas mask off the face, leaning back on her heels, looking down with a measured concentration.

"Male, fifty or so. Been dead quite a time. This sort of temperature and atmosphere makes it hard to tell."

"Days, weeks or months?" J.B. asked.

"Years?"

The black woman shook her head. "No, Abe, not years. Months? Probably not that. Weeks? Now we're inside the ballpark."

Doc had shuffled closer. "Positively mummified, isn't he?"

The face was pinched and leathery, the lips dried and peeled back off teeth that looked so perfect they were probably false. The eyes had already melted back into the withered sockets. The goggles had left deep furrows around the forehead and cheeks, and across the aquiline nose.

"Can't see any clue to what might've chilled him." Mildred shook her head. "You want a full postmortem, Ryan?"

He considered the question. "No sort of indication at all?"

"Heart attack. A stroke. Pneumonia. Doesn't look like he died in severe pain. Undernourished." She leaned over again and stared more closely at the wrinkled, dark face.

"What?" Ryan asked.

"Could be old sores around the mouth. Some kind of skin cancer, maybe. Perhaps one of the immune-deficiency diseases. Plagued the planet toward the end of the 1990s."

"Can we explore, Dad?"

"Yeah. You're right, Dean. Dead is dead. Let's move out."

CORRIDORS SHARPLY CURVED away in both directions so that it wasn't possible to see more than thirty yards either way. The ceiling strip lights were dim, and several had gone out.

Small vid sec cameras were fixed at points where walls met roof, most with their ruby eyes burning in the gloom.

"We're moving," Abe said. "Can anyone else feel it

Once it had been mentioned, everyone stopped, balanced, then voiced their agreement.

"It would support our hypothesis that we are on some sort of space station," Doc stated. "It would be the crudest and most obvious way of sustaining the false gravity."

"And if it's slowing down, then that would be why we all feel odd." Ryan touched his hand to the cold metal of the wall. "We're going around, somewhere up in space."

They continued on, discovering that most of the doors were locked in that section of the complex.

The group was strung out in a tight skirmish line, the bend of the passage meaning they had to be closer together than usual. Everyone was gripping a drawn blaster.

But it was becoming rapidly clear that they were the only living things in the area.

They came to a door that was half-open, an out-flung arm protruding into the corridor. The hand was curled, the fingers driven into the leathery palm.

"How come no rats or maggots?" Abe asked.

Mildred answered him. "When this place was built, and it must have been highly secret, they'd have purified it. Top to bottom hygienic. Not a bug anywhere. If they've been coming back to Earth through gateways, then they must have faced up to a serious risk of some kind of contamination. But they've probably got that sorted. With cockroaches up here they'd breed in no time."

"Thank God for that!" Doc exclaimed. "Tin box full of corpses is bad enough."

"What killed him?" Dean asked, pointing at the naked, blanched limb.

Mildred shook her head. "Woman. Long hair. Broad hips. Younger than the other one. No sign of what killed her."

"Could it have been a massive malfunction of the air system?" J.B. suggested. "Choked everyone at once."

"No. Would've been clinical signs. Got to be some sort of fast-acting sickness."

"Let's get off here, lover," Krysty said. "Gives me the creeps."

"Be good to try and find something out about it," he replied.

"All right. But the sooner we get out of this revolving drum and back into the gateway, the happier I'll be."

THE SPACE STATION was surprisingly large.

They finally found an observation port open on an upper deck. Abe was first to the immensely thick window, pressing his face against it.

"Judas Iscariot! Look at that!"

There was another ob port farther along, enabling all of them to peer out into the swimming velvet blackness.

"I have seen vids of the brave space travelers," Doc said. "I confess that I had never thought to be lucky enough to experience such a divine wonder for myself."

Ryan stared wide-eyed. It was a wondrous sight, stretching out ahead, below, above and all around them.

The darkness was so utterly intense that it was almost invisible, sprinkled with hundreds upon thousands of stars, glittering like the brightest of sparkling diamonds.

"Where's Earth?" Krysty asked, her arm across Ryan's shoulders, her cheek pressed against his.

"Probably behind us. We're in its shadow," replied J.B., whose multifaceted range of polymathic talents included a decent working knowledge of astronomy.

"I'm not sure I recognize any of these constellations," Doc said, his voice barely a whisper. "How about you, John Barrymore?"

"Now you mention it, Doc, nor do I."

"What're you on about?" Abe asked, spinning from the window.

"Just that this doesn't seem unduly like our own solar system," Doc replied. "Isn't that a remarkable thing?"

"Remarkable, you fucking triple stupe? How do we get back home?"

Ryan sniffed. "Same way we got up here, Abe. Don't worry."

A SLIDING SEC STEEL DOOR was marked: Bridge & Control Suite. Caution. Any Force Will Meet Maximum Retaliation.

"May the force be with us," Mildred said, grinning at the others. The merriment vanished. "Sorry. I clean forgot."

"Need plas-ex to blow that. Probably blast us all into space," J.B. said.

Dean stepped forward and grabbed the polished chrome handle and pressed down on it.

"No!" Ryan shouted.

But it was too late.

Chapter Three

Absolutely nothing happened.

"Locked," the boy stated, turning to his father with an impish grin, jerking the handle up and down a few more times.

"Leave it be." Ryan glanced around and saw three corpses, dressed in the cream-maroon-and-black uniforms. The companions had encountered dozens of corpses during their trek. These lay together in a corner of the passage, near another ob port. The only difference about this trio was that they'd obviously decided to commit suicide and had blown away most of their heads.

The Armorer had glanced at the weapons after they found the first corpse. "Standard Smith & Wesson, 9 mm automatics. Been repaired here and there."

"Let's get out of this floating meat locker," Ryan said.

"Dad!"

"What?"

"I heard something."

"What?"

"Sort of hissing noise."

"It's the door!" Abe exclaimed. "Must've been un-locked all the time."

The massive slab of titanium steel was beginning to move slowly and ponderously into the air, with the faint whispering sound of compressed air and the distant whirring of immensely powerful gears. There was already a gap beneath it of seven inches.

Ten inches.

A foot.

"Everyone back," Ryan ordered.

The door continued to climb, showing the floor of a brightly lighted room within. J.B. dropped suddenly to his belly and peered under it, shading his eyes with his left hand. His right hand held the 20-round Uzi, braced in front of him.

"Looks like the main control area," he said. "I see one chill. No, two."

Krysty shook her head. "Still can't feel any sort of life up here, lover. But the bad sense is getting stronger."

With a perceptible shudder, the door stopped, fully open.

"Dean! Stay out here," Ryan commanded in a whiplash voice, halting the youth in his tracks. "Don't move a single step, and keep watch back along the passage. Understand?"

"Sure."

It was the hub of the space station. Here, at its heart, the sensation of revolving was much milder than out on the perimeter. But the air was just as stale and thin.

They filed in, looking around at this amazing world of high tech wonders.

"Anything you've seen before, Doc?" Ryan asked, aware that his voice sounded muffled and flat in the eternal stillness.

"I was involved, as you know well, my dear Ryan, with Cerberus. Which was, in its turn, a cog within the bureaucratic machine known as Overproject Whisper. This in its own turn was a tiny segment of what was known in the Pentagon as the Totality Concept. Wheels within wheels within... And littler fleas to bite them, and so ad infinitum, if you see what I mean. No, you probably do not see."

There were all sorts of control decks, all with lights, dials and quivering liquid-crystal displays. One of the corpses was that of an immensely tall bald man. He must have been close to seven feet, but even in life he would have been skeletally thin. In death there was little but bone and strung sinews in the uniform covering.

On the shoulders there were two gold crowns, tarnished and dull.

"The skipper?" Abe asked, pointing at them. "Looks like he died at the helm."

The body was draped in a chair with padded arms, in front of the main console. Mildred bent and picked up a small bottle.

"Some sort of morphine," she said. "Whatever this last illness was, it looks like they knew it was going to take them all."

The other corpse in the control room was female, with a coarse mane of long blond hair turning to silver-gray. The woman appeared to have died of natural causes.

"Unless she took some of the tablets," Mildred suggested.

J.B. had been prowling around and he called Ryan's attention over to a small rack of pistols and carbines.

"Nothing worth taking," he said. "But there's ammo. Boxes of 9 mm and .38s. Help yourselves to them."

He took some for the Uzi, while Ryan filled his pockets with spare rounds for the SIG-Sauer. Krysty's double-action Smith & Wesson 640 also fired .38s, as did Mildred's rare target pistol, the ZKR 551 6-shot revolver.

Dean, who'd followed everyone into the control room, was already carrying spare ammo for his Browning Hi-Power. Abe had picked up an Uzi to match J.B., but he hadn't yet used any rounds for it, so he declined the offer.

Ryan threw one of the full-metal jacket rounds into the air, grabbed for it and missed. He marveled at how it seemed to hang in the air, revolving slowly around its long axis, giving him ample time to make a second snatch for it and hold it safely.

"Will a bullet go faster or slower?" he asked the Armorer.

"Yes" was the inscrutable reply.

'Some sort of files here.'' Krysty held up a dark blue folder "Says the station was called *The Enterprise*. This is the captain's log.''

Mildred laughed, the sound surprisingly loud in the dry suffocating silence. "Does it tell us what the last star date was? And everything about their mission to boldly go where no space station's ever gone before?''

"Let me look.'' As Ryan reached toward Krysty, there was a loud crackling noise.

"What!'' Doc exclaimed, jumping so much that his feet actually drifted clear of the floor for a second or two.

"No security pass code has been received at central control for admittance to this room. You have two minutes to comply.''

The voice was dusty, female, managing to sound both bored and bossy at the same time.

Ryan grinned. "Watch it, Dean. They'll be in to slap your wrist for this.''

There was another burst of electrical comm static, and the lights all flickered.

The voice came sidling in again, more insistently this time.

"Noncompliance with security orders is a serious offence. Nearest armed patrol to bridge. Comp-order nine. Now. Now.''

"Fortunate that all these security guards are now drilling to the beat of a different drum. Away in the marching band of the Lord of Chaos, Beelzebub.'' Doc smiled.

"Warning!" Now the woman's voice was shrill and querulous. "Intruders on base. Commence security countdown."

J.B. had finished methodically loading up with ammo, and he glanced across at Ryan. "Sounds like some sort of malfunction goin' down."

"Yeah. Slipping a few notches."

The voice was back, calmer, but somehow sounding more threatening.

"Intruders on space station are given their last ... their last ... their last ... warning. Autodestruct in operation at ninety minutes and counting..."

"Shit!" Abe looked at the others. "Goin' to blow us all with it. Let's go."

Ryan still held the blue folder he'd taken from Krysty, and he glanced down at it. "We've got an hour and a half. No hurry. We could get back to the gateway and make the jump in a whole lot less than that."

The stylized black lettering on the file told him that it was the log of the station for the previous six months. It was going to be amazingly interesting to see what he could find out about this uniquely secret establishment.

"Mebbe we ought to get out. Read that later, some other place." Krysty tugged at his arm, but Ryan was opening the thick file.

"Self-destruct mode operating at ninety. At eighty. At seven and seven and seventy minutes. One hour and counting. This is a practice drill. Not act...drill. Not. Fifty minutes."

"Fireblast! It's out of control. Let's go!"

Clutching the folder under his arm, Ryan turned and sprinted for the sec doors, everyone following at his heels.

If the pressure of the insanely smug voice hadn't become lethally dangerous, what happened would have been really amusing, like some old comedy vid with flickering figures tumbling and bumping into each other on a black-and-white staircase.

The alteration in the force of gravity on the space station threw all of their natural reflexes off kilter.

Ryan overcompensated and banged his shoulder into the edge of one of the consoles. His body slithered sideways, where he hit Dean, knocking the boy backward. As he floated across the chamber, the lad took J.B.'s legs completely from under him. The Armorer had been holding Mildred tightly by the wrist, and as he fell he pulled her after him, with a stretched, clumsy elegance.

Krysty would have made it, if Abe hadn't skittered into Doc. The old man dropped his sword stick, which somehow caught Krysty between the ankles. Her mane of hair sprayed out like a dazzling burst of radiant fire as she fell over to the right, toward the control panel of the sec door, clipping it with the heel of one of her dark blue Western boots.

There was the hiss of valves, and the slab of steel began to descend again, trapping the companions inside the control room.

"Destruct now forty and thirty and twenty minutes. Twenty minutes and counting. Nineteen and counting. Nineteen."

Chapter Four

"Roll under it!" Ryan rarely lost his self-control, but he noticed in passing that his own voice was screaming at the raw edge of panic.

The amplified message seemed now to have a hateful note of delight in it.

"Sixteen minutes and thirty seconds."

His rifle scraping on the floor, Ryan crawled under the slowly falling sec door. Dean scrambled alongside him. Krysty, eyes wide, was on hands and knees, coming out to join him in the passage. Doc, reaching for his fallen cane, seemed oblivious to the swelling danger.

"Doc!"

The old man glanced up at Ryan's yell and saw that the descending slab of metal was now less than four feet from the floor.

Abe was out, muttering a string of curses under his breath.

J.B. and Mildred scooped up Doc between them, the woman grabbing at the silver-topped sword stick. The three emerged into the corridor in a shouting tangle of arms and legs.

The sec door was less than two feet from the floor of the station.

"Fifteen minutes and counting."

"That file," Krysty gasped. "What'd you do with it?"

"Fireblast! Dropped..." He lay flat on the floor and peeked under the block of steel.

The blue folder was agonizingly close to the entrance. If Ryan stuck his arm into the shrinking gap he could probably almost reach it.

Probably.

Almost.

Such little words.

The door wouldn't bruise or break his arm. It would pulp it to a thin smear of tissue, a micromillimeter deep.

"No, lover," Krysty whispered.

"No."

"Fourteen minutes and counting." There was a demonic quality to the insistent voice over the loudspeakers. Though Ryan hadn't tried to check it, his guestimate was that the autodestruct system was operating at least twice normal speed.

Which gave them something around six minutes to retrace their steps and make the jump.

Ryan was on his feet, already panting from the thin air, steadying himself for a swaying moment against the cold metal of the door. It had reached the bottom with the softest breath of sound.

"Come on. Run ... Careful and slow."

There was an uncharacteristic snort of laughter from J.B. "Run careful *and* slow. Trader'd love you for that."

"Shut it and move."

He led the way, trying to follow his own advice. The experience in the doorway to the control room had taught him a vital lesson. With the low gravity, it was fatally easy to lose balance.

Time was dribbling away like sand through an hourglass, and a fall could so obviously be disastrous for all of them.

Dean moved ahead of his father, running in graceful, loping bounds, looking back over his shoulder in triumph. "Come on, Dad. It's easy."

"Eleven minutes and counting. Ten minutes and counting."

The two messages almost seemed to overlap each other, spitting out with a venomous menace.

Ryan could already feel a tightness across his chest, the dry air rasping in his throat. His heart was pounding, and he was painfully aware of the blood coursing through his ears.

"By the three Kennedys! I swear I have . . . have not felt so blown as . . . when I took part in a footrace up Mount Washington in my summer vacation. Before my sophomore year, I recall . . . it was . . ."

"Save your breath, Doc," Mildred urged, clasping a hand to her side as she jogged along with the Armorer.

"Eight minutes and counting."

Ryan felt as if a band of hot steel were being clamped around his forehead, and his sight was blurring. Tiny sparks of crimson fire were circling through his brain, faster and faster, like miniature insects of flame, whirling in a hurricane.

"Got to rest," Abe gasped. "Just for a minute or so."

"Seven minutes and counting."

"Keep moving or we all get blown into space. Can't stop." Ryan didn't even have the energy to look back at the man.

Dean had vanished around the next bend in the corridor, like a will-o'-the-wisp antic, luring them through a bayou to their doom.

"Can't be far." Ryan didn't even know if he'd spoken out loud.

He nearly tripped over a sprawled corpse. Trying to take a short step, he floated farther than he'd intended. His steel-tipped boot came crashing down, an ace on the line in the middle of the dead man's chest. Ribs cracked like broken twigs and the chest cavity seemed to close about Ryan's ankle, like a ghoulish trap. The body shuddered, withered arms and legs flapping like a gutter drunk struggling to rise to sing another verse.

With a wrenching effort Ryan got free, staggering wildly sideways for several steps like a demented crab. He bounced off the left-hand inner wall, nearly going in through an open doorway. His arms flailed for balance, and the Steyr SSG-70 bolt-action rifle across his shoulders smashed hard into the opposite wall, making him fear for the delicate Starlite night scope and the laser image enhancer.

But there was no time to pause and check for damage.

"We're there!"

Dean's shrill voice, cracking way up the scale, didn't sound too far away.

"Four minutes and thirty seconds and counting. Four minutes and counting."

Ryan raced through the control room, almost blacking out from the enormous effort of running in such a grossly diminished atmosphere. He skirted the last of the uniformed bodies, seeing Dean was ahead of him in the entrance to the gateway chamber.

"One hundred and fifty seconds. One-forty. One-thirty."

Dean was hunkered down, body trembling, his head resting on his arms. But he still managed a fragile, uncertain grin for his father. "We just made it."

Ryan sat in the armaglass doorway, the purple walls spinning around at the edge of his dulled vision. He seemed to have gone partly deaf, his son's words coming to his ears as if from an infinite distance.

Krysty was right at his heels, her boots clicking on the hard floor. Her green eyes stared at him, unfocused, as if she were looking through him.

"I'm nearly done," she managed.

"One hundred seconds."

"Come on," he hissed.

"Ninety seconds."

There were voices in the control room of the mat-trans unit, panting and exhausted.

Mildred entered first, her face drawn, bleeding from the lips with the strain.

Then came the uneasy troika of Abe and J.B., supporting Doc between them. The old man actually looked, for a moment, as if he were already aboard the black ferry, eyes rolled back in his skull, feet dragging.

"Eighty seconds."

"Get him in," Ryan rasped, lending a hand to help Mildred into the chamber. "Sit down and get ready for the jump."

"Could be a false alarm," J.B. said as he pushed Doc into the unit. "Then again..."

"Forty seconds."

Abe and the Armorer joined Krysty, all of them collapsing onto the smooth floor, lying anyhow. Abe was retching and coughing, doubled up, knees to his chin.

Everyone looked as if they'd just completed a jump rather than about to start one.

Unless the world blew up around them first.

"Thirty seconds."

Ryan reached for the handle of the door, to grasp it and slam it shut, triggering the mat-trans mechanism.

"Twenty-four, twenty-two, twenty..."

His hand was slippery with sweat, and he missed his hold, nearly toppling outside again, on top of the recumbent corpse.

"Eighteen, sixteen, fourteen, twelve . ."
Now he had it.
The door shut with a satisfying, solid click.
"Eight, six, four..."
"Two, zero."
Everything went dark and silent.

Chapter Five

One of the tail gunners on War wag One, known only as DeeTee, had once gotten hold of some bad jolt, buying it across the bar in a frontier gaudy house.

Ryan remembered the man, bearded and skinny, rolling around on his back in the middle of the camp, eyes wide, screaming and roaring like a bull under the gelder's knife.

Unlike some, DeeTee had come back to them after a couple of days and Ryan had asked him what had been so utterly terrifying.

After what had seemed an eternity of consideration, the man had replied that he had either taken a drug that had made him mad, or he was plain mad, or he was dead.

And he couldn't distinguish which was the most likely alternative.

Ryan didn't know if he was dead.

Or mad.

Or some place in between.

The jump had begun so quickly that he didn't have time to sit or lie down and compose himself, as he did with the usual mat-trans leap.

He'd been by the door, crouching as he readied himself to join the others on the floor.

The word "zero" from outside had been drawn out as though it lasted a hundred years.

Then came the rushing shroud of suffocating blackness.

HE WAS WATCHING HIMSELF in a mirror, a massive, convex disk of highly polished silver, set in an ornate frame of gold. Every few inches there was a carved acanthus, with an intricate rose of platinum next to it.

Ryan stared into it, seeing himself. He seemed to be lying naked on a large bed, with a goose-feather mattress. The room was lighted in such a way that he could make out nothing of his surroundings. The mirror was all that there was.

And all that there was in the mirror was his own face and body.

It was instantly recognizable.

And horribly different.

His face was swollen and puffed out, as if it had been stung by a thousand hornets. Both eyes, the good and the bad, had vanished behind mounds of puffy flesh, dappled white and a gleaming, obscene scarlet.

The nose was no more than a tiny dimple in the mass of his cheeks, and a puckered slit revealed where his mouth had to be.

Experimentally Ryan pushed his tongue between his teeth, but it met a firm, slightly soggy resistance.

Nothing seemed to be happening to the vacant face in the mirror.

No change of expression.

It occurred to Ryan to wonder how he could see his own reflexion in the mirror, when his face didn't appear to have any functioning eyes.

Yet he could actually allow his gaze to wander down his nude body, away from the dappled balloon of a face. His breasts were engorged, pendulous, ending in dark nipples that were surrounded with porcine tufts of wiry black hair.

The belly rippled from his sight like the Kansas plains, endlessly rolling. He could just make out his penis, semierect, with a tiny pearl of milky liquid hung upon its tip.

Beyond that Ryan gazed in wonderment at the twin columns of his legs, thighs diminishing toward the knees, the calves shrinking into ankles and tiny feet. There were what looked like septic ulcers along the fronts of his legs, raw and weeping, yet he wasn't aware of any sensation of pain.

In fact, there was no sensation of anything at all that he could perceive.

There must have been arms attached to him as well as the legs, but the strange angles of the mirror hid them.

Ryan could almost feel his entire body swelling and rotting, bursting with a foul corruption that was likely to make his flesh split open.

"Over, under, around or through." The voice was the Trader's.

Maybe he could help him, but Ryan couldn't speak. He fought against the pressure, but felt himself losing control.

"Over and counting."

"Under and counting, lover," said a voice that was unmistakably that of Krysty Wroth.

"Around and counting." J. B. Dix was as taciturn as ever, not using four words where three would be entirely sufficient.

"Through, Dad. Through counting. Through with everything, Dad."

The mirror was starting to vibrate, the surface shivering as if it were manufactured from a pool of quicksilver.

Ryan tried to scream, and sat up in the gateway chamber, eye blinking, blood trickling from where he seemed to have bitten his lip.

His heart was pounding and he felt deeply, gut-churningly sick.

For several racing heartbeats he sat still, mouth open, fighting to keep hold on the frail thread of sanity.

"Fireblast." He sighed.

The armaglass walls were crimson, a brilliant, startling color that flared at his eye like a bloody saber cut.

The mist had vanished from the chamber, and the disks in ceiling and floor had ceased to glow. The air was a neutral temperature and flavor, a little stale, as it was in almost every redoubt he'd ever visited, but nothing compared to the cold thin gruel on the space station.

Ryan looked down at his hand.

And nearly screamed.

It was scrofulous, with flakes of yellow skin peeling away from the back and the palm. A purple sore the size of a .38 round glistened on the wrist. One finger was lacking the top joint, with only a blood-dripping stump. Two other fingers had no nails at all, just soft, wrinkled flesh. The nail on the thumb was grotesquely furrowed, long and curved, like sharpened horn.

The middle finger sported a silver ring, with an archaic whorled pattern. The stone was an exact replica of a human eye, made from colored crystal, with every tiny detail perfect. As Ryan gazed at the ring, the eye began to move, winking at him. And he saw a knife coming toward the eye, held in the hand of someone he knew was his own brother.

Harvey Cawdor, blinding him.

The knife, hacking toward his own frightened face, waking him again.

The walls of the gateway chamber were still that vivid crimson.

Whatever was happening was worse than most jumps had been. Normally there was the brain scrambling and the nausea, but it passed and once you had consciousness it was easier.

But this was different.

Now there were hallucinations that were so real they transcended reality

Ryan closed his good eye and breathed slowly in and out.

Counting.

"Five and counting. Ten and counting. Twelve and count..."

He opened his eye, fearful that he was actually losing his mind.

His lips moved as he looked around, whispering to himself in a hasty monotone, his face angling from person to person.

"Abe. Don't know his other name. Gunner from War wag One. Last man to see Trader alive. Once badly injured and I left him. We left him. No, I left him. But he pulled on through. That's Abe, all right. Long thin face and a drooping mustache. Carrying an Uzi."

"Doctor Theophilus Algernon Tanner. Born in South Strafford, Vermont on February 14, 1868. Married Emily. Two children. Dean and... No, Dean's my son. That's him there. Mother was Sharona. Didn't know I had a son until he appeared. Ten years old. My son."

Doc coughed, his shoulders shaking with the spasm. His pistol rattled on the floor, sticking from the fancy hand-tooled Mexican holster.

Ryan concentrated as hard as he could. "Doc carries an ancient Le Mat, a .63-caliber scattergun round in one barrel, and nine .36s from the other. Doc was trawled in 1896, to the year of 1998. Then in December of 2000 he was sent forward again to our time. He had a couple of real young children.'' A pause. ''I've said that.''

Beyond Doc was a slightly built figure wearing a dark fedora hat. A pair of wire-rimmed spectacles stuck out from the top pocket of his worn leather coat.

''John Barrymore Dix. Known him for eleven or twelve days. No! Years. The Armorer. Five feet and eight inches tall. Weighs one-forty in his clothes, soaking wet, with all his blasters. Blasters.'' Ryan closed his eye and took three more long breaths. ''Got the Uzi like Abe. And the Smith & Wesson M-4000. Pistol grip and folding butt. Fires eight rounds of 12-gauge fléchettes. Twenty razored darts to each round.''

Oddly he was finding it easier to recover the details of the weapons than it was to remember things like the names of Doc Tanner's children.

''Rachel and Morgan. No. Titus. My father was . . . Jolyon, that was it.''

Next around the chamber, lying with her right hand gripped by J. B. Dix, was a good-looking black woman, short, stocky, with her hair neatly tied in tiny, tight plaits.

''Mildred Wyeth.'' He nodded. It was coming back more quickly. ''Mildred *Winonia* Wyeth. Thirty-six when she was frozen, after an operation for minor abdominal surgery went wrong. Ironic, since she was an authority on cryonics and cryogenics. Freezing people. Father was killed back in the middle of the 1960s in a firebombing by some bush-hiding, running-dog, white-hood racists."

Mildred wore a Czech target revolver in a rig under her quilted denim jacket. She was the best shot among women that Ryan had ever seen.

"Best shot of anyone," he amended.

Which wasn't surprising since Dr. Mildred Wyeth had won a silver medal in the last ever Olympic games in Atlanta, in 1996 in the free-shooting pistol.

"Came from Lincoln, Nebraska."

"That's right, Ryan," Mildred said, opening one bloodshot brown eye. "Like to go back there one fine day."

That only left Krysty.

"Krysty," he said, feeling the gray blanket withdrawing from his brain, bringing hope of sanity to him.

She reached out and squeezed his hand. "I was raised in Harmony ville, not all that far off thirty years ago. I'm an inch shy of six feet and weigh in close to one-fifty." Her voice was helping to complete the healing process. "Got eyes like grass after rain, and hair like the heart of a forest fire. You know about the rest of my body, lover."

Krysty's thumb and forefinger encircled Ryan's index finger, rubbing slowly and suggestively up and down it.

To his own surprise, he felt that familiar, pleasant tightening in the front of his pants. Ryan managed a grin at her.

"Yeah," he said.

Now everyone except Dean was coming around. The young boy still slept tight, but his breathing was regular and he didn't seem at all distressed.

Abe had taken the jump much harder than the rest of them.

His mouth hung slack like he'd been kicked hard in the groin, and his eyes were floating in their sockets as if he were recovering from a three-night bender in a pesthole gaudy bar.

"Don't think I'll do this again," he said, swallowing hard.

"Mebbe we won't have to," J.B. said, standing and straightening his hat, perching his glasses on the end of his nose. "Not for a while. Let's go take a look around, shall we?"

"Yeah," Ryan agreed. "Why not?"

Chapter Six

The outside light, filtering through the crimson armaglass walls, gave everyone the appearance of ruddy good health.

Ryan glanced around, ready to warn his people to get their blasters ready, but found that he didn't need to tell them.

Even Dean was up and ready to go, his big pistol gripped tightly in both hands. He caught his father's eye on him and winked.

"That jump wasn't so bad, was it, Dad?"

"You're kidding me," Ryan replied. "Like a frag gren going off behind my eyes."

"Fuckin' right." Abe coughed. "Don't know what death's goin' to be like, but it has to be better than making a jump."

J.B. WHISTLED SOFTLY. "Looks like we might have us a live one here," he said, looking across the usual small anteroom toward the main control area of the mattrans unit.

Ryan felt his pulse ease itself up a handful of notches.

Over the past couple of years he and his companions had found themselves in a variety of different gateways. After the nuclear apocalypse of 2001 had put civilization onto the back burner for the next millennia, a number of secret military complexes, known as redoubts, had remained.

Often deeply hidden, sometimes in remote areas of the country, less often within conurbations, the redoubts had been designated for a number of strategic military purposes. But the holocaust had been so astonishingly brief and so megadeadly that they had turned out worse than useless.

It was like a man preparing for a flood by digging a deep hole to hide in, then dressing in a suit and helmet of lead.

The redoubts that had survived contained the most highly secret of all of the Pentagon's crucible of arcane cunning: the ability to transfer a human being from one place to another in the space of a fraction of a second.

Sadly the ability to understand the functional capability of the matter-transmitter units had been lost in the freezing dark aftermath of the war—if the protracted deaths of most of humanity can properly be called a "war."

All Ryan knew was that you got into the chamber and shut the door and, after a great deal of mental and physical discomfort, you found yourself elsewhere. The only tiny piece of knowledge he'd also learned was that there was sometimes a control button that you could press marked "LD," for "Last Destination," that would return you to the place from whence you last made a jump.

Ryan's nightmare fear when they'd begun making the churning jumps had been that they'd eventually end up in one of the many redoubts that had been totally destroyed by direct missile hits, or as a result of the massive earthquakes and volcanoes that had remolded the map of the United States into the sparse atlas of Deathlands.

The idea of being reconstituted into a morass of mud or buried in brittle shards of torn granite had been truly appalling.

But there was obviously, Ryan had come to realize, some sort of built-in safeguard designed specifically to prevent anything like that happening. If a receiving gateway was seriously damaged or destroyed, then transportation wouldn't take place.

The one thing they still had no way of controlling was their destination. All the instructions and the coding manuals had been destroyed either immediately after the nuking began or by the ravages of time.

You shut the door and went someplace else. That was all they knew.

But there was a good reason for J.B.'s startled comment.

With only a small percentage of exceptions, every redoubt they'd ever jumped into had been totally evacuated and swept clear. It was rare to find even so much as a scrap of crumpled paper under a broken chair.

But this redoubt looked like it might just turn out to be different.

Every mat-trans chamber opened into a small room. Here it held a table and two plastic stools, colored a dull orange. There was a line of shelves, with several packages, cans and containers. A couple of paperback novels lay on the table, one folded back as though its reader had just slipped out for a moment and would return at any second.

Ryan pointed to the larger control area beyond, motioning to J.B. to check it out. The Armorer beckoned to Mildred, who held her target pistol cocked and ready. The two of them slipped through, while Ryan and Krysty covered them.

"Nobody. Sec doors safe shut."

J.B.'s words meant that everyone could relax for a while.

Blasters were holstered. In the relatively mild temperature, coats were thrown open.

"Look around," Ryan said, "but make sure you watch out for boobies. Could be all kinds of traps left around."

J.B. shook his head slowly. "Looks to me like these people got out in a serious hurry. Maybe they started some sort of orderly evacuation and then something happened to screw up the plans. Doubt there'll be any tricks left." He paused. "But we'll still make sure to be real careful."

Abe had gone to the shelves in the anteroom. His boots made the faintest crunching sound and he glanced down. "Looks like the roaches got here first," he called. "Lot of dead little boogers."

Mildred joined him, stooping and picking up one of the dusty carapaces. She examined it carefully, then dusted it off her palm.

"I'm no expert on dead cockroaches," she said, "but I'd be surprised if it had been alive within the last seventy or eighty years. There was hardly anything left of it."

"Caff sub," Abe read. "Milk sub. Tomato soup gran... What's that word, Mildred?"

"Granules. Fancy name for big bits of flavor-packed powder."

"Can we eat any of it?"

She reached out for a blue-and-white packet. "Says this was a freeze-dried huckleberry recon drink. Claims it's as fresh as tomorrow's sunrise and gives you the up-and-walking-good bounce of a Colorado dawning in the Rockies." She looked at it more carefully, angling it toward the overhead strip lighting to make out the small faded print.

"Sounds good." Abe grinned, licking his lips and wiping the back of his hand over his long mustache. "Try that."

"Wouldn't."

"Why?"

"The ingredient missing is anything that's been within a hundred miles of a huckleberry. Plenty of ad-

ditives, coloring agents, preservatives and gelling re-
actants.''

"Oh."

She patted Abe on the shoulder. "Don't worry about
it. It's also got a 'sell by date of June 2003.' " She
dropped it to the floor, where a small pile of pale pink
powder drifted lazily out.

Dean was fascinated by the foam cups that littered
the working surfaces of the desks and consoles, peering into each at the crusted black residue, as though he
somehow expected to come across one that was still
steaming hot and delicious, with cream and sugar.

"They really just walked off and left them like this?"
he asked his father.

"Looks that way, son. Just walked off."

Krysty sat in one of the chromed swivel chairs and
put her boots up on the next seat along. She leaned
back and smiled at Ryan. "Must've been sort of
strange working here in a redoubt."

"Guess so."

"Can't imagine it. Heard the stories and seen the old
mags. You worked from nine until five and you were
checked in and out. Went back to your safe little house
with hot water and light and instant food. Sort of envy
them."

"They died," Ryan reminded her.

Doc had gone to the books. Ryan joined him and
picked up the one folded open on the table.

"Give us a reading from the past, lover," Krysty
called.

He didn't look at the cover. " 'Her body bore a languorous sheen of ecstatic sweat turning the very core of her being into a love-ready delight. She gazed fondly at the sticky mixture that coated his erect . . .' Oh, forget it. Crap porno." He chucked it back onto the table, where its dried pages fluttered and crumbled into tiny white flakes.

"Shame about that diary on the space station," Krysty said. "Sex book like that is a sort of comment on what vanished, isn't it?"

Ryan stepped through into the control room, pausing in front of the large sealed sec door. The green lever was down in the closed position.

"Let's go take a walk into yesterday," he said, laying his hand on the control.

Chapter Seven

On the wall opposite there was a massive piece of graffiti, daubed in yellow on the rough concrete surface. Thick gobs of paint had streaked and run down to the floor where it lay in wrinkled, congealed lumps.

The letters were six feet high: SO LONG CHI-TOWN. A little farther up the passage was GOODBI WINDI CITI.

"Chicago," Doc said. "Looks as though we've arrived in that toddling town."

They walked on, everything functioning—lights, sec cameras, air-conditioning.

As was often the case, the mat-trans section of the rambling complex was situated in a distant corner, with all sorts of threatening warnings: Entry Barred to All but B15 and Above. Carry Your Pass at All Times. You Will Have to Show It.

The corridor curved to the left and ended in a wall of blank rock.

"We can go the other way," said Dean, unable to hide his excitement.

"Sounds like a good idea." Ryan turned to the rest of the group. "We'll try the other way."

THEY REACHED a large illuminated map set at the center of an intersection. Three other passages, slightly less wide, forked off in different directions. There was also a bank of elevators.

The seven companions gathered around the illuminated plan.

The first thing they noticed was that most of the sections had been amended. Nearly all the regions on the three-dimensional display had been altered. The word *cleared* had been superimposed over them.

"Looks like evac was well on the way, after all," J.B. said disappointedly.

"The mat-trans unit isn't shown as having been cleared." Krysty pointed at the area, way off to the right.

Ryan nodded. "Could be they left that deliberately till close to the end."

Armaments, Food, Janitors, Commissary, Medical and Pharmacy, Comps, Electricians, Housekeeping, Dormitories, Eateries, Stores, Transport Spares, Mechanics, Kitchens, Techno, Clothing, Communications, Records, Hospital, Maintenance, Library, Retrieval, Security Internal, Security External—the list was endless, and all were marked with the faint overtyping. Cleared.

"That bit doesn't say it." Dean pointed to a light green area near the top level, by one of the marked entrances.

"It's the outer garaging facility," J.B. said. "Could be that'd be one of the last the evac squad would touch."

Doc was squinting at a tiny box, almost immediately below the garage. "What in perdition does that say? I swear that my sight is becoming more erratic with every waking day!"

But everyone had turned away.

Abe and J.B. shared disappointment that the weapons section was no more. Mildred was upset at the clearing of the pharmacy and the hospital. Dean's face had fallen at the realization that there would be no fresh food supplies here.

"Shame about the library," Krysty commented.

"Records would have been good to see. Clues about what *really* went down here." Ryan shook his head, then realized that Doc was calling him over to the map.

"What is it?"

"What does this say, down here? It doesn't seem to have been evacuated like the rest of the complex, does it?"

Ryan found the faint lettering difficult to read. "No. Not cleared. It says it was the chron-temp section, Doc." He glanced sideways at the old man. "Doc?"

But he'd disappeared, falling to the floor in some sort of a faint or a fit, eyes rolled back to show the whites, mouth open, perfect teeth gleaming in the neon light. Stiff as a pine board.

THEY PROPPED HIM UP and J.B. supported Doc's head in his lap. Mildred quickly brought him around, slapping the old man gently across the face, talking to him.

"Come on, Doc. You're all right."

There was a convulsive shudder that made everyone jump, and the watery blue eyes opened, clouded with a look of fear.

"A feeble touch of the female vapors," he said, his voice shaky. "I must apologize to you all." He moved his head to seek out Ryan. "Did I understand you to say that this redoubt contains a section...a section with the nomenclature of chron-temp?"

"Yeah."

"Merciful saints."

"What is it, Doc?" Krysty was kneeling by him, holding a veined hand in hers. "Something to do with time?"

"Everything to do with time. With Chronos, dark lord of things temporal. But not spiritual. Chaos loosed from the abyss."

Ryan was struggling to make some kind of sense out of the babbling rush of words. "Slow down, Doc, slow down."

"Time present and past and time future are all .are all . . Tomorrow's just another now, my dear friends. It's the same, you see. What I endured, is here as well. Here."

"You mean this is a time-trawling operation, Doc?" Ryan turned to the others, his face showing his own amazement. "Hear that?"

J.B. shook his head and tapped a finger to his own temple. But Doc saw the movement and laughed. Not a crazed cackle of hysteria. But a sound of genuine amusement.

"You believe that I have mislaid a few of my marbles, do you, John Barrymore? Is there another person living on the planet who would know better than I what I'm talking about? Of course there is not. The trawling department was labeled chron-temp as its official name. Just like the mat-trans units for making jumps in space. Only these evil places were for making jumps in time."

"Why don't we go to the garage and find if there's any wags left?" Dean asked.

Nobody took any notice of the boy and he sulked off to the side of the passage, kicking his feet at the wall. He looked above him at some gray netting that seemed to be hung from the ceiling. It trailed off around a corner, along one of the other passages, and Dean began to follow it.

None of the others saw him go.

They were all much too locked into this amazing discovery

"It *could* be an amazing discovery," Mildred said cautiously. "Just because it says it hasn't been cleared doesn't mean it actually hasn't."

"Nor does it mean it's functioning." J.B.'s voice was a strange mixture of restraint and near wonderment.

The idea of finding a time-jump unit still here and working was too astounding.

I don't get it,   Abe muttered.

What, my dear chap?'' Doc asked.

'Time travel.''

"What about it?''

"I don't get it.''

Doc rose majestically to his feet, taking his cane from Krysty's hand. "But precisely what do you not comprehend, Abraham?''

"You saying you were pulled to the future?''

"Indeed yes.''

Abe nodded. "Right. I got that. But what if I go back in time?''

"What of that?''

"Suppose I meet myself? Can I tell me to be careful not to get an arrow in me neck in the Darks? Can I do that, Doc?''

The old man smiled. "Time travel is fraught with anomalies. Rife with absurd and fascinating contradictions.''

Krysty nodded. "Like if I go back and murder Mother Sonja before I'm born, then I won't exist. But if I don't exist . . .''

Abe boggled. "Then how can you go back in time to kill your own mother? Hey, that is amazing, Krysty. That one of those anomaly things you talked about, Doc?''

"Yes. It is perhaps the best known of them all, Abe. Yet we are wasting time here talking when we should be walking.''

But Abe was entranced. "I could stop my mother and father ever meeting."

"Know who they were, Abe?" Ryan asked.

"Yeah, course   No. The fact is, I don't know."

Ryan laughed. "Shouldn't be difficult to find the chron-temp section from this map. Sure you want to do this, Doc?"

"More than anything I've wanted in many a long month of living and partly living. Let us proceed."

"Why not? Everyone ready?" Ryan looked around. "Where's Dean? Nobody see him? Fireblast! He should know better than to go wandering off."

It was precisely at that moment the terrified screams began.

Chapter Eight

The spiders weren't *that* big. The largest of them was barely the size of a small mongrel dog, about eighteen inches in height and barely fifteen inches across the body, though the spined legs made it closer to two and a half feet from clawed toe to clawed toe.

But there were at least ten score of these spiders a hundred yards along the passage. A couple of hundred.

Ryan was first around the bend, seeing that the corridor had widened into a dome-roofed cavern around eighty feet high, with a number of side tunnels opening off it.

The initial impression was of whiteness, shifting, stirring whiteness, like a wind on a patio, blowing through mounds of dry, powdery snow, making it move and swirl as if it had life.

He also registered the strange fact that the distant ceiling was festooned with something that his eye took for mounds of Spanish moss, dangling pale and leprous in coils.

Against the right-hand wall, still screaming and yelling, was Dean Cawdor, his feet kicking and stamping, maintaining a small circle of clear floor away from the shifting bank of snow.

"Spiders," Ryan breathed.

Albino arachnids scuttled busily toward the trapped boy, their bodies covered in a sheen of needle-fine hairs, yellow eyes glowing in the overhead lights. Dozens more cascaded down the walls from their maze of linked webs that filled the roof void high above. All in uncanny, deadly silence.

"Fucking bastards!" Abe had arrived second, almost bumping into Ryan.

"Help me, Dad!" Dean had enough control and sense to know that any attempt to draw his Browning or try to use a knife would give the banks of creatures the opportunity to close with him. Once they reached his ankles it would only be a heartbeat before they had scuttled up his legs, over his chest, to attack his exposed neck and face.

He kept kicking and banging with his boots, making enough sound and fury to hold the susurration of spiders away from him.

But it could only be seconds before they overcame their fear.

Ryan was aware of everyone behind him by their indrawn breaths.

The appearance of the group distracted the spiders. Hundreds of eyes turned toward them, and for a silent moment the entire snowy army seemed to freeze into stillness.

"Dad," came a plaintive whisper.

That seemed to snap the cords of horror that had snared Ryan's combat brain.

"Put some lead into them and into the webs. I'll get the kid."

J.B. was fastest, firing single spaced rounds from the Uzi into the motionless morass of tarantulas. Krysty leveled her double-action Smith & Wesson 640, aiming and pulling down. Each .38 round ripped into the spiders, pulping flesh.

The cavern was filled with the roar of guns. Doc used the Le Mat's .63-caliber scattergun round with a devastating effect, clearing a gap the size of a dining table.

Abe pointed his Uzi upward and squirted off a dozen bullets into the ghostly webs, the 9 mm rounds igniting the frail, dry tendrils, turning the roof into a blazing torch.

Ryan didn't hesitate, throwing the rifle off his shoulders, hearing it clatter on the stone floor behind him, holstering the SIG-Sauer as he started to power himself toward his son.

"Stay there!"

He didn't try to jump over the living carpet, knowing that it would be terminally simple to slip in pulped corpses. Once down, it would be unlikely that he would ever rise again.

The bodies cracked and crunched under the steel combat boots, and Ryan was aware of an almost inaudibly high chittering sound. Bits of flaming web were already falling about him, some of it catching fire on the hairy bodies of the scuttling creatures.

Dean was facing him, mouth half-open, eyes staring with a barely controlled fear. His arms were lifted toward his father.

The spiders were scattering away from his rushing charge toward the boy. A few, bolder than the rest, tried to attack him, springing upward, knee-high. But Ryan was ready for them. As soon as he began his rescue bid he'd drawn his eighteen-inch blade from its sheath, hacking down to cut away any of the vicious muties.

Their blood was a colorless ichor that spurted from their sliced flesh, dappling his hand, burning like acid.

"On my back, Dean," Ryan called, half turning to give the boy a chance to vault onto him, balancing himself against the sudden jar of his son's weight, then turning immediately toward the relative safety of the rest of the group.

But the blanched creatures weren't done.

Despite the fire that was now falling like a biblical rain all over them, they were rallying in snowy clumps to try to bar his escape.

Ryan kicked out, trying to skirt the largest numbers. He heard the chatter of one of the Uzis and several of the prickled monstrosities disappeared in a gout of sprayed tissue.

Now more and more of the spiders were on fire, the long white hairs blazing with a magnesium intensity, the flames spreading from one to another.

But Ryan wasn't yet clear.

Half a dozen of the mutie arachnids, heavy as puppies, had gained hold on his pants, gripping with tiny barbed claws.

"Hang on my neck," he panted to Dean, finding that the boy was restricting his ability to use the big panga.

"Kill the bastards," the lad shouted, his own turquoise-hilted knife drawn and ready.

There was still the noise of firing, though the spreading flames were doing a better job than the full-metal jackets.

"Come on!" He recognized Krysty's voice.

A length of fiery web came drifting toward him and he parried it with the panga, finding that it stuck to his hand and arm. Ryan yelled with the pain, but the fire burned out quickly.

He hacked at two of the spiders, but suddenly another was by his neck, on the right side. Its hideous face was inches from his good eye, the serrated teeth parted to snap at his cheek.

There was a flash of silver, and the mutated horror disappeared from his shoulder, leaving only a smear of its poisonous blood across his jaw.

"Thanks, Dean."

"Okay, Dad."

Now there was only the disorganized fringe of the pack of spiders to be run through. One reared up, and Ryan kicked it so hard that it flew through the air and hit the wall of the cavern at least twenty feet in the air.

Doc gave a cheer, lifting both arms above his head, holding the smoking Le Mat. "And the extra point is good!" he shouted.

Now they were really safe and Dean slid quickly down off his father's shoulders, sheathing his slim knife.

On an impulse, Ryan leaned down and hugged the boy, touching his lips to the soft cheek. "Thanks again, son," he whispered.

Dean blushed.

It was impossible to see across the vaulted space, for wreathing coils of stinking smoke. The spiders had mostly vanished into the other narrow tunnels, leaving behind only their dead and dying in scattered, smoldering heaps.

Ryan picked up his fallen Steyr rifle, flashing a quick, sooty smile to Krysty. "Life's full of surprises, isn't it, lover?"

She reached out and clasped his right wrist in both her hands. "That was close."

"Yeah. Kid got one of the fuckers off of my face. Just in time."

She smiled. "What a horrible stench. Let's get away from it."

Once everyone had reloaded their blasters, they set off toward the chron-temp section of the huge redoubt.

Doc was off in the lead, despite Ryan's warning about caution. He was skipping and singing to himself, rapping the floor with the tip of his cane like an elegant vaudeville dancer.

Ryan had never seen him so happy

Chapter Nine

To Doc's frustration, they weren't able to go by the most direct route. Some of the sec doors were immovably down and locked, which meant they had to make frequent detours.

Fortunately J.B. had a virtually eidetic memory for maps, and was able to lead them toward their destination by other levels, up and down dusty staircases, through whole sections of the redoubt that had been stripped so bare it was impossible to even guess what they'd once held.

At one point they came near to the surface and the garage area that was, seemingly, not evacuated.

And it was there that they discovered the explanation for the parts of the redoubt that were still left untouched by the clearing party.

"THERE'S A SEC DOOR half raised," Mildred reported. She and J.B. had gone on a little ahead of the others.

"Or perhaps it's half lowered," Doc said sourly.

When they all reached it, around a dogleg turn in the corridor, they found it was actually about three-quarters of the way down, leaving a gap of two and a half feet to crawl under

There was a straight section of passage beyond, with a number of M-16s piled neatly along one wall.

"Twelve blasters," J.B. said.

Ryan swallowed, aware again of the flatness of the air, air that had been circulating in the sealed environment of the redoubt for a hundred years.

"They wouldn't walk away without their weapons."

Krysty had moved a few paces along, past the stacked guns, pausing in the open doorway of a room off to the right.

"They haven't," she said quietly.

"May the Lord have mercy on their souls," Doc murmured, turning away from the grim sight of the twelve bodies.

Dean stared, blinking in disbelief. "Dad?"

"What?"

"Did they..."

"Looks like they did."

Mildred and J.B. went into the room while the others waited outside. There was a long table with the desiccated remnants of a last supper, plates covered with a scummy crust of what could have been gravy or sauce or anything. There were the ubiquitous foam cups.

And empty bottles.

The Armorer picked up one of them and looked at the label. "Brandy. French. Armagnac, it says."

"And there's these." Mildred picked up one of half a dozen small mirrors that were lying on the table.

'Don't get it,'' Abe said.

Mildred held out a tiny bottle of brown glass, with a black screw top. She opened it and tipped it against her index finger, revealing a residue of white powder smudged on her skin.

"Jolt," Abe breathed.

"Nearly." Mildred touched it to her tongue. "Coke." She tipped her head on one side, eyes closed. "And *very* good coke. Pharmaceutical-quality cocaine. Uncut. Nobody stepped on this."

"More here." J.B. stooped and picked up a white glass bottle. "Must've held something like eight or nine hundred grams of the shit."

Mildred nodded. "They drank all this booze and then did huge quantities of coke... Not surprising what happened."

Everyone looked down at the long-silent circle of corpses.

Eleven were close together in a circle, all seeming to be male. But that was partly a guess since nearly all of them were missing most of their skulls. Eleven .45-caliber Colts also lay on the floor.

"Reckon we'd find they've all fired a single round." J.B. turned and looked across at the body that lay apart from the others, holding a Colt in the clawed remains of its right hand. "Except for that poor miserable bastard."

It wasn't that difficult to reconstruct the macabre scenario.

The men had been the last of what must have been a number of official evacuation parties, their job to finish off the clearing out of the final sections of the rambling redoubt.

They'd come close to the end of their task, with only the distant mat-trans section to work through, though it was possible that had been deliberately left functional as a policy decision. That had certainly been true of other gateways. The chron-temp suite was probably last on their list, then the outside garage in the rooms beyond.

But someone had found the coke in one of the pharmacy suites close by. Nobody would ever know where the top-quality brandy had come from. But the mixture had proved lethal to the soldiers.

It was impossible to even guess at precisely how things had gone down.

But one by one they must have become critically depressed, a condition exacerbated by the combination of drink and drugs. Probably they'd talked about what had been happening in the world in the past few hours—or days—guessing by then that it wasn't going to be like the old wars. This one would end it all.

There would be limitless, endless dying. By the time the dozen men reached their decision, they would almost certainly have been aware that their families—wives, children, parents—were dead. Or so critically rad-poisoned that death would be a needful mercy.

So they'd all had a last drink. Snorted a last couple of lines of coke. Ryan had picked up a crumbling five-dollar bill off the table, still rolled into a tight tube.

Then the twelve sec men had sat on the floor. J.B. had pointed out that there wasn't a single ordinary grunt among them. They were all special noncoms, with long-service insignia.

Each one had taken out his side arm and cocked it, placed it into the mouth of the next man along the line until the suicidal daisy chain was finally complete.

At the signal, every man had squeezed the trigger of his own gun and blown off his neighbor's head, in turn aware of a last moment of exquisite horror as his own skull exploded.

"All except for him," Abe said. "Looks like he mebbe tried to change his mind. Too late."

The lower jaw was missing from the twelfth man. It seemed as if the .45 round had angled away off teeth, ripping half the face, jaw, cheek and eye with it.

Mildred had been looking at the forensic evidence of the man's passing.

"I reckon that he must have been knocked unconscious by the shot."

"How long for?" Dean asked, staring around him with a ghoulish enthusiasm.

"Can't tell. Minutes. Half an hour. No way of knowing. Lost a lot of blood. You imagine what it must've been like to go out with the certainty that it was all over and done. Then to come around and find it wasn't."

Doc shook his head. "In truth it is a most doleful thought, ma'am. To recover in the worst agony, pur-blind, soaked in blood. Sodden with the gore, brains and bone splinters of your comrades. It is worthy of the pen of Edgar Allan Poe himself. Did I remark to you that my maternal grandfather once met up with him and... Once... What was I saying?"

Mildred smiled gently. "Just that you were real sorry that the poor guy had to recover consciousness to this carnage."

Ryan pointed. "See the black streak on the floor where he dragged himself over there? Then he fired a second shot to finish the job."

"Poor devils," Krysty said. "Can we get out of here, lover? Depresses me just being in the same part of the building."

J.B. WAS VERY EAGER to check out the nearby garage. "If there were twelve men going to get away from here, they must have had either three or four Jeeps. Or a truck. Or maybe even a small war wag. Got to be some supplies of gas as well. Could be good, Ryan, you know?"

"Sure. But there's time. Doc's hot to check out this time-jump place. Do that first, then come back up to the surface and see what the transport is. Yeah?"

"Yeah," J.B. agreed reluctantly.

His diminutive figure led the way, his memory taking them to the nearby section that had been shown as Chron-Temp.

Mildred fell back alongside Ryan. 'If this redoubt is supposed to be somewhere near old Chicago, then how come it hasn't been entered and ravaged?''

"Because there was once a big city here, it doesn't mean there's anything now. Look at whole slices of Newyork. And Washington went first. Nothing of that left. Big hole that glows at night for a hundred miles. We don't know what we'll find when we eventually get out of this concrete tomb, do we?''

She shook her head, the tiny beaded plaits clicking softly. "Guess not. How about in this time section?''

"No idea, Mildred.''

"Doc really is from the past, isn't he? I mean, it's not some kind of paranoiac delusion?''

Ryan stopped in midstep. He and the black woman were last in the group. Doc and J.B. had been matching each other stride for stride at the front, the others trailing along behind them.

"You mean that there's a possibility that Doc's made all this up? Wife and kids and... No, I can't buy that one.''

"Nor me, really. But it goes against everything I was ever taught. Then again, wandering around Deathlands with you wasn't in any of my textbooks, either.'' She smiled as they began walking again, after the others. "But it just seems that a place like this, with all its associations, could tip Doc over the edge again.''

"Over which edge?''

Mildred turned to stare directly into Ryan's eye.

'The edge of total, permanent, irredeemable madness, of course.''

There was an eager shout from Doc, ahead of them, and they both hurried to catch up.

Chapter Ten

The main sec doors stood open. Beyond them they could see another series of glass-topped doors, all closed.

One set was encircled with rubber sealing and looked as if they might be an air lock.

Above the doors was a red warning sign, more strongly worded than any that they'd ever seen outside the mat-trans units: No Entry to Chron-Temp Section. C-Passes Only. No Other Clearance.

Doc was gazing at the notice, his right hand gripping the lion's head atop his cane, the ferrule tapping nervously on the stone floor.

"This is... By the three Kennedys! This could be the fulfillment of my life. A dream come true. A shower of gold in my poverty. Honey in the desert. Water in the barren waste. A table before me against mine enemies."

He was oblivious to the great flow of tears that were sliding down his grizzled cheeks from his brimming eyes.

"Hey, simmer down there, Doc," Abe said uneasily. "Take it easy.'

"Yes, my trusty comrade, yes." He clasped the gunner by the elbows and smiled broadly at him. "I shall take it easy indeed."

J.B. coughed. "Well, if we're going inside, then let's go."

ONE SET OF DOORS was, as Ryan had suspected, an air lock.

There was the typical hissing as the outer portal opened. They crowded inside, while Ryan closed the lock with a firm click.

"Hope we won't finish up with Washington crossing the Delaware," Mildred commented, "or with a triceratops about to tread on us."

The inner door slid open and they were at the heart of the chron-temp complex.

They were standing in a large control room with a floor-to-ceiling window that opened into something uncannily like the freezing unit they'd seen twice before.

There were endless banks of computer consoles, occasionally changing as lights flickered across them. And there were three modules, about the size of hospital beds, with a clear plastic cover over each.

Doc pressed his face against the window, his tears smearing the polish. "Oh, my dearest loves," he whispered.

"Look over here," Dean called, already off on his own, exploring "Lots of vids."

Mildred and Doc were the only ones who didn't follow the boy. She was helping the old man to a chromed chair with padded arms, sitting him in it and talking quietly to him. She waited until he seemed a little more calm before leaving him and joining the others in the extensive video library.

Krysty turned to her from a display screen. "It's the records of all the trawling experiments they carried out here. And mebbe in other places as well. It's still geared up and ready to go. Just like they've all gone out for a mug of coffee and will be back in a couple of minutes."

Ryan had been trying to read the faded typed labels on row after row of videotapes. But Krysty's words made him look around. "You say it's all of the records, lover?"

"That's what the master file says."

He leaned over her shoulder, catching the scent of her hair, brushing her cheek with the tips of his fingers.

"How do you get into the files of this thing?"

"Access in through the keyboard."

"Type in whatever you want, Ryan," Mildred said. Her fingers touched several keys, producing streams of letters and numbers. "There. That's the central index. Thought they might have some sort of security code lock protecting it, but they haven't. Go ahead."

Cautiously, as though he feared that the pale cream keys were going to snap at his fingers, Ryan began to type: TANNER, THEOPHILUS ALGERNON.

Krysty pressed the main function key, and they all heard a faint humming sound The screen went blank for a few moments.

"Looks like they got nothing on No, wait, it's working."

Everyone crowded around. The yellow letters flick ered up on the dark brown screen.

Tanner, Theophilus Algernon. Doctor of Science, Harvard. Doctor of Philosophy, Oxford, England. Born South Strafford, Vermont, 2.14. 1868. Married Emily, née Chandler (qv), 6.17. 1891. Two children. Rachel, born 1893 and Jolyon, born 1895. Both children died 1896. Trawl date November 1896. Location at time of trawl, Omaha, Nebraska. Brought to chron-temp base in 1998. (See data in applicable file.) Became confirmed as a hostile and negative influence on the project, so sent forward in December 2000 to future date (restricted information).

Mildred pressed Scroll, and the flow of information rolled on. Most of it was technical, cross-indexed, giving runic strings of numbers and dates.

"Stop." J.B. had been watching. "Go back to the previous There. What's that bit say about Doc? About a vid?"

Mildred read it out loud. "Unique trawl video of subject seven days before trawl. Note: Quality poor. No sound."

"Do that mean what I think it does?" Abe asked. "A vid of..."

"Of Doc back in the nineteenth century?" Ryan whistled, glancing over his shoulder to make sure the old man wasn't watching or listening. "Let's take us a look."

The tape was easy to find from the computer's screen reference.

Dean ran to pick it off the rows of shelves, once his father had given him the position, taking out the white box and turning it sideways to read the label on it.

"Says 'TAT 11.7 1896. Highly classified and re-tricked. No, restricted is the word. What's that mean, Dad?"

"Means we shouldn't be looking at it. Bring it over here and we'll run it through the machine."

It only took a moment to slot it into the player. The screen in the TV immediately above took some time to come into hesitant life, a pattern of black and white spots crackling across it like a battle between crazed electrons.

"I don't believe this." Mildred shook her head. "I mean it's insane. We're going to see Doc Tanner in Omaha, Nebraska. On the seventh day of November, two hundred years ago. Custer wasn't twenty years dead, for Christ's sake."

"Here it comes," Dean squeaked excitedly, jumping up and down.

A woman's face, needle-sharp, came into focus. There was just enough of the neck and shoulders to

reveal a gray uniform, a collar and tie, severely masculine.

"If you are not specifically cleared to watch this
chron-temp vid then turn it off now. I repeat, turn it off
now. Security tabs will trace anyone attempting to view
illegally·" There was a long pause, while she simply
stared straight out at the camera.

"Come on, lady," Abe muttered. "You got all eternity. We don't."

There followed a long printed explanation that gave
the details of how and when the vid film had been
taken. And mentioned its extreme rarity.

Despite many subsequent attempts, it proved impossible to reproduce this experiment. Therefore,
the scarcity of this short piece of time-trawled film
cannot be overemphasized.

"Get on with it," Mildred said. "Look, it's maybe
better that Doc doesn't even know this exists. Could
push him..."

"Over the edge," Ryan finished. "He's resting con-
tentedly in the other room. It said the film was short.
We'll all keep an eye open for him. Then if he
should..."

The credits rolled: a project director, a rostrum
cameraman, a list of positions, many with long strings
of academic letters after their names.

Then came an orotund voice-over, against a sepia
print of a Victorian street scene.

"All that we know is all that you will now see. We know that the date is November 11, 1896. We had locked on to Theo Tanner as an ideal specimen to try to lift under the aegis of Project Cerberus linked to Operation Chronos. The time at the moment of contact is precisely 10:14:8 in the morning."

The scene changed to a distant view of a sprawling town.

"That's Omaha, Nebraska," Mildred whispered. "Lincoln, my home town, was only a hundred miles from there. I saw that photo in our school library."

The voice confirmed her words. "This is Omaha, Nebraska, about four years before our snatched moment of real-life video. Sadly, despite the most intensive research through local archive material and historical societies, we have not been able to accurately identify any other person or place on the film you are about to see."

A white-on-black countdown began from ten, running quickly through to two, one and zero.

Everyone was crowded around the viewing screen, utterly fascinated by the expectation of what they were about to see.

A man, tallish with shoulder-length hair, walked down the street, swinging a stick in his right hand. He wore a long overcoat with small buttons, belted at the waist. A high collar and a cravat were held in place with what could have been a diamond pin.

The film quality left a lot to be desired. It flickered and jumped, and it was in black and white. The background was fuzzy, but appeared to be a busy street. There were other people moving around, but the area of sharper focus was small.

The man had his arm linked with a tall, slender woman. She had on high-button boots and a skirt that swept the sidewalk. A long coat came to her knees, fastened right up to the neck, which made it impossible to see what she had on underneath. She wore a wide-brimmed hat with a long cluster of feathers on its left side.

The man's other hand was firmly gripped by a child. It was a girl, from the very long hair, but a scarf was wound around her face, concealing her features.

The woman was pushing an elegant wickerwork pram with a high back to it. It wasn't possible to see the infant inside.

A stout person came briefly into the shot and seemed to speak to one of the main players in the blurred drama. As they neared the camera the man hesitated as though he'd spotted something out of the ordinary. The woman also stopped and tipped back her head so that the sunlight illuminated her face beneath the brim of the hat.

And Doc Tanner gave a piercing scream, torn from the dark places of his tortured soul. "Emily! Oh, dear God, it's my wife!"

Chapter Eleven

It took all of them to restrain him.

Just as Mildred had predicted, the piece of vid film had driven Doc completely into raving insanity. Seeing himself with his wife and children, just before the twentieth-century scientists ruined his life forever, had knocked his fingers away from their fragile hold on reality.

He'd attempted to smash the vid viewer, screaming out a torrent of wild abuse at it.

Ryan had grabbed Doc by the arm but had been shrugged off with frightening ease. In his rage the old man seemed to have been given the violent strength of ten.

"Leave me alone, you fucking son of a bitch!"

"Calm down, Doc."

But Doc wasn't in the calming vein.

J.B. dived in and managed to get hold of one of Doc's legs, while Krysty dived onto his back, locking her strong arms around his neck. Ryan came again for another try, using all his power to knock the old man off balance.

Once they finally had him down, it wasn't quite so hard.

But it wasn't over until J.B. pulled out a length of whipcord from one of his capacious pockets and quickly tied Doc's hands behind him.

They all got off him, while Mildred sat on the floor and tried to quiet him.

"Doc, I understand how you must feel, seeing that vid of you and—"

"Oh, you understand, do you? You know what it's like to be torn from your wife and children? I believe that your own father was murdered, was he not? Yes, I thought so. Suppose you were to suddenly meet him after these long, lost years? How do you think you would feel, you stupid trull?"

"I'd feel a little like you do, Doc. Sick, bewildered and crazy angry."

"Oh, balderdash! Save your bedside manners for those who might need it."

But at least he was calmer.

Ryan rubbed at a sore place under the ribs where one of Doc's boots had caught him. "If we let you go, you promise not to break up the place?"

But the old man had begun to cry again, bitter racking tears that made his whole body shudder.

AN HOUR PASSED.

Doc had been released and had joined the others in a makeshift meal.

But he'd drifted away from them as they rested in the main room of the complex. Dean had followed, and reported that Doc was sitting watching the vid over and over.

"Got it on slow-mo. Triple pic freeze."

Krysty and Mildred both stood, but Ryan waved them back down. "Carry on with the delicious jerky and water," he said. "Don't want to spoil the meal. I'll go check him out."

He walked quietly through, seeing Doc hunched over the viewing screen. Though his feet had made no sound, the old man must have sensed him, and spoke without looking around.

"Jonathan Nolan."

"What?"

Doc laughed shortly. "No, Ryan, my dear friend. I've not gone totally off my trolley. Though I confess to being somewhat shocked at seeing my dear wife and children. A ghost in the mirror. A shadow upon the dream."

"You said someone's name."

"I did indeed. Look here. Jonathan Nolan. A scribbler in the popular prints. The man who comes up to me . . . just here."

It was the stout person, wearing a stovepipe hat. Doc had the machine set on ultraslow motion, and the movement was so frozen that it was difficult to make out any details.

Doc was smiling gently. "I remember this moment. A moment trapped here, like a fly in a piece of amber. Mr. Nolan had stopped to tell me that a book I had purchased had arrived in our local store. It was to be a gift for me for Yuletide from my dear wife. I never received that present, my friend. It is but a small tragedy among the other, larger ones."

Ryan laid a hand on Doc's shoulder. "Yeah. Life's a bitch."

"And then you die. I have heard that. The book was a first edition of Housman's 'A Shropshire Lad.' Wondrous verse. I have always loved those poems. They bring back with a painful clarity what I have lost."

"We figured it'd be good to have a rest now. Then take us a good look at the chron-temp section. The one through the big window. In the morning. That okay with you, Doc?"

But he'd lost the other man's attention. Doc had reached out to the control, easing the tape very slowly forward, just to the point where his wife lifted her face. The shaft of sunlight, two centuries ago, flared dazzlingly at them off the screen. Then the lens adapted to it and they watched an amazingly clear freeze frame.

"Oh, my sweetheart little girl. My dear Emily. My soft and comfy darling, Emily." The tears were flowing again as he looked over his shoulder at Ryan. "She was the most beautiful of angels, was she not, my dear and trusted companion?"

"She was very beautiful, Doc."

It was true. Emily Tanner had a serene, timeless beauty, a heart-shaped face, with dark eyes, and amid the bunched auburn hair, tiny pearl earrings that caught the November sun. There was a gentle smile playing on her lips as she looked up, seeming to stare straight into the hidden camera that spied upon her from the far future.

"I swear that I recall that moment. That day. That time. Only a week later I was plucked away forever." His face creased. "Forever?"

"It almost looks like she saw the camera there. Damned if I know what there might have been to see, Doc."

"Nor I. But she said later that she thought she had glimpsed something. A sort of quivering of the air, she said. Like the heat haze across a summer meadow in a hot July."

Ryan was fascinated. "But she couldn't really describe what it was?"

"I fear not."

"Guess at the time you thought nothing about it, did you?"

"No. Though, oddly, my sweet little Rachel said that evening, as she lay in her cot, that it had frightened her."

"What?"

"Something on the street. But the moppet was only three years of age, Ryan."

"How did she describe it?" He had the uncomfortable feeling that he was peeling layers of bandages off a ghastly wound, and that the final unraveled strip of sear cloth would release a hideous turbulence of infected blood.

Doc closed his eyes wearily, rubbing the back of his hand across them. "Before God, I am exceeding weary. A candle, Master Cawdor, to light me to my bed. No, you asked me a question. What... Yes, I remember. What did Rachel say?"

"Right?"

"That a big eye looked at her from heaven. Heaven! It was from hell."

"Let's go rest, Doc."

"Why not, friend. Cawdor shall sleep. And Glamis too, hereafter. And on the morrow I will go to see the cherry hung with snow."

THE REDOUBT WAS silent, except for the barely perceptible stirrings and vibrations of the ceaseless nuke power plant that ran the complex, keeping it lighted and heated, with all the main control consoles occasionally chattering to one another.

The chron-temp part of the redoubt slept.

Mildred and J.B. had bundled together in a side room. Doc had chosen the suite with the tapes and viewer.

Abe and Dean were sleeping in an office, the gunner's occasional snores resonating through the whole section.

And Ryan and Krysty occupied the office of the head of internal security for chron-temp.

The door was nearly closed. Both had stripped off their top layer of clothes, making sure their blasters were close at hand, though being in the deepest part of a lost redoubt was probably one of the safest places in all Deathlands.

As Krysty kicked off her boots, Ryan had come up behind her and kissed her on the back of the neck, the long strands of her burning hair brushing against his cheek.

"Hey, not more of your incessant demands?" There was a gentle laughter in her voice.

"Yeah, afraid so, lover."

The long stay at the Lauren spread had given them an unusual opportunity for prolonged lovemaking, without the threat of attack. They'd retired to their bedroom at least once a day, mostly at night, but on occasion in the sultry heat of the midafternoon.

Now they lay close together under their coats. The temperature in most redoubts was controlled in the middle seventies. Comfortable enough.

Krysty's strong hands roamed over his chest, touching his nipples. Her mouth nuzzled at his neck, her tongue darting in and out. He contented himself by lowering his head toward her breasts, bringing the fiery tips to an aching hardness.

"Oh, that's real nice, lover."

Her fingers wandered lower, across the hard ridged wall of his stomach, finding him sprung to eager life. Her left hand cupped his balls while her right hand began a steady stroking movement.

"This what you boys together like to call a real diamond cutter?" she teased.

"I hate to think what you girls together call this," he retorted, fingers moving rhythmically deep between Krysty's thighs, in her moist, warm depths, making her moan with growing pleasure.

She pulled him on top of her, guiding him in with her hand.

There was enough light filtering in from the corridor for him to watch her face as he thrust hard. Her eyes were closed, her lips slightly parted in a satisfied smile.

Afterward they lay close together until she wriggled down to rouse Ryan again with her mouth, swinging on top of him to spur him along toward a second pounding climax.

Only then did they fall asleep, locked tight in each other's arms.

IN ANOTHER ROOM, less than twenty yards away, Doc sat and watched the flickering seconds of black-and-white film.

Again and again.

Chapter Twelve

"You sure you're up to this, Doc?"

Ryan was rewarded with a wide smile, which showed the man's uncannily perfect set of large teeth. "My dear fellow, I am as chipper as a nipper and as spruce as a goose. Let us do it."

They had all met up in the early morning in the central zone of the chron-temp unit.

Doc looked in reasonable shape, though Ryan had already noticed that the old man's eyes were red-rimmed and sore.

But there was a desperate gaiety about him, like a young girl, mortally ill with consumption, determined to attend one last dance before passing out of this life.

Ryan could tell that Doc was on tenterhooks to get into the heart of the chron-temp section. But he was making a great play of not really being interested at all.

"Perhaps others among you would wish to pass by this place? I would be the first, yes, the very first to admit that it holds some of the grimmest memories possible."

"I want to take a look in the outer garage," J.B. said.

"Oh, but we can do that on our way out of the redoubt, can we not?" Doc said hastily, licking his lips nervously as he looked at the Armorer. His knuckles had whitened on the head of his sword stick.

"Yeah, I guess so."

Ryan almost smiled at the sweating relief on the face of the old man. "Come on, then, friends. Let's go see."

AFTER A HALF HOUR'S exploration, several of the companions reached more or less the same conclusion at more or less the same time.

It was Mildred who verbalized the feeling. "Am I losing my mind, or is this set up to go on an experiment?"

Krysty nodded, looking up from one of the comp screens that had engaged her interest. "Looks like that to me, too."

Doc was streaming with perspiration, unable to keep still, constantly darting from screen to screen, from console to console, reading streams of figures and nodding furiously to himself. His lips moved as if he were involved in some internal conversation. When the two women spoke he whirled around like a dervish, arms hugging himself.

"Yes! Oh, yes! You are correct, my dear, sweet ladies. Everything has been put in readiness for three separate trawlings."

"Who are they? And where do they come from?" Dean asked.

"Ah, now that may be more deeply coded and hidden. But we can access the references that will at least give us names and dates."

Ryan slapped the flat of his hand down hard onto the desk in front of him. "Hold it! Just hold it, will you?"

Doc froze, fingers poised over the keyboard. "What can be wrong, my dear companion?"

"Let's take this a short step at a time. You know how profoundly miserable your life has been made by those bastards pulling you out of your own time. So, you're thinking about doing this to three other poor devils."

Doc started to reply, hesitated, then looked away.

"Fair comment, Doc," Abe said. "These three that the machines are all set to bring into our time. What the fuck have they done to deserve that?"

"They did it to me," Doc replied slowly. "Why should I not be allowed to do the same thing to them?"

"Come on, that's no answer." Krysty's face was flushed with anger. "We aren't talking about the scientists who trawled you. They're all long, long dead and rotted. These are three others, minding their own business and getting on with life. Can you throw the switch on them?"

"Indubitably. Without the slightest pang of conscience. Most of the latter research, after a number of failures, was aimed at short-term chron jumps. If we check out who the three are and where they come from, I believe we might discover they are from the late nineties. Perhaps only days before sky-dark and the beginnings of the long winters."

"You mean they would've been trawled from the immediate past?" Mildred asked.

"The experiments were less than successful. I was about their only triumph. If that is the correct word. Some of the negatives that came through were . . . were less than whole."

Ryan rubbed at his forehead, trying to clarify his own thoughts. To actually get someone from just before the nuclear holocaust that destroyed the civilized world was immensely fascinating and had long been a dream of his.

"So, if what you say is right, it's probable that all three of these . . ."

"Victims," Krysty offered.

"Subjects," Ryan completed. "These subjects probably died within a short time of when the experiment was set. To bring them here would—"

"Save their lives," Doc concluded triumphantly. "Precisely, my dear Ryan."

"Show me the dates."

There was the clicking of keys on the computer board, and the screen went dark. Then it came up with three short paragraphs. Everyone stared at them as if they might somehow contain the missing answer to the riddle of the universe.

The first entry said Dolphin One.

"What's that mean?" Abe asked.

"The word the Chronos experts used for their victims. Trawled dolphins."

Dolphin One. Male. Aged forty-two. Then a string of numbers that Doc said was encoded information on the subject's height, build, blood type et cetera.

Graham Oswald Vair. Domicile: Mitford City, Wisconsin. Occupation: clerk in sports-equipment store. Parents deceased. Unmarried. No siblings.

"After the problems that they had with me, it was decided in future to only try to trawl single people with no living relatives. Generally friendless loners. But not always."

Ryan looked at Doc. "But these men had the unlimited authority and power to just pluck anyone out of the air?"

"Oh, yes, dear friend. They were above the law and beyond any reason."

The date shown on the screen confirmed what Doc had said about the potential victims being picked on trawl dates very late in the twentieth century. Graham Oswald Vair was slated to be lifted on December 30, 2000, at five in the morning.

Dolphin Two was female, aged thirty-nine. Dolores Mae Melville. Her residence was given as Tehachapi in California.

"I know that," Mildred said. "It's on the highway from Barstow to Los Angeles. No, to Bakersfield. Nothing much there except a big old penitentiary."

Dolores was due to be trawled the same day as Graham Vair, but forty-five minutes later.

The third of the time-jump subjects was due to be picked off another forty-five minutes after that.

Michael Brother was nineteen years old, from Nil-Vanity in California. His profession was oblate, and was expert in Tao-Tain-Do.

"What in dark night's an oblate when it's at home?" J.B. asked.

Everyone was equally puzzled, shrugging shoulders in bewilderment.

Except for Doc. "I believe it has something to do with a religious community. An oblate is a young man who's decided at an early age to dedicate himself to a monastic order"

"Doesn't matter what he does. What matters is that all three of them'll know lots about the world before the nuking." Ryan looked at the others. "What do you say? We going to trawl?"

Now the excitement was palpable and communicable, the objections mostly forgotten.

Krysty nodded. "Why not?"

Chapter Thirteen

Doc had shown a remarkable facility in handling the equipment. He caught Ryan staring at him and broke into a broad, slightly crazed smile.

"Remember, dear comrade of many adventures, that I passed some weeks of my half-life in an almost identical laboratory complex before they tired of me and pushed me from then to now. I watched and listened to what they did. Despite my occasional eccentricity, I have a good brain, you know. Once the fundamental principle of time travel is accepted, the mechanics of making it all function become quite childishly simple."

Everything had been programmed by the last occupants of the redoubt.

Ryan figured that the experiment would have been scheduled to take place around about the very day that the skies grew black with warheads and mankind finally began to die.

If the dozen soldiers hadn't decided on group suicide, then they would doubtless have completed their work by clearing out the chron-temp section of the fortress as well.

But they did chill themselves.

And it was all still there, waiting for the irony of Doc Tanner's finger pressing the green button

"THERE." THE OLD MAN leaned back in his swivel chair and steepled his fingers together in his lap. "There we go."

It was staggeringly quick.

From the moment that the process was initiated to the moment when a flux of light began to fill the nearest of the podlike capsules was less than ninety seconds.

Information was dancing across the multitude of comp screens at dazzling speed.

"It's going to work," Abe breathed, readying his Uzi. "We're goin' to meet someone from the fucking past."

"Something's appearing in there," Dean said. "Look, Dad!"

Everyone gathered around the transparent-topped container, peering down into the shimmering, misted interior

Krysty wiped the glass with a hand and stared at what was forming.

"It doesn't look much like   Oh, Gaia!"

Abe spun violently away and threw up all over the floor

Dean turned and looked at his father, his dark eyes frightened and bewildered.

J B. took off his glasses and polished them slowly, although they seemed clean enough.

Doc was nodding, seeming surprisingly unsurprised by what lay there. "Happened a lot, I believe," he said quietly.

Ryan glanced at Mildred. "Is it alive?"

"I don't think so. Not what you or I would call alive."

It was as if the contents of a butcher's slab had been poured out into the module, mixed in with the flayed remains of a mad pathologist's postmortem. There wasn't too much that anyone could have identified as being forty-two-year-old Graham Oswald Vair from Mitford City, Wisconsin. Even regular customers of the sports-equipment store where he'd been a clerk wouldn't have found much to recognize.

In the silence Ryan was aghast to realize that the trawled thing was making a sort of sound, a faint, muffled keening, like a tiny kitten trapped inside an old freezer.

"Can you stop it, Mildred?" Ryan asked. "Stop it making that noise."

The woman's face was slack with the horror of the moment. "How?" she whispered.

There was a hissing of air, and the thick cover of the capsule began to lift.

"Send it back, Doc!" Ryan grabbed him by the shoulder. "Now!"

The room began to fill with a noisome, sweet and sickly stench, the smell of blood, ripped flesh and torn intestines.

The old man moved quickly to the nearest keyboard and began to punch in a code. "Override," he said urgently to himself. "Upon my soul I believe that this will do it."

The movement of the lid ceased, and it began to lower again, clicking shut.

The container started to fill with smoke or steam, or the white fumes of complex chemicals. The churning vapors mercifully obscured the hideous spectacle.

When the mist cleared, thirty seconds later, the pod was empty again.

Abe wiped his mouth. "Doc?"

"Yes, my dear Abraham?"

"Got a question."

"I am ready to do my very best to answer it for you."

"That... The thing in... Whatever it was we all saw?"

"What the file records refer to as specimen Dolphin One, do you mean?"

"Yeah. Where's it gone?"

"Back to its place and time of origin, I would imagine. If that is the sort of explanation you would like to hear."

Doc was the calmest of them all, seeming unmoved by the temporal monstrosity that had appeared in their midst.

Krysty hesitated. "Doc?"

"Yes?" he replied, calmly as if he were discussing the delicacy of a sponge cake with the minister's wife at an Amish barn raising.

"Yes. Where's it gone? Will he... Will it go back like he was when he left, or will it be like it was here? You know what I mean?"

"My understanding of this sort of problem leads me to the belief that the answer to your question is simply 'neither.' Neither as he was nor as he became during the malfunctioned transmogrification through the ether."

"Then, where's he gone?" This time the questioner was J.B.

"Nowhere."

"What?"

"And everywhere."

"Come on, Doc."

"Allow me to hypothesize for a moment, my dear John Barrymore. Chronos was just about the most secret of all covert operations. There were errors. Many of them. People who disappeared in the past and never came back. That is an enigma and a mystery. People relish that sort of thing."

Ryan saw it coming. "And they didn't want aborted creatures like that thing we saw popping up all over time and space. That would have meant too many close questions."

Doc beamed and clapped his hands gently together. 'Excellent, Ryan. Your intellect is as acute as ever. Precisely right. So these wretches were... Let us say they were dispersed."

Dean had been struggling gamely to follow the discussion. "So, where's the monster gone now?"

Doc held out both hands. "Here   and there. Everywhere. Now and then. Up and down. In and out. Front and back."

"Maybe we should stop anybody else coming through," Abe said. "My stomach won't take any more of those fucking horrors."

Ryan glanced at the comp clock on the wall. "Fifteen minutes gone since that was triggered. Means the next one'll be coming in to join us in about thirty minutes or so."

"I can't cope with being a part of all this," Mildred said. "I know the Hippocratic oath might not mean too much here in Deathlands, but I still can't lend my word to this."

"Nor me," Abe agreed. "I'm goin' out the other room until it's over and done. Call me when there's no more of them."

Ryan insisted that Dean go and join them, much to the boy's disgust.

"Twenty-three minutes," J.B. announced, checking his wrist chron.

THE PROCESS WAS REMARKABLY similar to that of Dolphin One.

The whirring and the infinite speed of the displays on the screen was the same as before.

But the result when Dolphin Two came through was strangely different.

Chapter Fourteen

"Thank all the blessed saints!" Doc straightened. "It seems that the experiment has been successful this time around."

The mist was clearing, enabling the four of them to make out the shape of a human being lying in the capsule.

"What was her name?" J.B. asked.

Doc quickly checked the screen. "Dolores Mae Melville, aged thirty-nine. From Tehachapi, California. She worked as nursing auxiliary in a children's home in Los Angeles. No living relatives."

"What's she wearing?" Krysty shook her head. "Got a feeling about this, lover," she said doubtfully "Not a good feeling."

Now they could all see what the trawling device had delivered.

It was a woman, slightly overweight, with round cheeks and dimpled chin. Her hair was intensely black, cropped short to her nape. Her eyes were closed.

But what caught their attention was the bizarre way that Dolores Mae Melville was dressed.

Her feet were covered in little black slippers and her legs were bare to the knee. She had on a sort of nightdress of coarse linen material, pale yellow, with a dark green hem.

Over it all was a jacket of stiff black leather. It buckled around her neck, while another buckled strap disappeared between her plump thighs. At waist level there were chromed steel rings set immovably into the leather, with single wrist cuffs attached to them. The woman's hands had been pinioned tightly into those steel cuffs.

"Mildred mentioned something about there being an old prison at Tehachapi," Krysty said. "You think that's where—"

She was interrupted by the automatic lifting of the transparent lid, the noise and movement seeming to wake the trawled subject.

Her eyelids lifted, revealing tiny marbles of black jet that rolled around as she took in her surroundings and the four strange faces that were staring down at her

"Who are you? Where am I? Has Old Smoky already taken me?"

"Who's Old Smoky?" Ryan asked.

The woman's voice, little-girlish, faltered. "I don't know where I am."

Krysty leaned forward. "You're quite safe," she said. "We'll talk about it some more when you feel stronger."

A gentle smile blossomed on the prim, pursed mouth. "That would be nice. Can you let me out of this silly jacket, please?"

Doc started to reach in. "It would be my pleasure, madam."

"Hold it," Ryan ordered. "Just wait a couple of minutes, Doc."

"Just who..." she began, then stopped. "Have you rescued me?"

"Sort of." J.B. pushed his hat back. "Mind telling us who you are?"

"Don't you know?"

Doc was puzzled. "Of course. I don't understand why... Your name—"

"Let her tell us, Doc," Ryan interrupted.

"Melville. Dolores Mae Melville."

"Why've you got that straitjacket on?" Krysty asked.

There was a long moment's hesitation, and the little black eyes moved around the room. "Been ill," she finally said. "Real poorly. Fever. They thought—"

"They?"

The eyes met Krysty's. "The folk at the hospital wanted me not to hurt myself."

"The hospital at Tehachapi?" Ryan watched the woman carefully, aware that something wasn't quite right, but unable to pin down just what it was that was niggling at him.

"Hospital? Sure. Now, before we go for the sixty-four thousand dollars, can you get me out of here? It's real uncomfortable."

Doc looked at Ryan. "If you've quite completed the interrogation, my dear Ryan? I have the greatest personal sympathy for how she must feel after being trawled like this.''

Ryan hesitated, glancing over at Krysty, who very slowly shook her head.

"Just a minute longer, Doc.'' He leaned over the capsule, aware of the strong scent of the woman's sweat, rank and feral like a cougar's lair.

"You done with staring, mister? I don't know who you think you are, but there's laws even for people like—'' She clamped her mouth shut like a trap.

"People like you, Dolores? What are people like you? What kind of hospital was it in Tehachapi? How come they got you chained tighter than a triple-crazed mutie?''

The woman swallowed and wriggled in the cramped confines of the container. Ryan noticed that the tendons in both wrists were standing out as she braced herself against the steel of the cuffs.

"Just let me out, and I'll sing sweet as any sparrow. I don't know what's going on, I honest-to-God don't. You drug me and take me out of the . . . hospital, and bring me to this weird place. When my attorney hears about this, he'll start slapping writs on you faster than you can piss.''

The little-girl voice was disappearing, being replaced by something harder.

"Get some details on the screen, Doc,'' Ryan ordered. "Let's see about this hospital and why they got her trussed like this.''

"Let me go first." Now there was definitely a note of desperation and anger there, which even Doc picked up on.

"It should only take a short while, my dear lady. Be patient."

Again the old man's gnarled fingers pecked at the keyboard, like a flock of hungry birds.

"I was in the hospital. That's why I'm in this restraint."

"Want me to put this through a voice coder?" Doc asked.

"Yeah. Do it. Easier than all trying to read that little print."

"I feel sick. I'm goin' to faint if you don't let me out."

Ryan turned around. "Lady, close your mouth awhile."

The screen showed a "ready" instruction, and Doc pressed the Transmit key.

The voice was female, soft and gentle, each word allocated equal measure by the comp control, which gave it an odd, unworldly sound.

"Subject of projected Dolphin Two trawl is Dolores Mae Melville. Her age is—"

Ryan pressed the Stop key. "Take it forward, Doc. To where she's been and why she's there."

The voice resumed. "After sentence of death was imposed, the subject was taken to the State Penal Institute for Women at Tehachapi, southeast of Bakersfield, California.''

"Why?" Krysty asked. "Why was she sentenced to death? What did she do?"

Doc located that part of the information disk and accessed it.

Ryan was aware, though he didn't look around, that Dean, Mildred and Abe had reentered the control area and were standing listening in silence to what was going on.

"The first of the admitted twenty-six homicide victims, though the police authorities believe from forensic evidence that Dolores Melville's total score might exceed fifty, was Tony Lu. Aged nine, oldest of all the known murdered boys.''

Krysty's face was set like stone as Doc paused the computer. "She killed fifty little boys!" she said, her voice flat and cold.

"Just a little more, Doc," Ryan said, managing to control his surging rage.

"As with the other victims, it is believed that Dolores Melville abducted him from school. After extensive torture, involving razors and needles, she strangled the child. The corpse, like the others, was castrated either on the point of death or shortly after and the genitals preserved in alcohol. A label attached in the convicted woman's own hand gave details of the victim and date of his murder ''

"Fifty," Doc groaned. "Little boys. Oh, you monster ."

Behind them, the woman had begun to speak, spewing a torrent of violent, sexual filth, aimed at them all, the police, the judge, the jury, the prison.

It was an endless gloating sewer of vileness, of how she had taken her pleasures and how the children had suffered abominations at her hands.

Ryan pressed the key marked Cancel, closing off the screen and silencing the comp voice. He drew the SIG-Sauer from its holster and walked to the capsule, pressed the muzzle to the side of the raving woman's forehead and squeezed the trigger once.

There was a splatter of brains and bone, and the pumping of blood, slowing to a steady trickle, the noise loud in the stillness.

He holstered the automatic and glanced at the clock. "Twenty minutes to the next subject," he said. "Two down and one to go."

Chapter Fifteen

There was very little conversation while they waited for the arrival of Dolphin Three, last of the time-trawl subjects.

Mildred had gone across and lowered the lid of the capsule onto the corpse of the demented killer.

"I've seen crazy in my time, and I've seen some pure wickedness. I'm not sure I've ever seen them so combined in a single being."

As the clock ticked around, Ryan had gone to Doc and asked him quietly to check out some basic facts on the last of the time jumpers.

"We've already had a bloody pile of torn meat and a murderous crazie. Best we know a bit more what to expect this time."

Doc nodded. It was all too obvious that the previous arrivals had shaken him badly. All his febrile excitement had deserted him and he moved slowly, like a man trapped in a nightmare.

The screen cleared for a moment, then came up with a scant half page of information, more or less repeating what they'd already seen.

"Is that it?"

Doc tried alternative ways of accessing the files, but came up with nothing more. "Looks like it, I'm afraid," he said.

"Comes from way up in the high mountains. Be well snowed in at that altitude, the time of year he's trawled."

"An oblate from birth. A nineteen year old virgin."

THE INFORMATION WAS so absurdly limited that Ryan was puzzled. How had the Chronos Project team selected this young man as one of their victims? What was the basis for their choices?

To pick a convicted serial killer who was presumably under sentence of death made some kind of sense. But this Michael Brother was so wildly different. Why pick him?

The clock was showing less than five minutes before the final subject was due to make his appearance in the last of the glass-topped pods. Everyone was tense with the waiting.

"Mebbe this is wrong," Abe said, biting at the ragged corner of a fingernail.

"Wrong?" J.B. asked. "What do you think's wrong about it?"

"Don't know. God's laws?"

"God didn't know all that much about time jumping, Abe."

"Still, look at what's come through. The contents of a mammoth burger and the biggest triple sickie in Deathlands."

"This one'll be better." The Armorer nodded sagely at the lean figure of the gunner. "Trust me, Abe, trust me."

He got a laugh in response. "You remember what Trader said about someone who says that? Says to trust him? Trader used to say you trust him then you find that trust leads one place."

Ryan had heard the saying many times and he completed it for Abe. "To the grave."

"Sixty seconds, lover." Krysty took Ryan by the hand. "Know I had a bad feeling about that last one? Real bad?"

"Yeah."

"This time I got a good feeling."

"Fifty seconds," Doc said.

They all moved to circle the last of the row of capsules.

Ryan felt a wave of excitement. If only this one could be all right. A lad of nineteen would be well informed about what had really happened, and would be brimming with news about life in those lost days before sky-dark.

"Thirty seconds."

"I should've taken a leak."

"Go take one, Mildred," J.B. said.

"And miss the fun?"

"Fifteen seconds."

Ryan watched the digital numbers on the clock as they melted and reformed.

'Ten seconds.'' Doc was rubbing his hands together, making his knuckles crack in the tense stillness. "Five and four and three and two and one and zero.''

The machinery began to hum as it had before, and the interior of the module filled with a surge of white mist.

Ryan was fascinated by the unbelievably complex technical side of the process, wondering if this was what the interior of a mat-trans unit looked like during an actual jump. Certainly the mist seemed similar to ones that he'd noticed in the gateway chambers before being sucked down the twisting tunnels of unconsciousness.

"Something there,'' Dean said, pressing his nose against the glass. "And it feels bastard cold inside it.''

"Don't touch,'' Ryan said absently.

Now he could make out something appearing, seeming like layers of crystals forming one on top of the next at infinite speed.

It was a strange sensation, the reversal of a speeded-up vid of an animal decomposing and shrinking to nothing.

'Nearly done,'' Doc said, his voice hardly a whisper. "Looks like he's come through the transferral safe. Whoever he is.''

Now the mist was clearing and they could all make out the human figure that lay peacefully inside the container.

It was male, with a dark skin that might indicate some native Indian blood in the background. Long black hair was held off the forehead with a strip of crimson silk. The physical description seemed to be about right. Ryan would have put the young man at around two inches shy of six feet, and one-forty looked the correct weight. He was slimly built but fairly muscular.

He was barefoot, wearing a rough brown robe that came halfway below his knees. It was tied around his middle with a thick knotted cord. Ryan noticed that there was a slim-bladed knife sheathed on his left hip and another on the right.

"Least he looks normal," Abe said. "Strange clothes, though."

"It resembles the simple habit of a member of a monastic order," Doc replied. "Though twin daggers would hardly seem to be the apposite apparel of a true man of the cloth. A case of 'o tempora! o mores!' I suppose."

"What's that mean?" Dean asked, fascinated as ever by the old man's more arcane sayings.

"It means, young man, that the times they are a'changing, but they are not necessarily a'changing for the best."

The time lock clicked open, and the lid of the capsule began to slide smoothly upward.

"He's so clean," Abe said with a mixture of fascination and repugnance.

The top ceased moving and there was a moment of nothing.

The young man's eyes remained firmly closed, though they could all see his chest was rising and falling with a regular respiration.

"Michael," Doc said, "it's time for you to wake up."

The eyes fluttered but didn't open. But his lips moved. "Time for compline, Brother Athanasius? I'm afraid that I must have dozed off for a moment. One hundred Hail Marys for me."

"Open your eyes, Michael." Doc glanced at the others. "He'll be very shocked when he comes around."

Ryan nodded. "Sure." He raised his voice. "Wake up, Michael!"

The eyes opened, showing long lashes. A faint smile came to the young man's lips as he looked at the staring circle of faces.

"I see I'm not in my cell, sleeping, and none of you seem to resemble good old Brother Athanasius. So, who are you and where am I?"

Ryan answered. "Names come a little later. Your name is Michael Brother?"

The smile widened. "No."

"No?"

"No."

"Then, what are you called?"

"I think the questions should be coming from me. But, at least I'll solve this riddle for you. Not Michael Brother."

Krysty realized first. "Course. You're called Brother Michael, aren't you?"

The smile began to fade. "Yes, I am. But this is not the retreat. No part of it. You have drugged me and removed me from my own brothers. Are you demons of the netherworld?"

"No. We mean you no harm. Look, do you want to get up from there?"

"Yes. My thanks to you." Even lying flat on his back, he managed a courteous bow. He took Ryan's hand to pull himself upright, swinging his legs out onto the floor and standing without the least sign of discomfort.

"You feel okay?" J.B. asked.

"Okay? Yes, I think I feel 'okay,' as you put it. Thank you."

Brother Michael had a strange, slightly stilted and formal way of speaking.

"Best thing is that we go through into the other room here." Ryan pointed. "And we can tell you who we are. Where you are. What's been going down."

The young man nodded. "Though I am very much an innocent in the ways of the world, even I can tell that there is something strange about you and about this place. I shall be glad to hear your stories, brother. Very glad."

He glanced around him, with a wide-eyed curiosity As he started to follow Ryan he stumbled and nearly fell. Mildred went to steady him but he pulled away, knocking a chair spinning into the wall.

"No!" he shrieked. "I must not be touched by a woman! Not ever."

Mildred glanced at Ryan, who'd whirled around and half drawn his SIG-Sauer. "Looks like we'll have plenty to talk about," she said.

Chapter Sixteen

Ryan had done most of the talking, helped out by Doc on some of the more technical elements of the time-trawling operation.

Brother Michael sat and listened to them with a patient smile on his face. It occurred to Krysty that he would have put the same expression in place if he'd been humoring a band of fairly harmless lunatics.

The young man didn't speak at all, simply nodding now and then, glancing from face to face as if to reassure himself that everyone was going along with the same bizarre jest.

Finally Ryan had finished. He looked at the newcomer's bland disbelief, aware that he might just as well have been pushing water uphill for the past hour.

"That's it," he said to Brother Michael. "You know who we are, where we are and when we are. Anything you want me to run over again for you? Anything you don't understand?"

"I don't understand everything. I do understand nothing."

"Shall I go through it all again for you?"

"No." He shook his head and sighed. "We have been told of the Temptation of the Blessed Anthony.

Of the Torment of the Blessed Beubo of Ishmaelia. This must be something like that. But why I should have the honor of being so selected is something beyond my poor comprehension.''

Mildred spoke to Michael. "You've had a great upset. Probably you are, clinically, in deep shock right now. But you mustn't block out what's happened to you, son. Believe me.''

"Oh, I believe some things. I believe that your names are Ryan Cawdor, Dean Cawdor, J. B. Dix, Abe and Doc Tanner.'' He avoided looking at the two women. "And Krysty and Mildred.''

"Well, that's a start,'' Abe said.

"I believe that matins is followed in the day by prime. Prime is followed by terce. Terce by sext. And sext by none. None comes before vespers. And after vespers it ends with compline. So the day runs. And the one before it and the one after it. Every day exactly the same.''

"Those are what are known as the canonical hours,'' Doc explained. "Brother Michael's day would have been split up by those set periods for worship. Is that right?''

"Yes, it is. You have a certain wisdom beneath that grizzled pate.''

"Well, thank you, young fellow, for that wholehearted vote of approval.''

"I do not believe your evil lies about being taken from my own time and place to a ruined world, a hundred years in the future. I cannot believe that. I *will* not believe that."

Ryan realized that the teenager was on the brink of tears.

"Why should we lie to you, son?" he said gently. "When we get out of here, we should be somewhere near where old Chicago was. Then you'll see for yourself that we're telling you nothing but the whole, simple truth."

"The retreat of Nil-Vanity... where I was taken on the tenth day of my life and where I've lived ever since. You say it is gone. That Brother Athanasius is old bones. Wise Brother Cadfael sleeps now with the worms. Abbot Padraig gone. No."

Ryan reached to touch Brother Michael on the arm, but his hand was brushed away by the young man, moving with an unbelievable speed of reflex.

J.B. blinked. "You see that, Ryan?" he said quietly

"No. Felt him move but I never saw it. He's very fast."

"Of course I am fast. As a student of Tao-Tain-Do I have trained my body to do what I wish."

"Brother Michael?" Dean said.

"Yes, child?" He favored the boy with a broad smile. "What is it?"

"You think we're making up this about Death-lands? So, where do you think you are if we're making it all up?"

There was a flicker of doubt across his serene face. His eyes narrowed slightly "I don't know "

Ryan punched his right fist into his left hand. 'No point taking this further, Michael."

"I prefer my proper name of Brother Michael, if you don't mind, Ryan Cawdor."

"I don't mind. But we have to get moving out of this redoubt. Then, mebbe tonight, we can talk some more. And you can tell us all you know about the world you've just left."

"Nil-Vanity, you mean?"

"No, no. The world outside it."

Michael smiled, again with that patronizing expression of having to suffer fools. "Simply answered. I knew nothing at all about the world outside."

"Nothing?"

"Nothing."

"You never went outside?" Krysty asked.

"Never "

"Vids? TV? Books? Papers? Mags?" Ryan couldn't believe their rotten luck.

Brother Michael shook his head to every question. 'Knowledge of worldly matters was totally forbidden. I am as a child, and I see as a child and I think as a child. Only then can I properly serve the Lord God Almighty, Maker of Heaven and Earth."

Abe spit on the floor. "Boy!" he exclaimed. "Have we trawled us a triple dickhead!"

BROTHER MICHAEL was content to walk back with them through the vast, echoing emptiness of the redoubt, glancing from side to side, and occasionally shaking his head as if he were living through some involved private joke, until they neared the outer level where the garage was situated.

He stopped, holding up his hand. "I wish to pray for guidance," he said, his voice shaking. "I am beginning to believe your tales and that is foolish and wrong."

Ryan sighed. "Sure. If it makes you feel better, Michael."

The young man dropped to his knees in the center of the neon-lighted passage, revealing the dusty, hard soles of his feet, making it clear that he had probably never worn shoes in his young life.

"Blessed Father, guide my steps. I am lost in the valley of the shadow and I fear evil. Show me if these men and... These men are honest and are what they say. Lord, I beg you."

He stood and brushed flakes of dirt off his bare legs.

"Better?" J.B. asked.

"I don't know. I don't think I know anything, you see."

"Was there never any evil in the place you've come from?" Krysty asked.

"No!" came the shocked response.

"None, in nineteen years?"

"No. Apart from one or two times when the sin of theft had sneaked into our portals."

"That was all?"

"I recall a killing."

"One?"

"Two, I think. Perhaps three. And there have been occasions when lust and perverted depravity have encouraged the brothers into wicked ways." He paused. "Both with each other and, sometimes, with our animal kindred."

Abe laughed, the sound harsh and flat. "Does he mean what I think he means? Animals!" He slapped the youth on the shoulder from behind, but Michael dodged it easily. "Be better off with us than with thieves, killers and sheep shaggers, son."

RYAN AND KRYSTY had fallen to the back of the group, talking quietly about their new recruit.

"Wish there was some way we could convince him we're telling the truth," Ryan said. "Save him freaking off his head about us."

"If we really are near Chicago, then the ruins might make him believe that we're truly on the side of the angels."

Ryan didn't reply for a while. "I never seen anyone so quick with his hands," he finally said.

"Never 'saw,' not 'seen.' No, nor have I. Think it's this strange skill it mentioned on the comp screens? One with the funny name."

"Could be. If he stays with us, I figure we'll find out."

"Least Doc's happy. Look at him talking away there, nineteen to the dozen."

The old man was walking right alongside the teenager, head half-turned, speaking insistently to him.

"Looks like he's telling secrets." Krysty smiled.

"Right," Ryan agreed, unable to decide quite why he felt a pang of unease at seeing Doc locked so tight to Brother Michael.

THE INTERNAL SEC DOORS to the main outer garage in the redoubt stood wide open.

Inside was a fifteen-man war wag, fully armed and topped up with fuel.

None of them could believe their good luck.

Chapter Seventeen

Like many of the battered war wags that were still laboring their wheezing ways around Deathlands, this vehicle was an armored personnel carrier, based on the original M-75s and M-59s of the 1950s. Over the next fifty years there was a range of developments, involving aluminum and steel-hulled APCs.

Some more successful than others.

The chain of vehicles had been of particular interest to J B. after he'd come across a ragged book in an old store called Needful Things, near Vicksburg, that listed the models of the wags and all their variants.

It took J.B. only a couple of minutes of walking around the dark green-brown hunk of metal to deduce precisely what it was.

"The M-900," he decided. "Got four light machine guns, two front and back and one each side. They're Browning 50-caliber weapons and spew out five hundred rounds a minute. Accurate enough, up to about a mile or more if the wag's not moving."

"What sort of speed and range has the wag got?" Abe asked.

J.B. leaned a hand against it with a vaguely proprietorial air "Fifty miles an hour on a good flat highway Twenty or less over broken ground. Range probably around four hundred miles. More if you take it slower and easier "

"There's some cans of gas against the side there," called Dean, who'd been scouting around the cavernous building.

Apart from the single wag, standing four-square at its center, the garage was empty. Patches of oil stained the concrete, and the walls were chipped and scraped. But it looked like it had probably been evacuated by the soldiers immediately before their own group chilling.

"Are we going to ride in that tin box?" Brother Michael asked.

"You ever been in a wag?" Mildred queried. "No, I guess you probably haven't."

"I have heard about them. Faster than a man can run, though I have seen Brother Rupert in full flight and I can hardly believe a machine could go with more speed."

"You haven't lived till you've ridden a war wag at max revs over a ribbon blacktop," Abe said. "Right, Ryan?"

"Times with Trader I'd have changed places with those outside." Ryan grinned. "The heat and the oil and the fumes and the rocketing and bouncing. Not the best fun in the world."

Abe stopped smiling, glancing across the garage at Ryan. "You reckon he's gone? Really gone? Do you?"

"Trader?" he asked, though he knew who the middle-aged gunner meant.

"Yeah."

"Fireblast, Abe! How should I know? You saw him last."

"I know Know he looked like a man heading out to climb aboard that last train west. But he'd been ill for months."

"Years," J.B. interrupted, jumping down from the casing of the wag.

"Right, years. But when he walked off that last time, he   I don't know, fuck it! But he didn't seem off to buy the farm "

"Guess we'll likely never know " The Armorer turned to Ryan. "She's filled up. Keys in her. We can stock up with extra gas and be out of this place in five minutes."

"I'd like to go back to Nil-Vanity." Brother Michael's voice was trembling, and his lips quivered as if he were about to burst into tears. "If you've got me here, like you say, then you can send me right back. I'll miss the clam chowder and kedgeree for supper tonight."

"One thing you have to learn," Krysty said, "is that in Deathlands there's not ever any going back. Never."

"Just one time around and then they hammer down the lid on the box," Mildred added. "I'm afraid it's true, young man. I come from your time as well. That's a story that can wait. Occasionally I'd love to return and see my friends and folks. But I know it's impossible. Doc'd say the same."

"I have been talking to Brother Michael about that very subject, convincing him that I would do anything at all to go back to my dearest wife and children. Anything."

"But it's impossible," Mildred prompted.

Doc hesitated for the tiniest fraction of a moment before replying, and Ryan again felt the short hairs prickling at his nape.

"Yes, impossible."

A FEW MINUTES had slipped by while J.B. supervised the stowing of as many spare cans of gas as they could stock aboard.

"I'll stay here," the boy insisted.

"You die if you do."

Michael shook his head stubbornly. "Better that I pass to the realm beyond while still in a state of grace."

"Bullshit!" J.B. faced up to him, eyes narrowed with anger, cheeks pale. "You make me want to bastard puke! Religious crazies! I've had them up to here." He touched his chin. "Learn just one lesson today, you brainless prick!"

"Don't you speak to me like that!"

There was a spark of temper and the smooth face was furrowed.

J.B. nodded. "Better, son. More human than all that cant about heaven."

"What's the lesson I should learn?"

"That today's real. Yesterday's real. But you'll see a time when your tomorrow doesn't come and you're chilled. Cold meat. Dead. So you do the best you can for today. Understand?''

''Yes, sure.''

''So, no more crap about staying here.''

''Are you going to force me?''

''If we have to.''

Brother Michael shook his head. ''I do not understand. You take me from all I know and tell me I can't return. But when I wish to die, you prevent that. What do you want?''

J.B. grinned. ''Part of riding with Ryan Cawdor and company. Nobody ever knows what anyone wants. But I want to get out of this redoubt and on the road while there's still some daylight left.''

''I'll second that,'' Mildred said.

''And I'll third it,'' Dean shouted. ''Let's go war wagging!''

Chapter Eighteen

It was always a relief to find that the simple number coding was the same on all of the redoubts that they'd encountered.

The sequence on the main outer sec steel doors was five, three, two, reversed when you wanted to close them.

J.B. started up the engine, the deep-throated roar filling the concrete box of the garage and making Brother Michael press his hands over his ears with an expression of horrified pain.

"Is this the sound of the future?" he cried. "It is the triumphant screaming of the Lords of Chaos glorying as they mutilate and devour the babes of the earth."

"Lords of Chaos had their bite at the planet nearly a hundred years ago, Brother Michael," Mildred said bitterly.

"Come on," the Armorer shouted. "Get aboard and we'll roll."

Dean hopped in through the open doors of the rear of the smoking vehicle, followed by Abe. Doc stepped in with a surprisingly insouciant air, like a Regency dandy with his cane. Mildred went next, turning toward the young man, who shook his head.

"I would rather die here and now than travel in the belly of the Beast of Revelations."

"Then die," Ryan said. "Had enough. Sorry for what happened to you, but you're stuck here for the rest of your life. Stick with us, and we'll all do our best for you. Stay behind and you die of hunger. Mebbe thirst. Could last a week. Two."

"But you'd be insane by then," Krysty added. "Come with us, Michael."

"I can't be with a woman," he said, his voice shuddering with pent-up horror.

Ryan went to punch in the code by the sec doors, waiting a moment to be certain that the grinding of the massive gears had begun. He gestured to Krysty to climb in the back of the APC as J.B. began to move it toward the entrance, the tracks grating along the stone floor.

"Last chance, Michael. Fireblast! You have to take a chance now and again, lad."

The wag was moving at a slow walking pace, J.B. aiming it toward the center of the slowly rising sec doors.

"Better seal the doors in case there's trouble outside," he called, his voice crackling over the driver's amp mike.

Ryan peered out into bright sunlight, unable to see anything beyond a range of high walls. As the wag emerged, he followed it and immediately locked in the closing code of two, three, five.

The wag was stopped, engine ticking over, still belching oily smoke from its exhaust. Dean was on the seat nearest the rear doors, looking anxiously out toward his father. His gaze passed Ryan, focusing on the huge titanium-steel sec doors as they dropped closer to the floor.

"He's not coming, Dad."

Ryan shook his head, seeing that the barefoot teenager was still standing where he'd left him, his face immobile.

"So long," Ryan called.

Brother Michael made a gesture with his hands that could have been the sign of the Cross, but Ryan was already turning toward the wag and the rest of the group.

He was only a couple of steps away when Dean pointed behind him.

"Dad! Look!"

The doors, painted a mat gray, were less than two feet from the bottom.

Underneath them, it was possible to see the bare feet and the ankles of the nineteen-year-old, moving so fast he seemed to be a blur.

"Never make it," Abe said.

But he hadn't even finished the sentence when Brother Michael appeared, seeming to explode through the shrinking space as though a frag gren had propelled him outward.

"Upon my soul!" Doc exclaimed, his jaw dropping almost to his chest.

"Gaia!" Krysty glanced at Ryan, her face a study in amazement.

For a moment of frozen time, Ryan had a vision of Jak Lauren. The uncanny reflexes of the young albino boy had startled him when they first met.

But Brother Michael was even quicker.

It crossed Ryan's mind, as something to store away and examine later, that the stranger could possibly be some sort of mutie. Or even, perhaps, a kind of humanoid.

J.B. was holding the wag on the throttle, glancing back over his shoulder to see what was happening at the rear.

"He coming?"

Ryan jumped in over the low step, reaching out a hand toward the young man, who took it and joined the others.

"Yeah," Ryan called, "he's coming along."

As the one-eyed man sat down, the sec doors receding behind them, J.B. operated the control to close the rear entrance to the wag.

"Air-conditioning's fine," he said through the intercom.

"You got scanners? Pipe them to the screens in back here."

The engine changed tone as J.B. put it into neutral. "You come up here, Ryan. Check out the master dash and look after some of the stuff. I'll be busy just driving her."

There was good light in the back of the APC, and the ride was surprisingly steady. Ryan used the numerous handgrips to move past the others to the second driver's seat alongside the slight figure of J.B.

The windshield ahead was armored glass, with fine layers of protective wire set within it. There were also steel shutters that slid into place at a touch of one of the control buttons by the driver's hand. The dash was a mass of flickering lights, dials and gauges.

Ryan looked down at them. "You sure you can drive this?"

"Sure. Might take awhile to get good at it. Got basic panel like War wag One did. Think we ought to have the LMGs manned?"

Ryan squinted ahead. All they could see was a wide highway covered in heaps of old, dried leaves. It was lined by brick walls around fifteen feet in height, topped with the rusted remnants of coils of razored wire.

"Let's get to the top and see what we see. Then we'll see."

J.B. tapped down with his foot, and the engine faltered for a moment then roared again.

"Knew how to make them in those days," he said. "Just pressed the starter and off she goes. Been sitting in that garage for a hundred years, give or take. Waiting for us."

Ryan had been scanning the controls, finding the row of switches that operated the tiny sec cameras that were set into the front, back and sides of the wag. Their pictures piped into the rear compartment so that the soldiers could all see what was going on around them.

"I confess that this bears precious little resemblance to the Chicago that I once knew," Doc said.

J.B. pointed at a comp map showing on a green panel immediately in front of him. "Says Chicago on this, Doc."

"Believe half of what you see and nothing of what you read," the old man riposted.

"You ready to move on out?" J.B. changed into first gear.

Ryan nodded, bracing himself as they began to roll up the incline.

"THE MAP SHOW where we are?"

There was a tiny red blip shimmering on the map, near the bottom right corner. J.B. gestured toward it. "Sure. That's us."

Ryan bent and stared at it. "Can't read it. Looks like ant writing."

"Must be a mag button someplace."

"Oh, yeah. Here. Can blow up any part of the grid bigger."

He moved the cursor around, finding it difficult against the gentle rocking and rolling of the wag, eventually succeeding in magnifying the part that showed the bright dot of crimson.

"Lake Michigan behind us. No, more or less all about. We're on a kind of small island."

"Michigan seems more like a dream to me now," said Mildred, directly behind him. "It took me four days to hitch from... Damn! Can't remember what comes after that."

Ryan concentrated on the comp-graph map. "Looks like the redoubt was concealed under something called the Central District Filtration Plant," he said. "The main part of the city should lie more or less ahead of us."

"I feel sick." The plaintive voice was Brother Michael's.

Ryan turned in his seat and looked at the newcomer. His face was pale, with a sheen of sweat across his forehead and cheeks.

"Want to throw up?" Ryan asked.

"No. I shall draw upon my inner resources to heal myself."

Abe laughed. "I could do with some of that inner-resource shit next time I get skulled in a gaudy drinker."

The wag still rolled up the seemingly endless slope toward the bright sky.

"Ambient temp's just below fifteen," J.B. said, checking yet another of the liquid-crystal displays on the dashboard.

Ryan nodded. "Looks like we're nearly out of the perimeter."

"Can we have the machine guns manned, please?" J.B. said into his throat mike.

Krysty moved to the front blaster and Mildred took the rear-mounted weapon. Doc climbed up and steadied himself on the starboard side of the vehicle, bracing his shoulder to the butt of the LMG.

"Dad?"

"Yeah."

"Thanks. I'll give it a real hot ace on the line, Dad."

"Main thing is you keep the safety locked on until I tell you different."

"Sure."

This time there was a snap of anger in Ryan's voice. "Don't get casual with me, Dean. You've been around long enough to know that if one of us screws up, then we can all get screwed up."

"Yeah."

Ryan was still looking back at his son as he felt the tracks on the wag shudder to a halt.

He heard J.B. whisper, "Dark night, will you look at that?"

Chapter Nineteen

Back in the interior of the vehicle, only Mildred spoke.

"My God! Where...where's it gone? No, there's some mistake, John. Can't be Chicago. It can't be, I tell you. Can't."

Ryan stared out through the windshield at the vista spread before them. The fingers of his right hand were tapping out a slow rhythm on his knee, and he was whistling tunelessly under his breath.

It hadn't really occurred to him before that he'd never been close to Chicago. During the long years of riding with the Trader, they'd always skirted around the southern end of the big lake. Oddly he'd never thought to ask why.

Now he knew.

Out of habit he glanced at the tiny rad counter fixed to his lapel.

But it was shaded somewhere between the green and the yellow. At least they hadn't emerged into the middle of one of the diminishing number of hot-spot regions in Deathlands.

"Looks like a piece of charcoal twenty miles by ten," J.B. said.

The Armorer had never been known as a particularly imaginative man, given to picturesque images of the world.

What he said seemed to Ryan to be the absolute, simple truth.

Most everything they could see was black.

A landscape as dark as the wing of a raven, pitted and devastated.

"Where's it all gone?" Mildred was on the edge of tears. "We sure that we're in the right place, J.B.?"

"Comp map can't be wrong."

"Chicago?" Mildred had stood up and was leaning a hand on Ryan's shoulder, peering dumbly out of the windshield.

"Can I get out?" Brother Michael was fumbling with the locked doors at the back of the APC.

"Nothing to see." J.B.'s voice was flat and unemotional.

"Look at the screens," Dean said. "See everything there, all four sides."

Behind them was the ramp and the high stone walls leading down toward the hidden redoubt.

To left and right were patches of scrubby bushes, with glimpses of what seemed to be water glistening behind them.

And ahead of the wag stretched the vast, charred expanse of what had once been the Windy City.

"Chicago," Doc breathed, his voice hoarse with emotion. "Founded in the year of Our Lord, 1673. The French priests, Fathers Jolliet and Marquette, discov-

ered the river that the Indians—were they the Algon-
quin?—called the Checagou. Place of wild onions, it
meant. So the history books tell us."

Mildred was also on the edge of tears. "Remember
Carl Sandburg? 'Hog butcher to the world.' And Mrs.
O'Leary's cow. Started the great fire. The wonder years
of the Bears. I was here one January day with an uncle. An Episcopalian minister. Only time I heard him
use a profanity. Said that the wind off the lake was like
a whetted knife and it made him feel colder than a well-
digger's ass."

"I want to get out," Brother Michael repeated.
"These pictures in the boxes are a trick."

"Open the rear doors," Ryan said quietly. "Can't do
harm. Scanners are all negative."

"No place much for any hostiles to hide," the Armorer agreed, reaching forward to operate the rear sec-
door controls.

The fresh cold air surged into the APC and the interior grew lighter. The teenager scrambled eagerly out
and walked a few paces on the narrow blacktop to the
front of the wag. Hands on hips, he took in lung-filling
gulps of the morning air and stared out across the
dreadful blasted wilderness.

Ryan leaned his hands on his chin, aware that Krysty
had moved to stand right behind him, her head close to
his.

"Some kind of massive incendiary missiles?" she
asked.

J.B. favored her with a rare, thin smile. "Sure wasn't neutron nuking, was it?"

They'd all seen the odd phenomenon of centers of population hit by the more sophisticated Soviet weaponry during the shortest, and last, world war, neutron missiles that would take out all life-forms within thirty miles of ground zero but would leave every building standing.

The idea was that the winning armies would be able to invade and find much of their prize was still inhabitable, without any kind of lethal, lingering radiation.

Great idea.

Except that the Americans and their allies also had neutron missiles.

And nearly everyone was dead anyway.

So there weren't any invading armies left, and nothing very much worth invading, anywhere in the world.

"Kid's mebbe not going to make it," J.B. observed. "Shock's been too big for him to handle."

"Could make it with our help," Krysty said.

"Well built. Good shoulders on him. And he's triple quick."

Ryan agreed with J.B., nodding. "Can't just let him wander off. Some gutter scum'd slit his throat in the first hour."

The boy turned toward them, holding his hands out in a gesture of helplessness. The light wind was tugging at his black hair, rippling the hem of his long brown robe.

"Oh, Gaia!" Krysty pushed past Dean, who was jumping out of the back of the wag, and walked across the ringing highway toward Brother Michael.

From inside the vehicle, the rumble of the engine made it impossible to hear what was being said, but they could all see the woman, hair like living flames, leaning forward intently. Her hand gestured toward the midnight ruins of the city and back toward the watchers in the armored wag.

The young oblate was listening, occasionally shaking his head and half turning away from her, then returning his eyes to hers.

"I do not believe that any of you here can possibly begin to comprehend the madness that surges through that poor boy's brain."

"Mebbe we shouldn't have gone ahead with the trawling, Doc?"

"No, my dear John, I cannot agree with you on that. The apparatus had been set by other hands in other days. Science must step forward or it will atrophy and die. I would be the first to proselytize on its behalf, despite the scandalous results."

"What's that 'prostitute' word, Doc?" Abe asked. "You mean you been with whores?'

"The men and women who worked on Chronos project might well have merited such a title, my dear Abraham." Doc laughed. "Indeed they did. But they... What were we discussing?"

"Whether we should have trawled the kid," Ryan replied.

"Ah, yes. If you will permit me a small play on words, I think time will tell."

"We should have blown up the whole complex," Mildred said.

"No! Upon my... No. I think we should not."

"Look. Krysty's bringing him back." J.B. pointed through the shield.

Ryan rolled down the ob window on his side. "He still with us?"

The young man answered himself. "Just for a little time."

THE ENGINE FALTERED AGAIN as J.B. gave it the gun. He eased his foot off, allowing it to idle for a few seconds.

"Surprising it goes at all," he said. "Sure made them to last."

Ryan leaned across and studied the comp map that shimmered on the dash. "We going to go out across the ville? Or we can head north or south along the line of the lake?"

Doc cleared his throat. "I have been thinking, my friends. If the truth were told, I have scant interest in viewing the charred corpse of a once-great city. Perhaps you might drop me off here and I'll wait for your return to the redoubt? I assure you that I shall come to no harm."

Ryan turned and stared into the deep, wise, pained eyes. "You know the rules, Doc. Swim together. Sink together. No splitting up unless we have to. Been with us long enough to remember that, Doc." The response surprised him.

"You want to tell me why I have to obey your damned rules and bloody regulations, Ryan?" The old man had his hands on his hips, glaring at him. The knuckles on the lion's head of the sword stick were like hewn ivory.

The response was so unexpected that Ryan didn't know what to say.

J.B. turned around sharply. "You got a hornet in your pants, Doc?"

"No. No, I do not, thank you, John. But I am tired of being treated like some idiot cousin from a backwood holler. My opinions are valid and should be respected. If I wish to return to the redoubt, then I should be allowed to do so."

The trembling anger hung in the air.

Ryan sighed. "Sure. I won't even think of trying to force you to do something you don't want to do, Doc. But you still know the rules. You live within them or you die without them."

For a strange moment Ryan could actually hear the familiar voice of the Trader, saying those very words, on a hundred occasions.

Then, for the first time, it occurred to Ryan as a genuine possibility that his old leader might not be dead.

Doc sniffed and wiped his nose on his sleeve. "I admit that I'm not sure what came over me, Ryan, my dear old companion. Please forget that I ever said such foolishness. It was seeing the chron-temp unit all functioning. Ready to bring someone forward. Or take someone... But let that pass. Yes, let that pass, will you?''

"Sure. Pressure gets to everyone, now and then. Forget it, Doc.''

Ryan turned to J.B. "Let's go take in the town.''

This time the powerful engine roared without a moment's hesitation and the wag jerked forward into motion, past the lapping wavelets at the edge of the clean, sparkling water. On into the blackened wasteland.

Chapter Twenty

The firestorm must have been of the most ferocious intensity.

Ryan had once come across the tattered pages of an old magazine, with pictures and a story of the bombing of a town in a country called Germany, during one of the big twentieth-century wars. Dresden was the name of the place. He recalled that the bombing had been with ordinary hi-ex, but the effects of the saturation attack had been horrific.

Incendiaries had been used in the old part of the city, and the flames had spread and spread. And something the mag called a "firestorm" had begun. The conflagration had become so unbelievably intense that stone and metal had burned and the heat had sucked all of the air in for a distance around, feeding the insatiable fires and suffocating the hiding residents of the city.

Thousands had died, their bodies charred beyond any hope of recognition.

Chicago seemed to be a little like Dresden, but worse.

Infinitely worse.

As they drove up the sloping blacktop from the buried redoubt, there had been an air of excitement within the APC, a feeling that Ryan had often noticed when they emerged into some new and unknown part of Deathlands.

Now that was gone.

The lifeless expanse of black destruction chilled the soul.

According to the map, they had first hung a right onto North Lake Shore Drive, then a left on Pearson Street.

"One way here, J.B., and we're going the wrong direction," Ryan said, trying to lighten the leaden gloom inside the wag.

But the Armorer didn't even reply, leaning forward over the steering wheel, hunched up, eyes fixed on the rubble-strewn highway ahead.

Every now and again they would see what had obviously been one of Chicago's larger buildings. Whereas most had been reduced to level ashes, some stood like Jennison tombstones from the Civil War. Great black monoliths of scorched concrete and twisted girders.

At one point they passed by a series of low bridges, linked by drooping lengths of once-molten metal.

"That's the El," Mildred said.

"What was that?" Dean asked.

"A sort of railway. You know. Wags that ran along an iron highway through the city to take commuters and... Let it pass, Dean, will you?"

Every so often the road would be completely blocked with debris, sometimes piled five stories high. If there was no way around it or over it, then J.B. pushed the wag into reverse and ground back until there was a side route opened up.

"Sure brings back the old times, don't it, guys?" Abe said.

"Yeah," Ryan agreed. It was true. Rattling along on the steel tracks did recall so many occasions, both the good and the bad, riding the huge war wags with the Trader.

"Wish I'd known him longer. Better. Must've been an amazing man." Krysty was standing close to Ryan again, leaning on his shoulder.

"Yeah. Bright light went out that day when he walked off into the trees."

"Mebbe," Abe said.

"Mebbe? Don't give me that shit, Abe. Trader's deader than a beaver hat. You know it. Ryan knows it. I know it. And I can tell you, sure as shit, that the Trader knows it."

J.B. rarely revealed so much of his emotion, his lips narrowed, his eyes half-closed behind the polished lenses of his spectacles.

"Hey, you don't know shit, John Dix!"

The brakes came on, throwing everyone forward in their seats. "That so, Abe?"

"Yeah."

"Yeah?"

"Yeah."

Mildred laughed, breaking the sudden tenseness. "You're like a couple of snot-nose kids in a schoolyard, boasting about whose old man can knock the block off the other.''

J.B. sniffed. ''Shouldn't have fired half-cocked like that, Abe.''

''Hell, that's okay. But I still say we don't rightly know what happened to the Trader.''

''He died, Abe,'' J.B. insisted.

''Don't start again,'' Ryan warned.

''Sure. But what's your opinion?'' Abe was standing, gripping one of the roof handholds.

''I always thought that... Fireblast! He was real sick, old and tired. Just never thought he could still be living. No way. No way at all. We'd have heard, Abe.''

''There've been rumors.'' Krysty sounded uncertain. ''Haven't there?''

''Sure.'' J.B. agreed.

''Well...'' Abe began, obviously ready to carry on the argument.

''Shut it up,'' Ryan snapped. ''Two things. Trader's dead, like I believe. Or he isn't. If he still lives, we'll run across him one of these days. Until then, just get us going, J.B., will you?''

THEY SAW NOBODY.

The only occasional signs of life were some unusually large mutie rats, great big gray-brown brutes, bigger than cats.

They scampered among the charcoal devastation, some of them turning their questing muzzles toward the stationary vehicle. Ryan stared blankly at them, wondering what they found to eat in this sterile emptiness.

"Close to the Chicago River," J.B. commented, pointing at the narrow blue line on the comp map in front of him.

Ryan was looking away to the southwest. "My imagination, or you reckon there look to be some untouched buildings off that way?"

"Could be."

"I can lead us in prayer for salvation from this drear place," Brother Michael offered. But nobody took him up on it.

"Pray as much as you like." Ryan looked over his shoulder. "Won't do any harm. But it might not do any good, neither."

"Overheating," J.B. said.

"Need water?"

"No. Mebbe switch her off for a spell. Let her cool down."

Ryan nodded. "Sure. Open the doors and everyone can stretch their legs."

The sudden silence was startling.

Everyone climbed out of the wag, staring around at the bleak wilderness. The birds circling overhead began to shriek at the movement, a thin, keening sound, like the wind blowing between deserted tombs in a mountainside cemetery.

At street level, the devastation was overwhelming. The tumbled walls were streaked with deep scorch marks, seared into the concrete and brick. The remains of what must have been sidewalk lamps were sliced clear off, about eighteen inches from the ground. Their stumps ended in bubbles of once-molten metal. The powdered shards of thousands of windows still sparkled in the sheltered corners.

"Are all of the big cities like this?" Brother Michael asked.

"Newyork is worse, damn near nuked flat. Rivers broke in and flooded the low parts." Ryan looked at J.B. "Washington was wiped away."

"Yeah. That was where it all began."

"What?"

"Beginning," Mildred replied.

The young man looked puzzled. "Beginning? But I thought..."

"The end," she added.

"How's that?"

"The beginning of the end. You truly don't know anything about how the world was?"

"When?"

"When you were an... What was that strange word again, Doc?"

"An oblate. Brother Michael was an oblate up at the community of Nil-Vanity in the Sierras. But they kept themselves closed off from the rest of the civilized world." He paused. "The so-called civilized world."

The teenager nodded. "Right, Doc. Like I said, we had no TV or news. Supplies were left outside the gates. No strangers. No phone. No talking."

"You never heard about the problems with the Russians after their revolutions in the early nineties?" Mildred shook her head. "Amazing, isn't it? We trawl one of the eight people in the United States who knows absolutely, totally, utterly fuck all."

"Tell me. I'm eager to learn."

Ryan had been scanning the horizons, as far as that was possible with the piles of burned rubble all around them.

Now he turned to face Brother Michael. "You seem to me like you're believing where you are. When you are."

"I do, Ryan. I see and I believe."

"Well, sometime we'll fill you in on history. All you need to know is that a mess of bombs went off in Washington. So they say. Triggered the biggest firefight the world ever saw." He closed his hands together, then parted them slowly, like flowers opening. "Booooom," he whispered.

"So this dreadful war, when the seals were opened and the horsemen released, brought a sort of peace to the land?"

Ryan grinned. "Later, son, later. Right now—"

He was interrupted by the burst of semiautomatic fire.

Chapter Twenty-One

Everyone responded in their own way to the sudden attack.

Ryan was fractionally ahead of J.B., both men diving toward the cover of the open doors of the armored wag. Dean and Krysty jostled each other for third place, with Abe on their heels. Mildred was a splintered second behind the gunner while Doc's befuddled brain was, as ever, a few beats slower than the others.

But still hugely quicker than Brother Michael.

The slender monastic figure stood stock-still, jaw dropped, gazing down at the bright sparks that fountained off the highway close to his feet, staring in bewilderment at the scrambled disappearance of the rest of the group.

"Dark night!" J.B. had already gotten his hand onto the control for the rear doors.

Ryan was dropping the shields over the front screens. Doc, Krysty, Mildred and Dean were taking up their positions by the machine guns, waiting for orders. Abe was crouched near the back, squinting out at Brother Michael.

"Move it, shit-for-brains!" he yelled at the young man.

Ryan figured at least a half dozen were attacking them, probably within two hundred yards. Could be a couple of machine pistols and what sounded like old hunting rifles. The wag muffled and distorted the noise of the shooting, making the blasters much more difficult to identify.

Several rounds ricocheted off the steel plate of the APC, making the interior ring out like a temple gong.

And Brother Michael still hadn't moved a step to save himself.

"Leave him!" Abe shouted. "Get the fuckin' doors shut before we all get chilled!"

J.B. glanced across to Ryan, who didn't hesitate for a moment. "Close them."

"No! I shall rescue the poor lad."

"Doc! Let it lie!"

J.B.'s hand faltered above the control. He looked over his shoulder while Doc clambered quickly down from his gun position, almost falling over Abe as he climbed out into the open.

Ryan nearly ordered the Armorer to close the rear of the wag, condemning both Brother Michael and Doc Tanner to certain death or capture.

He had no feelings for the teenager and would have abandoned him without another second's thought.

But Doc was someone special.

"Hold it. Abe, get his LMG and put up some covering fire. You, too, Mildred. Krysty, watch out for the back of the wag."

J.B. had fired up the engine, putting the tracked vehicle through forty-five degrees to protect the open, exposed rear from the shooting.

There was an ob slit by the passenger's front seat, and Ryan was able to watch Doc. The old man kicked up his heels, dodging sideways as a burst of lead narrowly missed his ankles.

Now he was alongside Brother Michael, who looked at him with an expression of vague surprise, as though he partly remembered being introduced to Doc some years ago.

"Grab him," J.B. muttered, watching the vid screens.

The heavy blaster in the wag suddenly chattered as Abe spotted a possible target.

"Got one of the scum bastards!"

"Watch the ammo," Ryan warned. "Not like with Trader. Shoot that and there's no more."

His attention had been momentarily distracted from Doc's rescue bid. Now Ryan looked again and saw that the newcomer was following Doc toward the relative safety of the APC.

"Lousy shots," the Armorer commented. "Range is short and the cover's good. And they can't hit a couple of sitting ducks."

At that moment Ryan glimpsed the first of their attackers.

He was a raggedy man, slightly built, in patched furs, holding what looked like a trusty old M-16 carbine. He darted from behind a pile of rubble, trying to get across to the other side of the partly blocked highway.

There was a single shot from Mildred's LMG, the round puffing dust six inches in front of the running man.

"Short," she muttered. "Get him this time." She fired a second time, the massive bullet hitting him in the right thigh, smashing the femur, passing clean through, breaking the left leg and opening up the big artery near his groin. They all heard the scream, above the noise of the wag's engine.

The man went down in a clatter of limbs, the gun flying from his hands. For a few agonized seconds he tried to drag himself to cover. But the bright lifeblood was draining out of him into the dust, like water from a slashed goatskin.

"Don't bother with another round."

"Wasn't going to, Ryan. I can recognize a mortal wound nearly as good as you."

The vehicle shuddered as first Brother Michael and then Doc piled into it.

Ryan looked at J.B., but the doors were already closing.

"Why'd you just stand there?" Dean asked, first as ever with the question.

"I didn't know what was happening. They were seeking my death."

The lad's voice was calm and unflustered.

"You never come across bad people like that back in Nil-Vanity?" Krysty asked.

"Killers? Murderers? Those who slaughter against the will and wish of the Almighty? Moral perverts?" It was obviously an absurd query. "Why do they so detest me?"

Doc had flopped on a seat, fanning at his face with his hand. "They detest strangers, Brother Michael."

The shooting had almost stopped An occasional bullet rang off the armor plate, but the attackers had seen the wag's firepower and were now keeping themselves well out of sight.

Ryan swung around in the swivel seat. "It's a good welcome to Deathlands, Michael."

Abe cackled with laughter. "Sure is, son. Teach you to keep your ears and eyes open, and your mind clicking all the time. And your asshole sewn up tight as a goose."

"I only have two eyes and two ears, Abe. I was not thinking there would be such things. But . . ." He hesitated. "Every fact that any of you have imparted has proved true."

"Friend doesn't lie to another friend," Dean chirped.

"And you saved my life, Dr. Tanner."

"Just call me 'Doc,' will you? None of us are that impressed with courtesy honors and titles, Brother Michael."

"Of course. If I am lost forever to my time and my brothers, then I shall no longer use that name. I shall just be plain Michael."

"Most folks have two names, Michael," Mildred said.

"Call him Michael Stranger," Dean suggested.

"Michael Airhead," Abe sniggered.

"What's wrong with your own full name?" Doc asked.

"I have no second name."

"Two names. Just play the good old switcheroo with them."

Ryan smiled. "You mean call him Michael Brother, Doc?"

"Why not?"

"Sure, why not? What do you think about it, Michael? Like it?"

"I don't know."

"Yeah, it likes us real well." Doc grinned. "Folks, a good old Deathlands welcome to your friend and mine, Michael Brother."

There was a round of applause, led by Abe, and then everyone solemnly shook hands with their new companion.

THE FIRING CEASED.

J.B. used the main scanner to sweep the area, but the ruins were so extensive that it was difficult to be certain that their attackers had actually fled the area.

All that remained was the single sprawled corpse in the lake of congealing blood.

A couple of the bolder rats had come sneaking out of their deep hiding places, sniffing at the air, seemingly unworried by the rumbling of the wag's powerful engine.

"When do we perform the burial ceremony?" Michael asked.

"When hell freezes," Abe replied. "And not a single fucking second before."

"WHOLE CITY CAN'T HAVE been wiped into charcoal," Ryan said.

"Got a map. Go anyplace we want." J.B. shook his head. "There any point in this?"

"Trader used to tell us that the time you stopped getting curious was the time you got a bucket of dirt in your open eyes."

"Sure, sure. But look around us, Ryan. More life in a spent round."

The scanner display on the dash began to flicker. J.B. banged it with his fist, watching it steady for a moment.

Then the screen went blank, with a single tiny emerald spot of light at its center. That eventually faded away into blackness.

"Terrific," Krysty said, leaning against Ryan's shoulder again. "Now what do we do?"

"Still got the vid screens. Use them and the ob ports on the sides."

"But we don't know where we're going." Mildred laughed. "Feel like a hunk of tuna trapped in a nice safe can."

"Maps are luxuries." Abe slapped the black woman on the back, ignoring her angry glare. "Compass and a good sense of direction all you need. Am I right, Ryan? Or am I fucking right? Huh? You tell me that, Ryan."

"You're right. But we gotta decide. We can find our way back to the redoubt without much trouble. Got plenty of gas. Ammo for the blasters. No tires to get shot out."

"What will we eat?"

Dean grinned approvingly. "Yeah, Michael, yeah. Good question. When we going to eat, Dad?"

Ryan looked out of the side window. "We can head out due west. Then, if things don't get any better, we'll turn around and make another jump from the gateway."

"There's life in the ville, lover. I can feel it. Even inside this tuna can."

"What sort of life, Krysty?" J.B. had been just about to engage the main drive, but he stopped at her words.

"All kinds. The feeling's muffled, like hearing someone talking way down inside a cavern. But it's there, just the same."

"Wild animals in the asphalt jungle," Mildred stated. "Go loaded for lion."

The gears meshed and the dark-painted vehicle began to roll westward.

Chapter Twenty-Two

Gradually, very gradually, they moved away from the blackened ruins of the firestorm. When they reached the north branch of the Chicago River, though none of them knew that was the old name of the sparkling watercourse, they found a sturdy pontoon bridge, offering them the chance to continue their way toward the west of the city.

The wag rattled along the ancient Fifty-Six, passing the twentieth-century gangster citadel of Cicero.

"That devastated highway up to the left there must be the Eisenhower Expressway," Mildred guessed. "Looks like it got bombed out of sight."

"Buildings aren't in such bad shape out here. How far have we come, J.B.?" Krysty asked.

"Twelve miles showing on the clock."

The charred ruins slowly gave way to the more familiar sight of "normal" destruction.

They began to spot an occasional building that still retained part of its roof. There would be the glimpse of a window that actually had fragments of its original glass within its frame.

Abe was riding in the center, hugging the butt of the Browning to his shoulder. As there seemed little threat,

Ryan had agreed that they should risk having the upper hatch partly open, giving them the pleasure of fresh air circulating around the stuffy interior of the wag.

"Someone's moving." The gunner's voice came crackling from the throat mike he'd strapped on.

"Where?" J.B. eased back on the throttle, wary of running them into a trap.

"Green, thirty, one-twenty."

Ryan's side. To the right of the vehicle, thirty degrees off the line ahead, and about a hundred and twenty yards away.

J.B. aimed the vid in that direction, trying to pick up what Abe had seen, while Ryan looked directly out.

"Can't see it. Still there, Abe?"

"No, Ryan. Vanished into a narrow sort of alley between a couple of houses."

"Armed?" J.B. asked.

"Looked like some kind of harpoon gun. Spear. You know."

The sec camera wasn't showing them any sort of movement, just the featureless expanse of the ruined ville.

"Best shut that hatch." J.B. glanced sideways at Ryan for confirmation.

"Yeah. Close it down. Don't want somebody lobbing a frag gren in the top."

"Wouldn't get close enough. Spill their guts all over the pavement."

"Shut it anyway, Abe."

It clicked down and they heard the hollow sound as Abe threw the locking lever across.

"Secure," he called.

"STORM COMING UP," J.B. reported. He and Ryan had changed places as they rumbled slowly westward, allowing the one-eyed man to get used to the controls. If the blacktop had been clear of rubble they could have pushed on at five times the speed. But there was always the risk of the wag throwing a track in a pile of bricks.

"How's it look?"

"Heavy."

It had been three-quarters of an hour since Abe had spotted someone moving. Since then they hadn't actually seen anyone, though Krysty had told Ryan that she had a strong feeling that they were still being watched.

Now they were away from the blighted center of the city, into the suburbs. The houses were less damaged, and nature was creeping voraciously back. The highway had been rippled by earth movements, and lush weeds sprouted through.

Ryan pressed the button that lifted the screens over the shields, allowing him a clear sight of the region straight ahead of them. He touched the brake pedal, slowing their speed to something close to walking pace.

Now he saw what J.B. had meant by the threat of a storm. The sky to the far west was a dusky gray, streaked with slashes of purple and crimson clouds.

The sun had vanished, and the wind was rising. As he looked out, Ryan saw jagged lances of lightning, crackling silver against the darkness. He guessed the core of the bad weather was still around ten to fifteen miles away from them.

Closing fast.

"Sure looks like a chem storm." Krysty brushed a strand of fiery crimson hair back out of her eyes. "Hope this wag's waterproofed."

"Doubt it floats." Ryan opened up the throttle again, seeing that the highway ahead was relatively clear of obstructions.

"Could be trouble with the electrics," J.B. suggested.

"Find cover? Some of these duplexes got wag ports at the side."

"Might we not endeavor to locate a more substantial dwelling and then seek to pass the coming night within it?"

Ryan considered Doc's words. "Don't see why not. Anyone object?"

There was a murmur of assent. "Be good if you could possibly find us a house with some beds in it," Mildred suggested.

Ryan turned the wag off the main route, taking a quiet, tree-lined side street that rose in a gentle gradient. The houses were virtually undamaged, making him wonder whether the Russkies had used neutron bombs in some of the suburbs, taking out the population and leaving their homes.

It was strange to be tracking up these quiet roads in a military vehicle, past mailboxes and sloping lawns of waving grass. You almost expected someone rocking away on one of the white-painted porches, a glass of lemonade frosting on a table at his elbow.

"Nice house there," J.B. said, pointing directly ahead of them where the road divided.

It was Victorian Gothic, all gilt and gingerbread, with ornamented gables and balconies, the paint peeling and faded.

Some of the windows on the first floor had been smashed, but the upstairs casements were untouched, dark and somehow threatening.

"Looks spooky," Mildred commented.

"We going in?" Dean asked.

"Why not?" Ryan replied.

"IT MUST HAVE BEEN beautiful here once, don't you reckon, lover?"

They had parked and locked the wag around back of the building, close to what looked like it had once been a kitchen garden. And everyone had split up, exploring.

Krysty and Ryan walked past the garage to a side part of the huge area of grass and trees, which was massively overgrown. It was difficult to imagine cropped lawns and neatly pruned bushes. There was a section with bullrushes that might once have been a fish pond, and at the back, where the ground sloped away, they discovered a narrow stream.

It was set at the bottom of a steep-walled ravine of glistening black rock, where turbulent brown water boiled and raced.

"Wouldn't fancy your chances if you went into that," Ryan said, drawing Krysty back from the danger of the undercut brink.

It was difficult to see where the stream went as the undergrowth along its edge concealed its course, but it appeared to dogleg toward the right, away from the house.

"Looks like there's plenty of wildlife around here." Krysty pointed to the trodden paths that wound through the grass, stooping. "Fox. Small deer. Possum. Could even be beaver."

Ryan knelt at her side, examining the marks in the moist earth. "Not beaver. And..."

The cry of a bird came from somewhere among the trees on the far side of the stream, high, shrill and insistent.

Ryan straightened, reaching automatically for the SIG-Sauer on his hip.

"Listen," he said.

"Trouble?"

"Could be."

They waited, back-to-back, watching the shifting greenery all around them, but the birdcall wasn't repeated.

"Best get to the others. That storm's coming our way."

Ryan stalked through the long grass, the seed heads scattering around his steel-capped combat boots. Krysty was close behind him.

The day was darkening as the chem clouds raced toward them. By the time they reached the back porch the first heavy drops of rain were already beginning to splatter on the great slabs of York stone that made up the patio.

Doc was standing under cover, shading his eyes as he stared out across the garden. "Thought I saw someone coming after you," he said.

"Who?"

"Lost sight of them. If they were there in the first place. Probably an old man's imagination."

Now they heard the pealing of thunder, and the rain began with a serious intent. Dean joined them on the porch, looking at the downpour.

"Lucky we're dry and safe, Dad," he said.

Chapter Twenty-Three

Ryan allowed his son to take him on a conducted tour of the mansion, both of them ducking at a turning of the landing when a bolt of lightning ripped into a tall sycamore less than a hundred feet from the nearest window. The thunder was simultaneous, devastatingly loud.

The upper floor was filled with the bitter stench of raw ozone, and the panes of glass rattled in their frames.

"Shit a brick!" the boy exclaimed, grabbing at his father's hand, holding it for a brief, frightened moment as the building shook.

"Close," Ryan said.

It was no surprise that the imposing house had been ransacked, looted from the topmost attic bedroom down to the capacious cellars. Everything that could be eaten or drunk or traded or burned was gone.

But there was still a feeling of faded grandeur, rare in Deathlands, a sense of gracious living that Ryan had only read about in old books or glimpsed in flickering segments of vids.

"How many'd live in a squat like this?" Dean asked, letting go of Ryan's hand now that the immediate shock of the thunderbolt had passed.

"Three or four," Ryan replied, lifting his voice against the swelling of the storm. Rain was beating on the shingled roof immediately above their heads, battering on the windows.

Dean laughed. "You mean in this room. I mean the whole place."

"That's right. Could have had servants. Or slaves. Paid them to cook, scrub, wash and all that stuff. But mebbe only three or four."

"Wow! I seen places smaller than this one with about five hundred living in it."

The boy was exaggerating.

But not much.

DESPITE THE VENOM of the chem storm, the large mansion stood secure and dry.

The lightning was almost constant, pouring great bursts of pink, purple and silver brightness over the Chicago suburb. The wind had risen to near gale strength, whipping the tops of the trees and bending the trunks of the slender aspens like taut bows.

With the fallen branches of a tree out back, J.B. had built a fire in the hearth of what looked like it had been the main living room. The flames rose into the wide chimney, casting flickering shadows across the ornamented ceiling.

Ryan and his son had rejoined the others, sitting sprawled on coats around the blazing branches. When night finally came, he'd decided that they would post guards. That bird cry that wasn't from the throat of any bird he'd ever heard had put Ryan a little on edge.

Now, for a while, they could all relax.

Ryan lay down, Krysty close by him, letting his eye wander around the room, taking in the melancholy air of lost opulence.

The wallpaper was dark blue, heavily embossed with a pattern of silver vine leaves, with an occasional splash of acanthus. There were several rectangular discolored patches that showed where paintings must once have been hung from the sturdy iron hooks. The wainscoting and picture rail had mostly been torn down for kindling.

The only relic of the furnishings was a portrait in a battered gilt frame, leaning in a corner of the room, away from the windows. The glass was gone and the picture was smeared and torn. It seemed to be an elderly couple, the man with a trim beard, both wearing elegant jeweled coronets. Ryan didn't recognize either of them.

There were holes in the paper and plaster on the walls, where there had once been light fixtures. Bare strands of wire protruded from the center of the high ceiling, with a twisted piece of brass dangling from it. Two small, dusty, crystal prisms hooked on the brass revealed that it had once been a part of a splendid chandelier.

"Must've been beautiful, eh, lover? Bet you they had those great enormous four-poster beds upstairs."

Ryan nodded, smiling into Krysty's eyes. "Guess we'll have to do with our coats again."

"What's new about that?"

"Nothing new. But it's still about the most fun I know."

IN THE END they found that the reality of enforcing their defensive position took preference over their lovemaking.

The house was so large that it could be suicidal to split up into separate rooms for the night. Ryan had mentioned the strange call from the woods to J.B., and they'd agreed that double guards would be essential.

"Could do with hunting up some food tomorrow," the Armorer said.

They'd eaten the remainder of their jerky, washing it down with rainwater that had appeared among the stone flags.

"Plenty of tracks out toward the stream," Ryan replied.

"That stream'll be running faster than fast after the storm," Dean said.

Ryan stood, stretching his spine and sighing. "Wet weather always gets my joints," he said, looking out the window, the glass still streaked with water. "Think the wag'll be safe out there, J.B., without a guard?"

"Night patrol can keep an eye on it. But it's got all sorts of sec locks on it. If those guys back at the redoubt hadn't gone off together to buy the farm and left it open, we'd probably never have got inside the doors."

Doc also stood, his knee joints cracking like pistol shots.

"If it were only dampness that affected my poor old body," he said, groaning as he bent and rubbed at his legs. "Hot weather and cold weather and dry weather and wet weather. All make me feel a hundred years old, or more."

Michael had been quiet since they reached the house. Ryan had watched him, wondering if the young man had been considering taking his chance and breaking away from them.

Now he looked up at Doc. "I thought that you *were* over a hundred years old," he said with a quiet smile. "As am I."

"There's nothing to be done about that, I fear, my new friend."

"I thought that you said that if we could return to—"

Doc waved a hand. "No, no, no. I said nothing of the sort, Michael. No. We must both resign ourselves to our predicament."

"I was sure you—"

"Let us walk on the upper floor, Master Brother and I shall remind you of what I *really* said."

They walked off together into the gloom of the hall.

"What was that shit about?" Abe asked.

Ryan turned his head and stared at Krysty, who was looking vaguely puzzled, her green eyes blank and introspective, gazing into the tumbling flames of the crackling fire. She felt his unspoken question and half smiled.

"Can't tell, lover. You've known Doc long enough, know that his mind doesn't work like other people's. He's probably been telling Michael some tale or other from his past."

"Seemed more than that," Mildred said. "Like they had a secret."

Ryan nodded. "That was the way I saw it. Like the kid had spilled something Doc didn't expect him to mention. Fireblast! I don't know Just keep watch on them."

In the stillness they could all hear Doc's voice from somewhere above them. But they couldn't make out what he was saying.

NEITHER J B. NOR RYAN saw the situation as being a triple-red risk, which meant that they could divide up for the two-person patrols along social lines rather than deliberately picking pairs to maximize their combat skills.

There was a tradition on dark watch that the two most dangerous periods of blackness came just after midnight and just before the cold pallor of the false dawn.

J.B. and Mildred took the first of those two-hour watches. Ryan and Krysty had picked the last of them, through to first light. Doc and Michael were allocated the opening spell on patrol, and Abe and Dean were happy to share the couple of hours from two until four in the morning.

Doc stood in the eastern-facing attic of the mansion, his right hand gripping the butt of the Le Mat. His eyes were fixed out over the garden, past the rows of trees that moved gently in the night wind, toward the charred interior of the ville, where the redoubt lay still and secret.

He was so preoccupied in his vigil that he never noticed a flicker of light among the grove of oaks, toward the ravine.

On the floor below, the young oblate from the past was walking quietly along the corridors, stepping into each of the range of master bedrooms. Outside, the chem storm had cleared away to the far south, and there was a sheen of watery moonlight filtering in through the dusty glass.

He paused on the threshold of every room and stood very still, hands down at his sides. Despite Ryan's pressing him, Michael refused to carry any kind of blaster.

The things that the old man had been whispering to him had left him bewildered, unable to decide if they offered hope or doom.

The first of the two-hour watches passed without incident.

"WANT TO PATROL on your own, Dean? Or stick with me?"

"Mebbe better not to split up, Abe. If that's all right with you."

"Sure."

"Okay."

The moon was occasionally covered by a tattered shroud of high cloud, sending blurred shadows scudding across the empty rooms. Every now and again there was a faint creaking, as the old house settled into the cool of the night.

"Think there's anyone out there watching us?" Dean asked.

"You ask more questions than anyone I ever met in my whole life, kid," Abe replied.

They were in the hall, by the stained-glass panels of the double front door. The yellows, greens, scarlets and blues of the rich floral patterns that decorated the leaded glass were dappled all around their feet.

"Could be someone out there," Dean insisted, holding the Browning nervously in his hand.

"Open the door and take a look." Abe grinned. "If there's someone there, tell him to shove off and go someplace else."

"Think there is?"

"No. Doubt it."

They froze at a faint noise from the living room, where the others were sleeping. They could just make out the reflected glow of the dying fire in the dark doorway.

"What was that?"

"Log breaking up into ash," Abe replied. "Cool it, will you? You're making me jumpy."

"Sorry, Abe."

"Open the front door and chase off anyone you find there."

"Sure."

There was an iron bolt at the bottom that opened easily, another at the top that Dean had to stretch to slide back, needing help from Abe, and a thin brass chain that the boy unhooked.

He pulled the door toward him, going along with Abe's joke.

"Get out of—" he began, smiling broadly into the blackness.

Chapter Twenty-Four

The cry of shock tore through the mansion, jerking everyone awake.

As the door swung open, Dean was already grinning over his shoulder at Abe. So he first glimpsed the crouching mutie out of the corner of his eye, bathed in the spilled moonlight.

The creature was hunched over, holding a long thin-bladed knife, point up. Its lipless mouth was open in a soundless snarl of bloody hatred, its pinpoint eyes glaring at the boy It wore an assortment of torn rags and furs, and its head was totally bald, pitted with suppurating sores.

The knife lunged toward the boy's throat, held in a gloved fist.

Dean's bizarre upbringing had developed his reflexes so that he could almost match a striking rattler

He slammed the door as hard as he could, catching the mutie's forearms. There was a crack of splintered bone and the knife dropped to the floor of the hall, where Abe stopped and picked it up.

As the hand was pulled away, Dean pushed the door closed again, jerking the two bolts across to hold it shut.

The whole incident took about five seconds from opening the door to clattering home the iron bolts again.

By the time that Dean turned away toward the living room, his father was already standing there, his powerful blaster in his hand. J.B. was at his shoulder, Krysty close behind the Armorer.

"Muties," Abe said. "Just seen one. Kid broke its arm. Must be others."

It was a fair judgment from an experienced fighting man. Muties didn't go around on their own. They lived and raided in groups, anywhere from a half dozen to a half hundred.

"I'll take the top floor." J.B. headed toward the stairs. "Watch all sides." Mildred appeared. "Come on with me," he said.

Doc and Michael came into the hall together, the young man slowly knotting the cord around his waist.

"Are we under attack, my dear friend?"

"Yeah. Stay here and watch that front door, Doc. Anything moves, wipe it away with your cannon. Michael, keep out of the way."

They all heard the sound of breaking glass and ripped wood from somewhere at the back of the house.

Doc shook his head. "What a deal of sprick-sprackery noise."

Abe stayed with the old man while Dean joined Krysty and his father, racing along the narrow passage toward the kitchen quarters of the house, past the row of silent bells that hung on the wall, each one still bearing the faded label of a room in the mansion.

Ryan was conscious of a dim hubbub of shouting and yelping from outside the house. He guessed that Dean had discovered the muties' attack only moments before they had been about to launch it. But those moments had given an edge to the defenders.

Now each of the three groups faced different problems.

J.B. HAD HIS Smith & Wesson M-4000 cradled in his arms, the heavy 12-gauge cocked and ready. As he darted along the corridor on the second floor, past the row of silent rooms, his eye was caught by a glimmer of movement. The master bedroom. With the ornamental balcony.

Someone was hunched over on that balcony, using a broad dagger to pick at the window catch.

The Armorer paused in midstride, bracing himself and firing from the hip.

The blaster gave its booming cough, the twenty Remington fléchettes held in each round exploding in a lethal hail. The inch-long arrows exploded through the glass and ripped into the unsuspecting mutie at chest level.

Five or six of the darts penetrated clean through, emerging blood-tipped, driving on to embed themselves in a tall larch fifty yards away from the house. Some struck bone and angled sideways, twisted and distorted, slicing through skin and flesh, reducing the heart to rags of pulsing muscle.

The impact of the fléchettes tipped the dying mutie backward, over the black iron railing, where its body landed on top of three other attackers, knocking them sprawling in the long, moonlit grass.

"I'll take this side!" Mildred shouted, running toward the broken window, the target pistol ready for action.

J.B. didn't hesitate, slotting another round into the chamber of the scattergun, looking for a vantage point where he'd be able to shoot from cover into the swarming muties.

Behind him he heard the light snap of the ZKR 551, then a second shot. He had enough faith in Mildred's skill to be certain that two more of the enemy would now be down and done.

He found a narrow chamber, the holes in the black-and-white tiled floor showing it had once been a bathroom. The window looked out to the side, where the wag was parked. J.B. wasn't surprised to see a group of the muties, clustered around the locked APC, hammering on its armored steel flanks.

Two more rounds from the Smith & Wesson left one dead, three more severely wounded.

On the second floor things were going well for the defenders.

RYAN BURST into the scullery, seeing the kitchen ahead of him. The back door was swinging wide, and there were at least eight or nine muties between him and the open night.

There was little light and it was impossible to make out any details, just a group of figures, chattering and waving knives. That first glance didn't show Ryan any blasters.

He leveled the 15-round SIG-Sauer P-226, and without a heartbeat's hesitation pumped ten rounds into the mass of bodies directly in front of him.

The gun bucked in his hand, but the built-in silencer muted the sound of the shots. There were screams, and a thrown knife clattered against the door frame, inches from his throat.

"Back in the hall," he shouted to Dean and Krysty, who were at his shoulder

Krysty's pistol snapped three times at the muties, and Dean's big Browning boomed once.

In the back of the mansion, things weren't going too badly for the defenders.

DOC STOOD AT THE BOTTOM of the stairs, the Le Mat in his right hand, the silver-topped sword stick held negligently in the left.

Abe was gripping the mutie's knife, head darting around to watch the pools of shadow that swam in the corners of the hallway

Michael was standing between Abe and Doc, hands at his sides, a faintly curious expression on his face.

'They wish us evil?'' he said.

"Do bears shit in the woods?" Abe spit. "You triple stupe, course they want us dead. Probably want the wag."

There was the sound of the scattergun from up the stairs, and then the lighter explosions of Mildred's pistol. Almost simultaneously the three men heard a burst of gunfire from the back of the house on the first floor.

"Be coming our way any—" Abe began, his warning interrupted by the double front doors crashing inward in a cascade of brilliantly colored glass and splintered wood.

Half a dozen muties stood poised on the threshold, like a pack of nightmare hunting animals. All were totally bald, with scarred and pitted faces. All were slavering and frothing at the mouth with the death lust, moaning as they saw three of their intended victims before them.

All had knives or axes.

"Greetings, gentles all," Doc said with an infinite calm, leveling the Le Mat at the invaders and squeezing the trigger.

The .63-caliber shotgun round ripped into the group of muties at head height, the pellets starring out across the hall. The leading attacker took most of the impact, its face disappearing into a smear of blood and torn bone.

Two of the others were also hit, staggering backward into the front driveway, tumbling down the flight of steps.

But the muties had concentrated their main attack at this part of the big house, a dozen more appearing in the doorway, screaming their hatred.

It took too long to convert the Le Mat to a normal 9-round .36-caliber revolver. Doc stuck it calmly back into the hand-tooled Mexican holster at his belt and unsheathed the slender steel blade from the center of his cane.

"En garde, mes amis!" he called, whipping the rapier from side to side, making it sing in the silvered darkness.

"Come on, shit eaters," Abe hissed, dropping into a crouch.

Michael still hadn't moved.

Things weren't going so well for the three defenders by the front doors.

IT WAS AT THIS MOMENT that Ryan came running along the corridor from the kitchens of the building.

He saw the trio of friends, facing a charging mob of yelping muties.

It only took a moment for Ryan to empty the SIG-Sauer at them. Then he stuck it into his belt and drew his long panga, readying himself for the bloody hand-to-hand combat.

Krysty grabbed Dean by the elbow and jerked him back out of sight, behind the ornate banisters of the staircase.

'Wait," she snapped.

Ryan's instincts told him that this was likely to be a triple-close one.

When it came to chilling, Ryan's instincts weren't very often wrong.

Chapter Twenty-Five

J.B. and Mildred had heard the screams and shooting as the main body of the muties attempted to break into the house through the vulnerable front doors.

They raced to the top of the broad staircase into the hall and looked down into a scene of chaos and carnage.

There were dead and dying muties near the smashed doors, kicking out and moaning in a welter of spilled blood.

A number of separate battles were being fought in the half-light below them.

Doc Tanner had slipped into a world of his own, where he wore the gold and crimson of the king's musketeers, fighting for his life with D'Artagnan, Athos, Porthos and Aramis at his shoulder, against the sweating mob.

"Aye, sirrah, and that and that!" he was shouting. "Take this message to your master, the treacherous Cardinal, writ in your own blood!"

The rapier flashed and danced, holding four of the muties at bay with the dazzling arc of hissing death. All of the attackers were wounded, blood streaming from chest or arm or face. But they still pressed the old man, panting open-mouthed, their own knives pecking toward him.

Abe was in a bitter struggle, backed into a corner where he was tussling with two muties. One of them was unusually tall, grappling with him, trying to hold his knife arm.

Ryan was swinging the panga, trying to fight his way toward the gunner to help him out, though the brawling press of numbers was telling against him.

But J.B.'s eyes were caught by the newest recruit to their group.

Michael was in the shadows, stock-still, and had only just attracted the attention of the attackers.

"Dark night!" The Armorer leveled the scattergun down into the hall, but the angle was poor and the risk of hitting a friend rather than an enemy was far too great.

Mildred had also raised her target pistol, but the melee of bodies swirled and shifted in the pallid gleam of the waning moon.

"Can't," she said, caught in a hopeless moment of quiet desperation.

All they could do was look on, helplessly, as the clawing knives of the muties stabbed toward the young man.

Michael took a quick breath, holding it in, his eyes staring at his opponents. If any of them had looked at him they might have hesitated, turned away, for his dark brown eyes held a dreadful, cold threat.

Michael had a slim dagger strapped to each hip, in doeskin sheaths.

Suddenly they were drawn.

Their whirling steel caught the silver light, dancing and sparkling, moving so fast that J.B. and Mildred were dazzled.

He had been confronted by four muties, pushing at one another to be the one to relish the delight of butchering him.

Now they had vanished, each kneeling, falling or rolling on the floor.

Three of the four had their throats slit clear across, giving the appearance of an extra, ghastly, grinning mouth, red-lipped, spouting great fountains of blood.

The fourth had been stabbed with immaculate accuracy through the very center of his left eye. Clear liquid seeped over its stubbled, pocked skin, dripping over its chest.

The quadruple slaughter tipped the balance in favor of the defenders.

The muties lost heart at their appalling losses. One gave a piercing cry that rasped at the ears of the listeners. The rest echoed it, ululating as they retreated toward the front porch.

J.B. aimed the Smith & Wesson, finger tight on the trigger, but it would have been a waste of a valuable round to fire into the backs of the muties as they ran away.

Doc thrust at the neck of the last of his opponents, drawing a shriek of pain and fear

Ryan stood still, looking at the blood-slick panga in his hand, wiping sweat from his forehead with his sleeve.

Krysty and Dean were emerging from the passage to the kitchens.

Michael was looking at the mayhem around him, as if he were puzzled at who might have killed the four dead muties by his bare feet, feet that were literally covered in sticky crimson.

Abe was the only one of the companions who wasn't yet done.

He'd ripped open the guts of the smaller mutie with the borrowed blade, but the much taller man was giving him a hard time.

As the rest of the survivors fled, Abe managed to slice at the arm of the mutie, sending him staggering away.

"I'll take him," Krysty called, leveling her .38.

"No, I'll finish the—"

The mutie had been scrambling away, Abe close on his heels. But the gunner slipped in the lake of blood and nearly went down. His opponent sensed a chance and hacked at him with a dagger so long it was almost a sword.

It cut Abe deep across the forearm, drawing an instant thread of blood, secming almost black in the moonlight.

"Shithead!"

Krysty fired, but the mutie was already on the move again and the bullet missed by a good yard, smashing in a cloud of white plaster into the wall to the right of the open door.

"Gaia!"

"Let him go, Abe!"

But Ryan's warning shout was too late. His arm dripping blood, the enraged Abe was after the mutie, both of them vanishing into the front drive of the house.

"Always was hasty," J.B. stated, picking his way down the stairs, avoiding slipping on the blood that was spilled everywhere.

"Better go after him. Doc, come with me. Rest of you get this place. What the firedark are you doing, Michael?"

The young man was kneeling in front of his four victims. He'd dropped his daggers and had his hands clasped to his face.

"Fastest thing I ever saw in my life," J.B. said wonderingly. "If that's the Tao-Tain-Do you spoke about, then I'll have me some."

The ex-monk wasn't listening. His lips moved as he pattered out a prayer.

"Blessed Lord forgive me for having taken life against all your laws and accept the souls of these poor wretches into your safekeeping forever and ever."

"Amen," Doc said.

RYAN LED Doc into the front garden. The Le Mat had been recharged, and Ryan had reloaded the SIG-Sauer he held in his right hand. The mutie blood had been wiped off the panga and the blade resheathed at his hip.

"Which way do you think the ungodly have fled from our righteous wrath?"

"Toward the stream and into the trees out the back."

In the stillness of the night they could hear only the faint sound of the breeze through the branches of the wood and the distant roaring of the water, as it tore along the steep-sided ravine.

But Ryan's keen hearing caught another noise.

A voice, raised in a cry of anger.

Or pain.

The moon was veiled behind a bank of low cloud, making it difficult to move quickly through the undergrowth toward the thunder of the turbulent stream. Doc stumbled as he tried to keep up with the agile, pantherish speed of the one-eyed man.

"By the three Kennedys, Ryan!"

"You all right, Doc?"

"As right as rain, my dear fellow. Speaking of which rain, it sounds rather as though it has swollen that diminutive watercourse to something approaching a full-blown torrent."

The noise was certainly louder.

Ryan ducked under a dripping thorn bush, snagging his sleeve on it. As it sprang back behind him he heard a muttered curse from Doc.

"Sorry."

Now the shout was repeated, nearer. It was Abe's voice, angry.

Ryan started to run, his boots swishing through the long grass.

Behind him he heard Doc trip over the exposed root of an elderly quince tree and measure his length on the lawn.

"Fuggerbugger!"

But that was behind him, and Abe, in trouble, was close by ahead of him.

The moon broke free of the restraining chains of cloud and spilled its icy light across the rambling garden.

It showed Ryan that he was within thirty yards of the brink of the drop to the stream. There were only a few sparse bushes between him and three figures that were struggling together, close to the edge of the ravine.

Abe had his back to Ryan, stabbing at a mutie that was lying down, clawing up at his legs, trying to bring him to the earth. A second creature—the very tall one that had wounded Abe in the house—was wrestling with the gunner, its long arms tangled around Abe's waist.

There was no chance of a shot at that range and in that light.

On the run, Ryan holstered the blaster and once again drew the panga with its razored eighteen-inch blade.

As he drew closer he saw the mutie on the ground suddenly let go of Abe, hands clutching at a ferocious gash that had been opened in the side of its throat. The mutie then toppled away, legs thrashing, a bubbling scream bursting silently from the begging mouth.

"Break clear and I'll take him!" Ryan yelled, realizing instantly that the overwhelming noise of the river was drowning out all sounds.

But the tall mutie had seen him coming out of the undergrowth. Spitting in blind rage toward Ryan, the creature exerted all of its strength and heaved the much smaller Abe from his feet, clutching him around the midriff, ignoring the knife that Abe plunged once, twice, three times into its chest. The mutie took two staggering steps and vanished into the blackness of the rocky abyss.

Carrying Abe with it.

A half minute later Doc joined Ryan, finding him standing on the slippery edge of the glistening crevasse, staring into its deeps.

The water foamed, frothed and raged over the jagged boulders at a fearsome rate. The moonlight barely penetrated into the bottom of the ravine, but it gave enough illumination for them to be able to see that Abe was gone, whisked away in the sullen stream, locked together with the mutie.

The killer and the killed.

Together.

THEY ALL SEARCHED AGAIN at first light, scouting along both sides of the water. The level was already dropping, but it still foamed westward at a furious rate.

Dean accompanied J.B. for a full mile downstream, but they came back with no good news. The water flowed into a great underground culvert, which was partly barred.

"Never had a chance," J.B. said sadly.

"Took a mutie with him." Dean shook his head. "Good way to go."

Ryan patted him on the arm. "Wrong, son. There's never any such thing as a good way to go. Never."

Chapter Twenty-Six

The sun refused to show its face, and the morning was dull and dank. A cold mist hung over the tops of the trees, draping down across the leaves like wraiths of Spanish moss.

J.B. went out hunting with Dean, but they came back with only a single small rabbit to show.

Krysty found Ryan standing in one of the attic bedrooms, staring out across the overgrown garden, toward the hidden stream.

"Fistful of jack for your thoughts."

"Not worth the spit off a leper's nose."

"Abe?"

He nodded. "Yeah. Seems that every time I cross his path the poor devil gets bad wounded. Now he's gotten himself chilled."

"We all do, lover "

"Sure. But Abe was so sure that Trader wasn't really gone."

"Now he's gone himself."

"Yeah."

She put an arm around his neck from behind, face against his, her sentient hair seeming to caress his

cheek. "Think we should go on back to the redoubt?
To the gateway?"

"Make another jump?"

"Why not?"

He sighed. "Because I'm tired, Krysty. Tired of always running and fighting. Tired of seeing my friends
dying around me."

"Come on, Ryan." She straightened and turned him
to look directly at her. "Stop walking, and you just fall
over."

"You want to settle."

"Sure. Sure I do. Want that more than anything in
the whole damned world."

"Kids."

The word hung, flat and dull, between them.

Krysty broke the silence. "Yeah. That too. Before I
get too old. Don't want you in your eighties before
they're teenagers."

"Them?"

"Six."

"All boys?"

She smiled. "Three of each."

"Why not?"

She kissed him on the mouth, her tongue probing
very gently between his lips. "Let's go downstairs,
lover."

"Why not?"

"WHICH WAY?"

The engine on the wag was coughing and spluttering. J.B. had struggled to get it to fire, and there had been an anxious wait of nearly five minutes before it finally caught. Even then the sound was worryingly irregular, spitting out great clouds of greasy blue-gray smoke.

"Damp plugs?" Mildred asked.

"Just old age and not turning over for about a hundred years."

Krysty smiled. "Reckon you might struggle and cough some if you didn't get turned over for a hundred years, lover."

It was the only light spot in a dreary and miserable morning.

The disappearance and death of Abe hung over them all like a bad dream.

Death had been a constant companion for Ryan from a very early age. It didn't matter how cunning and cautious you were in making sure the hooded man with the scythe only picked on enemies. Every now and again a friend would embark on that last train to the coast.

It never got easier.

"Which way?" J.B. repeated.

"Go a little farther, until we reach open country. Take a look around."

"If you like, my dear fellow, you could allow Michael and myself to return on foot to the redoubt. I am cognizant of the entry code to get through the security doors."

Ryan looked around from the front passenger's seat. Doc was staring pointedly out of the half-open back of the armored wag, ostentatiously not catching his eye.

"What are you up to, Doc?"

"Nothing, my dear chap. The nothingness is most important, my esteemed chum."

Ryan glanced at Krysty, who shook her head and shrugged her shoulders.

"Why, Doc?" he asked.

"Food is in short supply, is it not? Two less aboard will help that."

"No. We stick together, Doc. We won't go far. Sounds like the wag might give out under us. But if all's well we can be back before dark in the redoubt. That please you?"

"I suppose it must, Ryan."

THE ROAD WEST, which paralleled the course of the stream, dipped into a tree-lined valley that was still brimming with early-morning mist.

"Looks like a good place for an ambush," J.B. stated, wrestling with the gears.

"Be an idea to close the rear doors and man the LMGs."

The Armorer followed Ryan's suggestion, and the vehicle was sealed against any attack.

There were sizable pools remaining at the sides of the street from the previous night's storm, the water hissing and splashing under the tracks of the APC.

The road slewed to the right, across a narrow bridge, then straightened again, going downhill with trees jostling in on both sides.

Ryan peered through the screen, the wipers going to clear away the rain that dripped from the overhanging branches.

"Doesn't seem to be much life around here, J.B. commented, steering them along the faded white line toward another bridge.

On the right they could both see the glint of water as they came down to the stream's level. It was running brown and fast.

'Must've gone through that culvert and come right on out the other side." Ryan wiped condensation off the inside of the shield. "Wonder where Abe's body finished up?'

"Probably halfway down the Sippi by now. Dark night!" The gears made a hideous grinding noise, and J B. wrestled with the controls.

"Mebbe we ought to turn around and head back toward the lake and the redoubt." Ryan settled himself in the bucket seat, trying to find a position that was less uncomfortable.

Their speed had dropped to less than walking pace as they approached a very sharp corner, with the road narrowed to a single lane.

It crossed Ryan's mind that if the muties were still in the area, then this would be the time and the place for them to try to spring a trap. A tree felled in front and one behind, and they could all be in some serious shit.

He and the Armorer spotted the pale figure emerging slowly from the dense undergrowth at exactly the same moment.

The brakes slammed on, bringing the wag to an instant shuddering halt. Nearly everyone was taken by surprise at the stop and both Doc and Mildred actually fell over.

Ryan had his pistol drawn, the combat reflex cutting in even before he'd recognized the skinny, naked man standing thirty paces in front of them, holding up his right hand.

Krysty recognized him from the vid screen. "It's Abe."

ONE OF THE LOCKERS inside the wag contained several items of clothing, and Abe was soon huddled inside a camouflage jacket and pants, with a pair of steel-capped boots on his feet. A stainless-steel Colt Python .357 was holstered at his hip.

Using a plug-in heater, Ryan had boiled some water and reconstituted some packs of insta soup he'd found. Abe was hugging a steaming mug, teeth chattering, body still trembling. Mildred had given him a once-over, patching up the superficial wounds with the first-aid kit from underneath the front passenger seat.

He was a mass of cuts and bruises. Livid patches of purple covered his chest, where Mildred suspected he might have cracked at least two of the lower ribs. A huge bruise marred the temple, and another circled his right thigh. A flap of skin hung loose off his shoulder, and Mildred had managed to stitch it up. Dried blood was caked in Abe's hair and around his mouth.

"Want to talk about it?" J.B. asked. "Last we saw was you and the tall mutie going over the edge into the water."

"Last I remember."

Dean was sitting next to the gunner, staring intently into his lined face. "You chill the pig?"

"Wouldn't know, son. Told you. Him and me went in the river a thousand miles an hour. Dived under. Hit my chest, and that's all she wrote."

'You must've gone into the culvert that carried the stream underground," Ryan guessed.

Abe nodded slowly, eyes far away. "Seem to remember trying to hang on some iron bars. Got tugged off. Dark. Fucking dark, friends."

"Still, now you're back safe with us, Abe." Mildred smiled. "Few days to sort of convalesce and you'll be good as new. Better than new."

"I don't know.. ."

J.B. patted Abe on the shoulder in a rare display of emotion. "Good to have you back safe, bro."

"Yeah. Good to..." Again, the words trailed off into the stillness inside the wag. Up front, the engine coughed again.

"Screw this," Ryan said. "Turn her around, J.B., and we'll head for the redoubt. No point going on any farther."

Abe put down the empty mug and stood, a little shakily, and drew the gleaming handgun ''No, he said. ''Not going on.''

Chapter Twenty-Seven

Ryan shook his head. "You must've got a bad knock on the head, Abe."

"Yeah, I did. But that's not all I got. Want to talk to you, Ryan. Outside."

"You need the blaster for that?"

Abe laughed. "Shit, no. Just took it out to sort of show I could look after myself. Once I get going on my own again."

"Where?" Dean asked.

"I'll tell your father, kid." He slid the 6-round revolver back into its holster. "You coming out for a moment, Ryan?"

"Sure."

Outside the air smelled cool and green.

Ryan leaned a hand against the cold, damp metal of the wag, his eye raking the trees for any sign of life. The Trader used to say that you didn't trust anyone, especially not yourself. It was possible that Abe was going to betray them.

Not likely.

But possible.

"Yeah?" Ryan prompted. "So, tell me."

"I got saved."

"I know. You wouldn't be standing here if you were chilled, Abe."

"I mean *saved.*."

"By what?"

"By who."

"What?" Ryan felt his head spinning. The conversation was slipping out of his control.

Abe sighed. "Look, I mean that someone came along and plucked me from the dark night."

"You said you didn't remember anything. So how come you—"

Abe rode over him. "Will you fucking shut your trap and listen, Ryan?"

"Sorry, Abe. Go on."

"It was dark. I was drowning. Under for the twentieth time. Sucked down. Ready to give up." He punched his right fist into his left hand. "No! I'd already given up."

"And you got saved. Sounds like... No, carry on with it."

"Someone came and grabbed me. Pulled me out. Told me to get my shit together and stop whining and feeling sorry."

"Who could've—"

"Said to me that a man who's ready to give up is ready to buy the farm."

Ryan's good eye opened wide and his jaw dropped. "Trader?"

"Man around his early fifties. Black pants, black shirt. Black boots. Grizzled hair. Holding a battered

Armalite. Just tell me who the fuck that was, will you, Ryan?''

"Trader."

"And he still had the bastard cough. You know? Way he used to bring up blood?''

"Toward the end."

"Yeah. Looked me right in the eye. Like he was going to chew rocks and shit sand."

Ryan grinned. Abe's description was an ace on the line for Trader. He was the toughest man that Ryan had ever met. Or ever expected to meet.

"Then what?"

"Pulled me by the hand. Hauled me up to the night air.''

"You dreamed it."

Abe looked at him for a long half minute. "Mebbe."

"Trader's dead."

"I told you I heard different."

"I heard the rumors as well, Abe."

"So?"

"So what? Fireblast! Stories around the fire late at night. Man as big as Trader buys the farm, and everyone in Deathlands gets to hear about it. Like the king or the president in old times."

Abe stepped in closer, dropping his voice to a whisper. "Tell me the truth, Ryan. No bullshit or lies. Truth."

"What?" Knowing in his heart what the question would be, knowing with a chill that he truly didn't know the answer

"You certain Trader's dead?"
"No."

ABE STOOD by the passenger's side of the wag.

The engine was, for the time being, running smoothly, ticking over in the morning quiet. The sec doors were sealed tight, and the wag was pointing toward the east again, back toward the charred heart of the old ville of Chicago.

The farewells had been said, hands shaken, kisses exchanged, a tear or two shed.

The armaglass window was down a few inches, so that Ryan and Abe could share a last moment through the narrow gap.

"You could stay with us, Abe. I told you. We hear anything more than just a rumor, or a drowning man's dream, and J.B. and me'd be alongside you, tracking Trader down."

"I know that."

"But you're going." It was a flat statement, not a question.

"Got to go look."

"Yeah." He reached out and the two men clasped hands.

"Been good meeting up again with you, Ryan." He nodded to the driver. "And you, too, J. B. Dix." He waved to Krysty, Doc, Mildred and Dean, and finally to Michael, who'd taken no part in the conversation about the Trader. "Look after them all for me, Mike," he said.

"I will so do, God being my helper," came the young man's voice.

"See you around," Ryan called.

He turned to J.B. "Let's go."

He watched the small, lonely figure diminishing in the rearview mirror of the wag, until they eventually turned a corner and Abe vanished from sight.

Chapter Twenty-Eight

The engine cut out forty-five minutes later.

It had been sounding raggedy the entire morning, despite J.B.'s best efforts to nurse it along. The ignition was irregular, and the gears were grinding and missing.

"Noise like two muties duelling with powersaws," Krysty said.

"Not healthy," Mildred agreed. "Hope our insurance is up-to-date."

"I don't imagine that you are cognizant of the ways of the internal combustion engine, are you, Michael, my dear fellow?"

"Sorry, Doc."

"Can you repair wags?" Doc amended. "No? I rather thought not."

"Any idea what's wrong?" Ryan asked.

J.B. sat at the wheel, staring straight ahead of them at the highway. "Yeah. It hasn't turned over for a hundred years, and now we turned it over too much. Needed running gently for a few minutes. Bit more next day. So on."

"Can you start her up again?"

'Who knows?''

"J.B., can we get out? Once the engine stops, then it gets real stuffy in here."

"Sure, Krysty. No sign of anyone around is there? Ryan, you see anyone?"

"No. I heard this used to be one of the biggest villes in the world. That right, Mildred?"

"Yeah. Where'd they all go? So many millions of them."

"Food." It was Krysty who answered the question.

The Armorer had opened the sec doors at the rear of the APC, letting in a surge of fresh air. One by one they began to climb out.

"Food? You mean they starved?"

"Some places were better than others. That's what I heard from old-timers. Those whose parents lived through the nuke nights. Some places the missiles wiped out virtually everyone. They were known as the lucky ones."

Ryan was standing near the front of the wag, looking around at the endless suburbs of the ville. Many of the houses were in decent shape, but there wasn't any sign of life.

Many of the really big villes he'd visited, like Newyork, still had some kind of population in their devastated centers, often engaged in barter or in crime, often muties or breeds.

Apart from the roving gang that had attacked them during the night, he still had seen virtually no trace of a living soul at all, which was probably something to do with the center of the city having been wiped away in the firestorm.

Krysty and Mildred were both looking eastward, to the smudge of darkness that lay between them and the lake.

"So, after the nuking, civilization virtually collapsed overnight." Mildred shook her head. "Like a horror novel."

"Worse," Krysty said. "This was real. They used to have all these stores for food and drink. But the highways were wrecked, and so was all the power. Food rotted in warehouses and the people couldn't get at it."

"Farmers must have done well."

Krysty looked at her. "Think so? You got a starving child and a sharp knife. Man tells you he's got a load of food, at a price. What do you do, Mildred? You pay him?"

"You open him up from groin to throat. Yeah, I see what you're saying."

"Ma told me that there were big fights after the dark nights started. And the long winters." Dean was picking up stones from the pavement and flicking them underhand at a row of tilted mailboxes, hitting most of them.

"I believe there were floods of desperate people, an exodus on an unbelievable scale. But the country was stripped of food. As they walked they starved. And as they starved, they died." Doc blew his nose into his swallow's-eye kerchief. "So I have been told, my friends."

Krysty nodded. "True. Stench from tens of thousands of rotting corpses lasted for weeks. No sunlight, crops withered and dead. Nightmare."

"Why?" Dean asked. "I never understood that. Asked Rona, but she didn't know. Why did the end begin? Whose fault was it?"

But nobody could tell him.

RYAN AND J.B. were working on the engine, trying to fault-find backward from the poor ignition. They weren't having any success.

Krysty was lying on her back, eyes closed, beneath the shade of a widespread yew tree, catching up on the lost hours of sleep from the previous disturbed night.

Doc had walked into one of the nearby houses and come out with a frail, faded paperback book that he'd found hurled into a corner of the ravaged living room. It was the collected poetry of Bob Dylan and he sat on the stoop, immersed in its wonder and beauty. Occasionally his lips moved as he read out some of his favorite lines.

Dean had hung around with his father until Ryan shooed him away.

Michael sat cross-legged in the long grass of a lawn that ran down to the edge of the street. He had laid his hands, palms up, on his thighs and was staring blankly toward the watery sun that hung low in the eastern sky.

Mildred had been checking through the first-aid kit from the wag, occasionally slipping an item into her pockets. One of the ampoules was a fast-acting anesthetic, and she held it cautiously up to the light, agitating it before adding it to the rest of her collection.

"What are they, Mildred?" Dean asked.

"Drugs."

"Any jolt?"

"No."

"Any crack?"

"No."

"Dreem?"

"No, Dean, nothing like that at all. These are drugs to make you feel better."

"Any runners? Purples?"

"No, I told you."

The boy stood in front of her. "Bet you got some good stuff, haven't you?"

Mildred leaned forward, making him take a wary step away from her anger. "I told you what I've got. Nothing that'll interest you, Dean. Not unless you go and get sick."

"Yeah, all right, all right. Geez, you're a sorehead, Mildred."

He shuffled away, dragging his feet in the gutter, picking up another handful of stones and resuming his game of chucking them at the mailboxes.

"Why don't you go and do that some other place," Krysty called, not even bothering to open her emerald eyes.

"Why?"

"Because I'll pull off your head and spit down your neck if you don't."

The boy laughed delightedly. "You and Mildred must both have your monthlies. That's why you got so itchy and mean. Rona was always like that when she had the curse."

"Don't criticize what you can't understand," Doc said without looking up.

"I'm bored. You got any brainies or bursters in those drugs, Mildred?"

"Look, I'm not—"

Michael uncoiled himself from his meditation and walked toward Dean, who backed off nervously, making a gesture to threaten the teenager with his pebbles.

"Hey, you better leave me alone or I'll bust your face open."

"How many of those mailboxes can you hit? Say, out of ten throws?"

"Ten," he replied quickly. "Well, around six or seven."

"I'll hit ten."

"Crap."

"Ten."

"You mean ten shots at the same box? That what you mean, Michael?"

"No. I'll start with the nearest."

"Red flag on it?"

"Yeah. Powell family."

"Ten stones at the next ten along. Up to the one nearly falling over?"

The young man looked and nodded. "Burke. That one."

You can read the lettering that far off? You got eyes like a hunting hawk." The boy whistled. "Dad, you hear that?"

Ryan was chest-deep in the engine compartment of the wag, trying to fix a wrench on a recalcitrant and unreachable bolt. He didn't answer his son.

"Dad, you hear me?"

"Sure, sure. Just keep quiet and stay out of everyone's hair, will you, Dean?"

"Come on," Micahel said quietly. "I say I'll hit all ten with ten stones. What do you say?"

"I say you're a liar."

"Suppose I do it?"

"Suppose the cow jumps right over the moon, huh?"

"Suppose I do it, Dean?" the young man repeated. "What then?"

"Oh, like a bet?" He dropped his voice so that Mildred, who was closest, couldn't hear him. "You mean like suck your dick or something dirty?"

Michael narrowed his eyes in surprise. "Why would I want to do that? No. If I do what I say, you can just say you're sorry for not believing me."

"That all?"

"Of course. Back in Nil-Vanity, where I was raised from a little baby, that was how we would all play this game."

"Sure. Go on, then. Get your stones."

Michael wandered into the street, walking slowly, occasionally peering down at the assortment of rocks and pebbles. Twice he picked up one with his toes, balancing easily on the other bare foot.

The rest he collected into the pocket of his brown robe.

"I'm ready," he said.

"Go."

Dean blinked. He hadn't seen Michael's arm move at all. But he'd heard the snap of the wrist and a high, whirring sound, followed by a clunk as the rounded pebble struck the center of the Powell family mailbox, leaving a silver dent.

"One," Michael counted.

"Yeah, one," the boy agreed.

The next three stones were thrown with such awesome speed and accuracy that they rang on the boxes only a bare heartbeat apart.

"Four."

"Right."

Doc had laid down his tattered book and was staring down into the street.

Mildred was watching what was going on with an intent fascination.

Krysty had opened one eye.

Ryan and J.B. were still buried under the hood of the malfunctioned wag.

"Five, six, seven, eight."

The mailboxes of Floyd Thursby, Simeon Rack, Jemima McPhee and the Houston family all rattled in quick succession.

"Shit," Dean breathed.

Doc stood. So did Krysty. Mildred called out to Ryan and to J.B., attracting both men's attention.

"Two to go," Michael said. "One without a name on it and then Burke. Ready?"

Dean nodded. "I don't believe this," he whispered.

"What's going on?" Ryan asked.

"Michael just threw stones at eight mailboxes in a row," Krysty replied, "and hit all eight. Now he's going for ten out of ten."

Ryan glanced down the suburban street. The farthest of the boxes was at least two hundred feet away, partly in shadow. It would have been a fair shot with a handgun. With a stone it would be exceptional.

"Ten out of ten," he said.

"Watch him, Dad." Dean's voice broke and squeaked in his excitement.

"Nine," Michael said, his wrist snapping forward, the stone hissing in a low, flat trajectory.

The box was knocked clean off its post by the force of the stone striking it.

"Want to bet he gets the tenth one as well," J.B. said to Ryan.

"I was going to ask you the same question. Wouldn't lose jack against his doing it."

The young man turned to look at the watching faces. For the first time since he'd been trawled, Michael seemed happy. There was a smile haunting his lips. He tossed the last rounded pebble into the air and caught it again.

"Ten for the ten bright shiners," he said.

The stone flew, a tiny dot in the shadows beneath the overhanging trees. The Burke mailbox gave out a dull thud and rocked on its support.

"Ten!" Dean whooped.

"That's good." Ryan clapped his hands together.

"Best I seen," J.B. agreed. "Kid could knock the balls off a diving hornet."

"Marksmanship that would have brought the yellow tint of jealousy to the very eyes of William Tell himself," Doc said, runic as ever to most of his companions.

Ryan turned back toward the engine. "Get this going and we'll be off to the redoubt, make a jump someplace else."

Doc had his thumb marking a page in the book of poems. He peered down into it. "Someplace else," he said quietly. "Like the man says here, should we not consider ourselves to be a morning too many and apart by a thousand miles?"

Ryan didn't understand what Doc was saying.

Not then.

IT TOOK THREE FULL HOURS to get the engine of the wag to start again and run for more than thirty seconds.

Krysty had been sleeping most of the time, and Mildred had eventually joined her, after making sure that her little trove of medicine was tucked safely into her pockets.

Dean had been running up and down the street, firing stones from the hip at the windows of the houses, yelling delightedly at the occasional crashing sound of broken glass.

Ryan eventually stopped him from the pointless destruction.

Doc and Michael had been talking on the porch of the nearest house.

As the APC's exhaust finally belched bluish smoke, Ryan stood by the rear doors and shepherded everyone inside the wag.

"Come on, brothers and sisters!" he shouted. "All aboard."

"For a trip around the bay," Mildred added, following Krysty and Dean. "Where have Doc and Michael gone? They must've heard you shout."

"Yeah." Ryan looked around. "They must've heard the engine. And me shouting. Must have."

Chapter Twenty-Nine

Ryan went with Krysty and Dean and searched carefully along the northern side of the street, blasters drawn and cocked.

Having spent all that time and energy in getting the wag to run, the Armorer slipped into the driver's seat and switched off the ignition.

Then J.B. walked with Mildred on the south side, going through all the houses, calling out for their missing friends.

Their voices rang through the silence, but there was no reply.

Because the whole region was a maze of crisscrossing paths, porches and streets, there was no hope of tracking them down.

Ryan quickly discovered that the two had simply walked through the nearest house and out the back door, across the garden and past a rotted gate into a rear alley. Then they headed into the vast, wandering silent suburbs of Chicago.

"We could chase them, Dad," Dean offered. "Can't've gone too far."

"Nobody's seen them, for sure, for at least an hour and a half. Could be two hours. Might be anywhere within a radius of seven or eight miles from here. No, it looks like they planned all this and went of their own free will."

"Where?" the boy asked. "Why'd they run away and leave us?"

Ryan shook his head. "I've felt something up with Doc for a while. Since we trawled Michael. Thing is, with that old son of a bitch, you never quite know for certain what's going on inside that scrambled head of his. But I'm sure he had some plan. Just don't know what."

Krysty solved the puzzle.

On the porch, where Doc had been sitting and reading, she found the book that had preoccupied him—the collected poetry of a singer from the late-twentieth century, called Bob Dylan. It was a fat volume, printed on thin paper, that had grown dry and frail and brittle over the intervening century.

"Turned over the corner of a page here," she said to Ryan.

"What?"

"Doc's folded a page over, where he was reading. Must have been just before he and Michael went off hiking."

J.B. had just reappeared with Mildred after their fruitless search along the other side of the street.

"Not a sign."

"No. They went out back of this house here. Vanished into the path behind it. You can't pick up any tracks. Hopeless."

"Where on earth do they think they're going?" Mildred asked.

"After Abe?" J.B. shook his head, answering himself. "Why would they do that? No. Doesn't make any sense."

"Krysty found the book Doc was reading before he went."

J.B. turned to her. "Any clue on that page he marked?"

She looked up, her face solemn. "Think so. He's underlined one bit of one poem. Near the front of the book."

"What's it say?" Mildred asked.

"It's a line about trying to find old friends, if they're still around."

"Old friends," J.B. mused.

"Fireblast! Old friends! He and Michael are going to the redoubt. The chron-jump unit. They're both trying to get home."

Chapter Thirty

"One shouldn't lose touch with old friends. The skillful Mr. Dylan is quite correct, you know, my dear Michael. Keep in touch while they're all still around."

They had hidden, at Doc's suggestion, less than a quarter mile away from where J.B. and Ryan were laboring to repair the wag.

"Once they find us missing they'll search. But they will swiftly give up. Can't track on bare stone. I have learned that, Michael."

"Should we not have run away as far and fast as possible?"

"No. I do not know how long it will be before we are missed. But they can move faster than us. We might get caught in the open, and then we should never be able to follow through with our plan."

"Your plan."

The old man nodded. "Indeed."

They'd been in the front bedroom of a trim duplex, three streets from the rest of the group, sitting quietly on the faded linoleum floor beneath a broken window. Waiting and listening.

THE AGONY of seeing himself with his wife and children on the dark, flickering vid film had been one of the most difficult and painful experiences of Doc Tanner's life.

The disturbance of being trawled, years ago now, had left him permanently damaged. There were times that his mind was relatively balanced and normal. Times that it became deeply disturbed.

Few people knew better than Doc what an erratic and unreliable procedure the time-trawling had been. He had gradually become reconciled to the fact that he would never again be able to see Emily or the little ones.

Never.

Then they had come across this unbelievable jewel in the heart of the abandoned redoubt. A chron unit, fully functioning and ready to go.

All he had to do was to get back there, have a few hours of secure privacy to check everything out and make the necessary computations, then, if the gods smiled upon him, he could hazard the jump back to November 1896.

It was like a dream. A dream that he'd lived with ever since he was lifted and jerked into the horrors of the present. A dream that could, just possibly, now become a reality.

The arrival of Michael Brother had been a kind of trigger for him to act.

Now there was someone else in the same boat. Someone he could help at the same time as helping himself. And someone who could lend a hand with setting and operating the complex range of controls for the chron jump.

Sitting on the floor, locked into his thoughts, Doc was smiling.

Very distantly, like something half-remembered on waking, they heard voices calling their names. But the searchers never got within a block of the house where they were hiding.

Michael giggled, shoving his fist into his open mouth.

"Shhh," Doc warned. "Maintain self-control, my dear boy."

"Sorry, Doc. We used to play hide-go-seek back in the sanctuary and I was always skillful at it."

"This isn't a game, Michael. If Ryan and the others find us, then our chance of returning to our own time and our own friends may well have vanished from us forever."

"Why wouldn't they help us?"

Doc hesitated. "They are the bravest and best of friends. But they might decide to follow the lords of chaos and prevent us from leaving Deathlands. Do you understand?"

Michael shook his head. "I can't honestly say that I do."

A large cockroach, antennas quivering, picked its unsteady way across the floor of the bedroom, vanishing into a jagged crack in the plaster beneath the opposite window

Now the shouting had drifted away into the still-ness. Doc stood and risked a glance outside, his face flattened against the dusty glass.

"No sign," he said.

"Then we can go?"

"Why not?"

A LIGHT COVERING of high cloud drifted across a sky of pallid blue. A gentle breeze blew in from the south, bringing the scent of oranges with it.

Doc led the way down the stairs, avoiding the jag-ged remnants of the banisters. "I think we should make our departure through the back entrance, like the tradesmen that we are."

"What if we get attacked by the evil-hearted ones without hair?"

"Then I'll use my Le Mat and you'll have to draw your trusty steel again. But if we are cautious, I hope that we shall make our destination safely"

"When?"

"By dawn tomorrow. If not before dusk this very day. Ryan generally advises against traveling after dark in a hostile ville."

"Hostile ville? Is this place hostile toward us, Doc?"

The old man grinned, showing his fine, strong teeth. "A valuable lesson in this dark land is that everything and everyone is hostile. I believe a man called the Trader used to say something very similar"

The rear garden lay before them, luxurious and overgrown.

Which way   the young man asked.

'East,' Doc replied with a massive, splendid confidence.

Leading the way at a fast stride in the general direction of north.

Chapter Thirty-One

They'd been walking for some time, zigging and zagging as the winding side streets dictated, occasionally having to stop and cut across acres of undergrowth where houses had been burned down and the ways blocked, roads vanished.

"Listen." Michael held up a warning hand, stopping Doc in his tracks.

"What is it? I confess that my hearing is not, perhaps, as acute as once it was."

"An engine. Like the truck we rode inside. That armored box."

"The wag? Where? By the three Kennedys, I wish I could hear as well as you."

"Who are the three Kennedys?"

"Men from my past. Our past. John who was president and was shot. Bobby who was like a panther in a hurricane and would have been president, had he not been gunned down."

"That's only two."

"There was a third brother but I disremember much about him. Times past hardly worth the trouble of forgetting. But you hear the wag?"

"Yeah. Behind us." He pointed with his finger "Sounds like it's moving roughly from right to left, as we look toward it."

"Then they're going south. I wonder why that is? I thought..." Doc hesitated and Michael caught onto the doubt.

"You sure we're going east, Doc? I wouldn't know myself."

"Of course. Let us check. Moss grows on the south side of trees. Young Jak Lauren taught me that." A long pause. "Or, might it possibly have been the north? I'm a trifle confused, I fear."

'Sun rose over there and seems like it's setting over that way."

Doc nodded. "That would be the west. I think I have led us a little astray, my boy. The foolishness of a dotard."

"I can't hear the wag engine anymore, Doc. I think it stopped."

'Fireblast!"

"Dark night and triple damnation!"

"Gaia! Wish we'd never got started in this wag in the first place."

Mildred stood, waiting for J.B. to open the rear doors of the APC again. "Let's get out and get under," she said.

"Sounded terminal." Ryan swung out of the driver's seat.

"Think we got a major oil leak." J B. joined him outside.

The engine temperature needle had been hovering well into the crimson sector for the past fifteen minutes. That, combined with the hideous grinding, crunching noise every time the throttle was opened, made the Armorer's pessimistic diagnosis seem the probable one.

Once they investigated the latest stoppage, it was obvious that the condition of the vehicle was terminal.

Thick brown oil was smudged everywhere, stinking and burned.

J.B. pointed silently to a large crack that was also seeping a turbid black sludge.

"Bad news?" Krysty peered over Ryan's shoulder. "Oh, yeah. Bad news."

"Worth trying a repair? Just to get us back to the redoubt?" Mildred's voice betrayed her doubts.

J.B. whistled, pushing the fedora back off his forehead. "Don't know Think we might do better trekking it."

Ryan looked around. They'd made comparatively poor progress since dawn. There'd been the search for Doc and Michael and now yet another mechanical malfunction.

"Not all that far to sunset," he said.

"Haven't seen any live ones today." J.B. slammed the hatch shut on the engine. "Think we could get back to the lake before dark?"

Ryan shook his head. "Straight march with no problems and you and me could do it easy But if anything goes wrong, then I don't fancy holing up for the night in that mess that used to be the center of the ville."

"Think there's ghouls there, Dad?"

Ryan laughed. "Want to meet some?"

"Met some once. Rona and me hid in the ruins above an old ville. Indian ruins. They come after us. Two of them with sharp teeth. She tracked them away from me. One tried to fuck her, so she cut his balls off. Other ghoul ran off."

"Serve them right," Mildred told him. "Only way to treat a ghoul, Dean. Cut the son of a bitch's pecker off."

J.B. wasn't smiling. "We're down to five, Ryan. Small number for a foot patrol."

"I know it."

"Got plenty of firepower. Wish we knew that Doc was safe."

Mildred squeezed J.B.'s arm. "That old goat could fall in a pile of shit and come out smelling of lilies, John."

THEY AGREED that they'd move a little closer into the heart of old Chicago, going in an extended skirmish line to minimize risks.

Ryan and J.B. took turns at point and rearguard, the two isolated and vulnerable positions in any patrol.

J B. had his Smith & Wesson scattergun at the hip, finger always on the trigger Ryan kept the Steyr bolt-action rifle slung across his shoulder, the SIG-Sauer in its open holster

Mildred, Krysty and Dean alternated in the center of the quintet.

They kept off the buckled remnants of the freeway, working their way slowly eastward along side streets and quiet avenues.

There were storm clouds gathering to the west, with thundertops rising thousands of feet into the evening sky. The sun had dipped behind them, out beyond the plains of Iowa and Nebraska, bringing a sullen chill to the air.

They'd come across a region that looked as though it had been a target area for more-conventional low-yield nukes. Probably Russkie multihead missiles that fragmented as they sliced through the upper atmosphere. The American defences had been able to knock down nine out of ten, but some got through.

There were old craters, some of them four or five blocks across, many filled with stagnant, swampy expanses of water.

Suddenly they started to see more wildlife around them. An enormously long cottonmouth slithered out of a patch of jimson weed, curling among the purplish-white trumpet flowers. Dean drew his Browning, drawing a careful bead at the questing, shovel-shaped head, but Ryan turned to the boy and hissed an urgent warning.

"Let it be, son. Quiet evening like this and a shot'll carry three or four miles."

The snake wound its leisurely way toward the nearest water, sliding beneath the oily surface with hardly ripple.

And there were rats.

One darted across the rubble-filled street ahead of J.B. when he was out on point. It was a normal-size rodent, skittering belly-down, jaws gripping what looked like a scrap of meat.

Within the next fifteen minutes they saw more than a dozen rats.

One of them was a bizarre, mutated creature, eight-legged, twin-headed. It was the size of a small dog, its teeth like yellow tusks that curled over its upper lip. The skulls moved separately on two necks, watching both ways at once.

"That's one of the most repulsive things I ever saw in my life," Mildred said, her voice thickened with disgust and loathing.

Her voice attracted the attention of the mutie rat, and both heads swiveled toward her, the four yellow eyes glistening wetly. The lips curled, and a long hissing breath slid past the fangs.

"Don't shoot it," Ryan warned, drawing his panga and taking a step toward the grotesque parody of an animal.

It made a mewing sound, and its double row of legs shuffled untidily, almost as though half of them wanted to go forward and half of them back. When Ryan stamped his steel-heeled boot on the pavement, it finally retreated.

"Who needs ghouls with something like that around?" Mildred asked no one in particular.

"This much animal life means there's food around the ruins," J.B. observed.

"And that likely means people." Ryan looked behind them at the darkening sky. "Could be a good time to find a place for the night."

"Yeah."

THREE-QUARTERS OF A MILE to the northeast, Michael kept looking over his shoulder. "Big storm coming, Doc."

"Figure we should find us a safe place for the night. Don't like all these damnable rats. If only half my coat were rad and half were yellow."

The young man laughed delightedly. "The Pied Piper. I know that poem."

"Well, we could most certainly utilize his pest-control talents around here."

"I could kill them with my knives."

"No, I think not. Better not to antagonize the pests. You might kill one and then find a thousand come boiling out of some vast burrow beneath the ruins."

Michael shuddered. "We had rats in Nil-Vanity. Hated them."

Doc leaned on his sword stick, breathing heavily. "I am too old for this sort of activity." He sighed. "Time was, my dearest Emily and I would—" He stopped, shaking his head, crystal tears tumbling from his rheumy eyes.

"You'll be seeing your wife and children again, Doc. And me my friends."

"Yes, yes, of course we will. I wish we had made better time and not wandered off our true path. If Ryan and the others get to the place of the chron jump first..."

"Maybe we should keep moving through the night," Michael suggested.

"Why not? Excellent idea." Doc slapped him heartily on the back. "Brother Michael, the confined monk with the unconfined mind."

At that moment the first heavy drops of rain began to splatter around them, glittering in the dusk light like new-minted coins.

"BE RAINING any minute." Ryan looked around them. A feral cat, as skinny as a razor, was slinking along the front of a row of abandoned stores, its golden eyes shining in the gloom.

"Think Doc and Michael are okay, lover?"

"Until you can spit in the eyes of the corpse, you better figure it's living."

"One of Trader's?"

Ryan nodded. "Course. I reckon they must be ahead of us. Could possibly have reached the redoubt, but I don't think so. Moving fast over broken ground was never Doc's strongest card." He paused. "And he's not so hot at navigating."

Krysty looked up at the black sky. "I'm seriously worried about Doc and Michael going to the chronjump unit, Ryan. Got a bad feeling about it. Suppose they get there before us and try to go back to their own times?"

He looked at her. "If they do, then they will. From what we know, the odds are huge against them. If they try it, I doubt we'll ever see them again."

There was a distant rumble of thunder, and the first spots of rain began to splatter around them.

"Best get cover," Mildred said, hunching her shoulders.

"Those stores." J.B. pointed with the muzzle of the shotgun. "Be safe in there for the night. Easy to defend."

"Hope there's no ghouls inside," Dean muttered worriedly.

Chapter Thirty-Two

The end sections of the row of a dozen stores had fallen in, leaving piles of wind-washed stone and rusting iron.

Several more units had lost parts of their roofs and were already awash with flat pools of dark rainwater. Only the two in the center were still reasonably solid and weatherproof. All of them had lost their main windows a hundred years earlier, but the pair in the middle had been boarded up.

The names could still be made out, silhouetted against the stained concrete. One had been the F.M. Baby Emporium. The other had been called, mysteriously, Vinyl Daze.

Once the five friends were huddled inside, the rain teeming outside, Ryan asked Mildred if she knew what the name meant.

"Vinyl Daze? Yeah, I can guess. You know that you told me you've seen, occasionally, music players that used a CD?"

Ryan nodded. "Little disks. Patterns like rainbows on them."

"Right." She wiped rain off her plaited hair. "Well, before these CDs came along, there were records. Ordinary disks, twelve inches across, of vinyl. Lot of people loved them, but the big companies came along and said that they were phasing vinyl out so's everyone had to buy the CDs."

"That's a double bummer," Krysty said. "I heard Uncle Tyas McCann talk about it once. He got red in the face and big purple veins swelled in his forehead."

"All the sort of minority music, like blues and country started to disappear. Then you got specialist stores, like I guess this was, and they flourished. So, despite the worst they tried to do, vinyl never died after all."

Dean yawned. "That's dead boring, Mildred. Who cares about music? Not me."

The black woman shook her head slowly and sadly. "You can't believe what it used to be like, kid. Music was big in the lives of young people. What you got to replace it? Not books or movies. All you got is keeping alive. Keeping warm. Keeping food in your belly. Chilling the other guy before he damned well chills you. Not the same. By God, it's not anywheres near the same, Dean."

Doc AND MICHAEL had also holed up against the storm.

They'd come across a small complex of business units, with one six-story office block still standing at its center. Every single window had vanished in the days of dark nights, but the center staircase was still secure and the inner rooms were dry.

It seemed perfect to Doc.

If Ryan or J.B. had been there, they'd have pointed out that the building constituted a perfect trap. One set of stairs up and down. No rear exit. A single proficient man with a handgun could clear it out from basement to roof at virtually no risk to himself.

Others had been there before them.

The largest of the rooms had three stained and dusty mattresses lined neatly along one wall, and the dark remains of an ancient cooking fire sat in the middle of the floor.

"Got the last of some jerky," said the old man, lying on the nearest mattress, knees cracking like hazel twigs.

"Plenty of water outside." Michael squatted next to Doc, looking out across the corridor to where rain was pounding in through a broken casement. His bare feet, as hard as horn, were tucked comfortably beneath him.

They rested in silence for several minutes, lulled by the hissing of water and the occasional distant roll of thunder.

Doc broke the stillness between them. "You are sure you want to do this with me?"

"Yes."

"I would not wish to pressure you or to draw skeins of wool over your eyes. This is immensely hazardous, and we may both die in the most unimaginably horrific manner."

"I understand that."

Doc rolled onto his side and fixed the young man with a piercing glare. "You realize I am not talking of death No man knows what happens during a chron trawl. Where the molecules of your body and soul fly to. And how they reform. Or don't reform. If the process fails, you may not be here. Nor will you be back at Nil-Vanity, Michael. You will not be anywhere. In the vast coldness of inner space. And you will be there for all of infinity."

"It's worth the risk to get out of Deathlands. I haven't seen a thing to make me want to stay here any longer."

Doc sat up. "Oh, do not be deceived, brother. There is much good in this place. Much courage and honor and simple Christian values. If I were to pick the manner of my passing, I would not wish for anyone but Ryan and the others for company. They are truly heroic, Michael."

"Yes, but I want out."

"Think of being an incorporate entity throughout eternity, my dear boy. Do you have any understanding of eternity?"

"I guess not."

Doc took a deep breath. Michael lay back and closed his eyes, allowing the rich, sonorous voice to wash over him.

"Imagine, my boy, a sphere of solid brass, highly polished, floating in darkness. It is a thousand miles in diameter. A thousand miles across. You have that in your mind's eye?"

"Yes, I've got it."

"Now imagine a small white dove, fluttering upward toward that sphere. It does this once every hundred years. It brushes the tip of a wing feather against the polished brass just once every century. Think of how long it would take to wear that immense ball of brass away to nothing. That, Michael, is an approximation of eternity."

He looked across the gloomy room. The slender teenager was lying still, hands folded on his chest, his breathing steady and regular. Doc watched him for some time, smiling gently.

The old man's lips moved, and he whispered to himself in the dank darkness.

"I'm coming, Emily, my darling love. Soon now we'll be back together again. You and me and the dear little ones. The pain and suffering of our separation will be over."

THE RAIN CONTINUED unabated until the streets were teeming rivers. Ryan decided that they might as well stay in the old record store for the night. If Doc had gone straight back to the redoubt, then they would be too late anyway. If he hadn't, then he and Michael would probably have holed up somewhere against the storm. The old man had never been too keen on getting himself wet.

They'd finished off the last of the dried meat, washing it down with rainwater collected by Dean in a battered tin.

Night sidled in from the tempest that was blowing itself hoarse all about them, darkening the store. J.B. scavenged around and found some dry wooden laths from under the cracked ceiling and kindled a small fire near the front door, so that most of the smoke drifted out into the starless blackness. There was a through draft from the back door that hung askew on broken hinges.

"We move at first light," Ryan said.

"Guards?" The Armorer was methodically field-stripping his weapons and cleaning them with rags that he plucked from his capacious pockets.

"We've been seeing animals. Rats. Cats. Means there's probably people someplace close. Rain'll keep hunters away."

"Won't they smell the smoke and track us from that?" Mildred was sitting close to J.B.

"Rain stops that as well. Makes it hard to trace us." Ryan sniffed. "But it'd be stupe to take a chance. Yeah, we'll set a watch."

Despite his protests, Dean was forbidden to take a turn.

"There's only five of us." Ryan said, kneeling by his boy. "You never want to have anyone on guard on their own. Not in a situation like this here. Needs pairs. Means four hours on and four off."

"Why not me?"

"Because you're the youngest. If we had a round number here, then I'd be happy to have you take your share of watching out. It's not that I don't trust you, son."

"Truly?"

"Yeah, truly."

RYAN HAD WANTED to make love with Krysty, but she'd pleaded that she was too tired and cold.

"And please don't try the old line about warming me up, lover."

They'd pressed close together under the blanket as the fire died away, hearing Mildred and J.B. walking their patrol quietly outside.

Ryan was conscious of his own swelling need, moving gently against Krysty's buttocks, hearing her murmured laugh.

"All right," she whispered, hand coming around to feel inside his pants and grasp him. Her strong fingers circled the shaft, easing it out.

He wriggled Krysty's own pants over her hips, touching her and finding her roused for him.

"You lied," he said.

"Yeah."

Their coupling was long, slow and tender. Ryan took her from behind, reaching around and helping her to her own climax.

Afterward they dozed in the low-ceilinged rectangular room. Ryan was aware, around midnight, that the rain had finally stopped and the moon had broken through.

It seemed like a few seconds later that J.B. was kneeling by him, hand resting on his shoulder. "Time for your turn, bro."

"I'VE GOT TO PEE," Krysty said as they stood together, just inside the back entrance to the record store.

"Sure. I'll wait here."

"Won't be a minute."

She vanished, moonlight flaming on her hair, toward a low wall that was close by on the fourth side of the row of stores.

Ryan leaned against the door-frame and waited.

Chapter Thirty-Three

Krysty didn't have anything approaching J.B.'s fanatic expertise on firearms. But she knew enough about blasters to be able to recognize the Ruger SP-1010 .38-caliber revolver that was pointing at her face from a range of six inches.

"Blow yer fuckin' head clean off yer fuckin' shoulders. One word is what it'll take. Please say one word, cutelet."

The whispering voice was panting and hoarse, the breath in Krysty's nostrils sour, reeking of stale, rotten fish.

There was the unmistakable chill of another gun barrel pressed hard against Krysty's nape. Her sentient hair curled instinctively closer to her scalp, as though trying vainly to protect her from the threatened bullet.

"Very still, lady," said a thinner voice, less tense, somehow less threatening. "Very still and very silent."

Krysty knew in her heart that the initial speaker already had her trigger finger trembling, first pressure taken up, quivering with a barely controlled eagerness to squeeze down the last nanometer and explode Krysty's skull into brains, blood and shards of whirling bone splinters.

The moonlight was bright enough to dazzle Krysty, coming out of the total gloom of the building. She'd walked around the corner of the four-foot wall, belt already loosed, ready to drop her pants and squat to relieve herself.

And they'd been there.

Six, all women.

In the shadows Krysty couldn't make them out that clearly, but she was sure they were muties. The skin on their faces seemed unusually pale, gleaming in the silver light like the belly of a fish. And their eyes were protuberant, as if someone had their thumbs stuck behind them.

One surprising thing was that they were well-armed, though not with the usual mutie array of self-mades and cobbled together old muskets. The blasters that Krysty could see were all in good condition. She could catch the clean scent of oil from the Ruger. All the weapons were handguns.

Apart from the big Ruger, she noticed a 9 mm Llama Large Frame, a Walther P-88, an Astra A-90 parabellum and a white-painted Colt Commander.

The mutie women all wore black clothes, from their leather boots to the high-necked shirts. Three had on dark woollen caps, and four had mud smeared across their cheeks.

Krysty was aware of a tautness and discipline in the group.

"Move out." It was the woman behind her giving the orders.

"Where?" Krysty asked quietly.

Just another fuckin' word and yer rat food.'' The woman holding the Ruger pushed the muzzle forward until the chromed steel was actually touching Krysty's lips.

"Freddy means it. Just one more word from you and you're blown away. Move over there, toward those buildings."

The land dipped away giving them dead ground in that direction. Even if Ryan happened to be looking in her direction, he wouldn't notice anything. Less than thirty seconds had passed since she left him. It would be another two minutes, at least, before he started to worry.

And she knew she couldn't stall her captors for that long.

"Keep your head down. Six blasters on you. Get going."

Krysty did as she was told. She'd lived close enough to death to realize that her life now truly hung in the balance.

There wasn't even a chance to leave Ryan any clue to what had happened, and no hope of trying to draw her own concealed Smith & Wesson 640.

As they scurried off, Krysty wondered what the gang of women had been doing there. Had they smelled the smoke from J.B.'s fire and been getting ready for a

bloody raid? Or were they satisfied with a single prisoner?

'Earth Mother, I beg your aid,   she murmured to
herself.

RYAN WAITED a little less than two minutes before becoming apprehensive. The short hairs at his nape began to prickle and he drew the SIG-Sauer, dropping
from habit into a crouch. He didn't call out. It would
be a futile and probably dangerous thing to do.

After another crawling minute had gone by, Ryan
ghosted out from the deep pool of darkness in the
doorway, moving one cautious foot in front of the
other, avoiding the fragments of brick and glass that
littered the area around the stores.

As he neared the low wall, Ryan hesitated, going
onto hands and knees. He shuffled forward to the end
of the obstruction, inching his head around the rough
stone until he was finally able to see behind it.

"NOT A SIGN. Moonlight's not good for tracking, but
there was enough to make out marks of at least four
sets of boots."

Mildred, J.B. and Dean were all awake now, listening as Ryan told them the sorry news of Krysty's inex-
plicable disappearance.

The ground had been wet from the heavy rain, and
the footprints were deeply indented into soft mud. But
they overlapped one another to such an extent that it

wasn't possible to be sure of how many there had been in the raiding party.

"Anything about the marks?" the Armorer asked. "Give a clue to what we might be dealing with."

"Small."

"Women?" Mildred asked.

"Possibly. But not likely. They were all small. I never heard of gangs of women killers going around any-place."

J.B. took off his fedora and wiped his forehead, straightening his thinning hair. "Nor me. Knew a baron near Waycross ville had him a sec force of gaudy sluts. Liked watching them torture prisoners. Not the same as this."

"If they got Krysty away without her being able to give us any warning, then they gotta be good." Ryan peered out into the night. "Tracks'll be easy enough to follow at first light."

"Why can't we go now?" Dean stamped his foot in anxiety. "They could have chilled her by now, Dad, couldn't they?"

"Mebbe. Chilling silently isn't easy. They took the trouble to lift Krysty, then they did it for a reason. Odds are she's still living."

"Then, why'd they steal her?"

"Wish I knew, Dean. I wish I knew." He paused. "If all goes well in the morning, we'll quickly track them down and save her. Then we might find out just what's going on."

"MOVE YOUR ASS or you'll get a slapping!" One of the women, her fat body reeking of long-unwashed sweat, pushed Krysty in the back, making her stumble and nearly fall.

"Careful, Frankie!" snapped the lean mutie who seemed to be their leader. "Don't want her spoiled. Not after the trouble to get her."

They were a half mile away from Vinyl Daze, moving more slowly through the empty streets, with greater confidence.

"Why have you all gone to so much trouble?" Krysty risked asking.

"You were seen a day ago. One of our patrols. Trailed you since. Been waiting long for someone special like you."

"Special?"

The woman grabbed a handful of Krysty's amazing, fiery hair. "Special," she repeated. "No more talk. Just move."

MICHAEL SLEPT flat on his back, not all that far north of the others. He dreamed that he walked through the endless corridors of a vast cathedral, its vaulted roof soaring mistily above him. A choir was singing the Mass for the Dead in a side chapel, invisible to him for the tracery of stonework all around. There wasn't a single living person to be seen.

The air was thick with incense, and light flowed through a magnificent stained-glass window at the north end of the nave, spilling gules and azure, deep vermilion and bold porphyry amethyst and onyx all across the pale stones of the aisle.

The high, pure voices of the young boys filled the air and made his head spin with their cold, ethereal beauty

Above the altar he could see the figure of Christ crucified, life-size, so skillfully carved that it seemed almost human: the sinews, strained and agonized under the suspension of the execution, the glittering nails driven deep into the frail flesh, head thrown back, spittle drooling from the parted lips. There was blood dripping from palms and feet and from the gaping spear wound in the side.

Michael drew closer, his bare feet silent on the flagstones. He knelt before the altar and gazed at the face of Christ.

He turned to look at him and His mouth opened. The voice of the Lord spoke to Michael, far away and infinitely weary.

"Return to me, my son."

Michael started awake, trembling, finding his face bathed with perspiration, his limbs stiff and cold.

Doc lay at his side, his body moving as though he were consumed with some dreadful fever. The old man's fists were clenched, and he was mumbling a string of inaudible words to himself.

The teenager stood and walked out of the windowless room, standing in the corridor, stretching, pondering on the meaning of the dream. At Nil-Vanity they had been very strong on the interpretation of dreams. Brother Raymond would have told him.

Michael's ears caught a faint sound from the street outside. He inched to the nearest window and peeked out through shattered glass into the moon-bathed darkness.

There were three women there, all wearing black, their faces unusually pale. All were holding guns.

The tenseness of their body language told him immediately that they were hunters.

Just for a brief moment Michael wished that he owned a blaster like Doc and the others. But that moment passed.

One of the women turned to stare straight up at where he was hiding and he moved back. There'd been an impression of protruding eyes, searching him out. But when he looked again the three women were beginning to walk slowly away toward the south.

At that moment Doc, in the room behind Michael, cried out in his sleep, loud and shrill. "Emily!"

The trio of armed women immediately raced toward the main entrance to the building.

Chapter Thirty-Four

In the seconds after he startled awake, Doc Tanner hadn't the least idea where he was, or what was happening. Nor could he recall anything beyond the vaguest outline of the nightmare that had awakened him. He knew that Emily had been in it, and there had been a threat against her, something involving bright golden sand that she'd fallen into, so swiftly that only her hand, in a white lace glove, torn around the thumb, was visible to him.

"An anxiety dream," he muttered. He'd once read that all dreams were anxiety dreams in one form or another. Ever since he'd read that, Doc had discovered that all of his dreams really did seem to conform to some sort of worry.

"Michael?"

"Shut up." The voice came from just outside the abandoned office, in the passage.

"Michael?"

The young man appeared in the doorway, his bare legs ghostly pale. "Some women are coming in. They heard you call."

"Then I shall ready myself to welcome them as befits a gentleman."

"No, they're—"

Doc wasn't listening. "Perhaps they are some friends of dear Emily, calling for tea and wafer-thin cucumber sandwiches."

"No. I think they're coming to kill us, Doc. Let's find some way out."

"Kill us?" He heard the sound of boots, clattering up from the first floor. "The boots mount the staircase...." he whispered. "Poor old Marat. Poor old... To kill us?"

"Think so. Come on."

But there was only the one way up and down. A fire exit door beckoned at the farther end of the corridor. Michael pushed on the security bar, nearly tumbling to his death as it swung open onto dark space, an empty void waiting where the fire escape had once been.

Now the noise of running feet was louder, closer, one floor below them.

"Stay there," Michael said, pushing the old man into a pool of black shadows in the far corner of the passage.

"They may be friendly, might they not? Do not be too hasty, young man."

Michael padded to stand near the door into the room that they'd just abandoned, hands loose at his side, waiting.

The three women came out onto the landing, staring toward him. All of them were holding drawn, cocked pistols.

"Look what we got," said the first, a tall woman with a sloping forehead.

"Rat in a frock."

"Rat in a trap, likely."

Doc, in the darkness, slowly drew his Le Mat. His muzziness had gone, and he saw that he and Michael were in peril. If he cocked his own blaster now, the women would hear him and he'd fall dead before he could squeeze the trigger. He waited.

Michael had disappeared.

"Where's he gone?"

"That room."

"No doors or windows there."

"Rat in a trap, like I said."

"Have some laughs before he visits endless night," said the leader of the hunting trio, licking her narrow lips with a lascivious excitement.

"Yeah," the others echoed.

"I'm in here," Michael said, his voice calm, perfectly under control.

"Cheeky prick."

"Won't have a prick to be cheeky with. Not in a couple of minutes."

"Stick his prick in his cheek."

"I'm still waiting."

"Coming, ready or not."

The women had seen that the slender young man in the loose robe didn't appear to be carrying any sort of blaster, just a couple of little knives. Real easy picking.

They actually pushed and jostled one another in their eagerness to get at their victim. But the doorway was only wide enough for them to go through it one at a time.

As the last of them vanished from sight, Doc took a deep breath and eased back the hammer of the Le Mat revolver

He heard a scuffle, a long sigh, and something like a fountain being switched on, water pattering onto stone. Doc paused a yard from the door, his eyes screwed up as he tried to peer into the gloom, hesitating to draw attention to himself by calling out to Michael.

He jumped as a voice in the darkness whispered his name.

"All right, Doc."

"Michael?"

"Sure."

Now he could see something seeping into the passage by the toes of his knee boots, a thick liquid that appeared black in the moonlight.

As his eyes became accustomed to the gloom, Doc was able to make out two bodies. No, three corpses, lying sprawled and still, one of them on top of the other pair.

Michael was stooping, wiping his daggers on the jacket of the tallest of the women, straightening as he saw Doc watching him.

"All dead," he said.

"How? They all held revolvers. Three of them. How, Michael?"

"By using the skills I have been taught. Speed and simplicity. I cut the throat of the first with the knife in my right hand. The second with the other blade. The artery beneath the ear. The third stumbled, and I turned a little to the side and broke her neck with a kick from my right foot. It was not difficult, Doc. They helped me to do it by their vicious and eager foolishness."

"I see." Doc holstered the Le Mat. "They may have friends, Michael. I think we should consider making a move from this location, do you not?"

"I agree, Doc."

THEY LEFT THE TRIO of bodies where they'd fallen.

Michael hesitated, looking at the three handguns, then he turned abruptly on his heel and let the weapons lie.

He and Doc spent the remainder of the night in a small wooden shed at the bottom of the garden of a house in an adjoining street.

They both came quickly awake as soon as the first light of the eastern dawning broke through the dusty window.

"A new day, my dear young man. A new day for making dreams come true. I had a dream," he said in a loud, orator's voice. "And soon, very soon, we shall both witness that dream of eternal happiness reaching its climax. Today "

RYAN WAS AWAKE before first light.

After Krysty's disappearance he hadn't honestly slept at all. He lay on his back, under the blanket they'd been sharing only an hour earlier, the SIG-Sauer in his hand.

Part of the time he was trying to look ahead, planning how they might travel, whether he would send Dean to the redoubt to wait for them there. But he decided almost immediately that he wouldn't do that. The risk of the young boy's being chilled out on his own in an unknown ville was extremely high. And the other factor was that they would likely need every blaster they had.

"Women?" he murmured.

Perhaps a gang of women who were good enough to take Krysty out without leaving a single clue. She could only have been a few yards away from him, yet they prevented her from passing on any sort of warning.

It was, he thought, remotely possible that they had been a gang composed entirely of very small men, or children.

The Trader used to say that as long as you had an explanation that was possible, even though it was unlikely, then there was no point in worrying about anything else.

The tearing pain of being separated from the only woman Ryan had ever truly loved was folding over his mind, making it dangerously hard for him to think about logistical planning.

He was only too aware of how potentially lethal that could be, both for Krysty and for himself and the others.

"Put your heart in front of your brain and you don't get happy. You just get dead." Ryan half smiled in the dark of the old record store. "Right on, Trader."

Chapter Thirty-Five

Michael Brother had seen madness before. Despite his youth, and having lived in a closed community virtually since birth, he had considerable experience of the range of oddities that constituted human life.

Brother Antony had mysteriously bled to death after falling heavily in the courtyard on an icy morning. Only later did Michael hear the whisper that the brother had been walking with a large, empty bottle inserted into his rectum.

Brother Gerald had been found hanging in his cell one April morning, dressed in a garish parody of a woman's clothes. It seemed that it had been some sort of experiment in perverse and forbidden pleasure that had gone awry.

Brother Owen had been so consumed with the sin of insane pride that he thought he was infallible and could do no wrong.

He had attempted to prove it by walking out of his window on the top floor of the enclosed community. Michael had seen him moments after the impact in the stone courtyard. Both thigh bones had been driven clear out through his shoulders.

But the way Doc was behaving was unlike anything the teenager had ever seen.

He was striding along toward the distant lake with the swagger of a man who's just won a fortune in a gambling game and was returning home to tell his wife the good news.

Doc's head was high, the light wind ruffling his shoulder-length silver hair. His teeth were clenched and he was whistling, occasionally breaking into song in a fine, strong voice.

Michael trailed along a few paces behind the old man, eyes constantly raking the surrounding trees and houses for signs of any threat. If Doc had been preceded by a uniformed marching band blasting out "Hail to the Chief" he couldn't have made them any more conspicuous.

"I think you should keep your voice down a tad, Doc," Michael said. "Might be danger around. Remember what happened last night. Want me to walk in front?"

"A servant in front of his master. With two masters. Master of Ballantrae. Walk in front. Walk this way. Walk, don't walk. Walk, don't run. If I could walk this way, my dear Michael, I wouldn't need . . ." He stopped in his tracks, the cane falling from his fingers, lying unregarded by his feet. Both hands went to his face. "What am I doing, Michael? Where are we going? What am I saying? How when is up?" His eyes were filled with horror. "Oh, blessed Lord! Am I going insane? Emily, I need your love."

Michael took Doc by the arm and stooped to pick up the lion-headed sword stick.

"Want a hand?" he asked.

"No. My thanks for that offer. I owe a cockerel to…to nobody. My cane, I believe. I will see you again in the coffeehouse on the corner of Barbary and Ape. At ten in the forenoon if that proves convenient for you."

He set off at a fine rate again, head turning to smile over his shoulder at the young man. But the nuking had caused earth movements in that part of the city, and the stone had rippled like satin. Doc caught his toe and fell, twisting his ankle beneath him.

He gave a cry of anguish, trying to sit up, clutching at his leg. "It's broken, Michael. I felt it snap. How shall we reach the redoubt now before Ryan and the rest catch up with us?"

Michael was mainly aware of a strong feeling of relief that the accident appeared to have restored Doc to his senses.

For the time being.

THE CHURCH WAS SMALL and cramped, nothing like the wonderful edifice of Michael's recent dream. The roof was half-gone, with the jagged fangs of broken and blackened rafters silhouetted starkly against the sky. The pews had been removed, and the plain windows along the flanks of the building had all been blown in.

There was no crucifix.

No sign of life, but an overwhelming stench of stale urine.

Doc managed to hobble inside, one arm around the young man's shoulder. But it was obviously extremely painful, and he collapsed on the filthy floor with a moan of distress.

"Broken, Doc?"

"Help me off with my boot. Gently. I said gently! By the three Kennedys, can't you—"

"It's too tight to come off easily. The ankle's really swollen. Want me to try to cut it off for you?"

"No!" he shouted, then added more quietly, "No, Michael, I think not. I have had these boots for two hundred years and I have no wish to start breaking in another pair just yet. Leave it a moment."

"Did you feel it break?" Michael knelt at the old man's side.

"No. It turned, and now if feels like a small needle of white-hot steel jabbing at the joint, every step I take, every move I make, every breath I . . . Perhaps a severe strain."

"Can you walk?"

Doc sighed and shook his head. "I confess I find myself close to tears, my dear boy. To be so close to making a chron jump and to fall, literally, at the final hurdle."

"Maybe Ryan and the others have had something happen to slow them down."

"And pigs might fly, Michael. No, I fear that they will most definitely return to the redoubt before us."

"That mean you can't get me home?"

"It means it will be a damned sight more difficult. Not impossible." He slapped his hand on his thigh. "If only something could have happened to slow the others!"

TRACKING WAS SIMPLE.

At first.

Since no more rain had fallen in the latter part of the night, the trail was easy to pick up across the broken, muddy ground.

"Six of them," Ryan pronounced after only a hundred yards. "And all in small-size boots."

"And Krysty in the middle of them," J.B. agreed.

"Where do you think they're taking her, Dad?" Dean asked.

"I'm not a seeing mutie or a doomie, son. Tracks lead toward the heart of the old ville. That's all we know."

"Think we should've destroyed the wag?" Mildred glanced behind her as though she half expected to see it rumbling toward them.

The Armorer shook his head. "No point. Engine was wasted. Nothing worth raiding for."

"You got the drugs and medical stuff out, didn't you, Mildred?"

"Sure, Ryan. Nothing of a whole lot of value to us. I got that syringe with the instant knockout anesthetic in it safe in my pocket. Might come in useful if we get attacked by a raging gorilla or something like."

THE FARTHER IN they went, the more difficult it became to follow the raiders.

The group seemed to be heading directly into the charred heart of Chicago, to their den somewhere amid the hulks of the great skyscrapers, around the ruins of the civic center.

Ryan held up a hand to stop the other three. "Seem to have passed out of the region that had all those rats. Doesn't look to me like anybody could live around here."

It was simply the biggest area of utter desolation that he'd ever seen.

The earth, mud, grass and trees had virtually disappeared, replaced by molten stone and rusted iron. It was a place where the unimaginable intensity of the heat had actually fused the earth into a glittering expanse of crude glass.

"Tracks stop here." Ahead lay nothing but raw rock, with little that would carry a boot mark. Both Ryan and J.B. had moderate skill in reading a trail, but there were limits.

"Where do you reckon?" J.B. cast around, head down, eyes screwed up behind the polished lenses of his spectacles.

"Thought about it during last night. I got me a theory."

"Underground, Dad," the boy suggested.

Ryan looked at him in surprise. "Yeah. That's my guess, too."

"We were in places, me and Rona, that was total shit above. And whole villes underneath."

Mildred stared. "In cellars and basements? That would make sense. But how do we find the way in?"

"We wait and we watch," Ryan said. "Let's find a good place for that."

A THOUSAND YARDS AWAY, Krysty was being offered the first food of the day, by a woman who seemed oddly in awe of her. It still didn't make sense.

Chapter Thirty-Six

"A cherry hung with snow."

Michael jumped. He'd been staring out of the back door of the small church, across a miserable little yard with high walls. A padlocked gate blocked access from a street at the rear, and the corpse of a large dog, its belly swollen and burst, with two legs gnawed off, lay in the corner by a pile of cans so rusted that they hardly existed.

"What's that, Doc?"

"My sweet little child, Rachel. One cold morning she was wrapped all in white—a long shawl of Flemish lace—and her precious face was red with the chill. I recall now that she seemed much like a cherry hung with snow. I cannot imagine what brought that memory to me."

"How's the ankle?" Michael asked, wanting to change the subject away from the old-timer's past.

"Poorly. It is no more swelled than an hour or so ago. But even with my cane I do not believe I can yet walk any distance."

"I could go look for Ryan and the others. Get you safe."

''No, I think not. It has occurred to me that it might not be a disaster if they return before us. Ryan could give us up for lost. We creep into the redoubt and into the chron section. They would not think to search there. Then you to Nil-Vanity and me back to Omaha, Nebraska, and my family. Familiar family. Famished family. Famous family. A famulus was the attendant of a sorcerer or warlock in medieval days. You, the oblate, are my famulus.''

Michael sighed, turned and sat on the floor, tucking his feet under him. ''Yes, Doc,'' he said wearily.

Chapter Thirty-Seven

Despite the angry objections, Ryan insisted that his son stay with him on one side of an open plaza area.

They remained on the west. J.B. took the north, and Mildred concealed herself on the southern flank.

"Let me go and I can take the east, Dad. Then we got all ways covered."

"Best not, Dean. Likely their patrols are going to be heading out toward us and coming back past us. That's why we need to have double blaster coverage up here."

"We goin' to chill these bitches?"

Ryan shook his head. "You got to make sure your brain's in gear before you set your mouth off running, boy."

Dean blinked as though his father had slapped him across the side of the face. "Why do—"

"Women aren't bitches. You wouldn't have liked to hear a man call Sharona, your mother, a bitch, now, would you?"

"Guess not," Dean replied sullenly

"Second, we don't know for certain they are women. Could be muties with small feet."

"Yeah, but you and J B. both said   "

Ryan grinned at the solemn expression on his son's face. "We could be wrong. We said we *thought* it might be all women."

"Yeah, I get it."

"No, Dean, you don't. Third thing is that if we chill them, then how do we find out where they've taken Krysty?"

"Well, it's not easy to get all three wrong out of three, is it?"

Ryan couldn't help laughing quietly at Dean's irrepressible cheekiness. "Just shut up and watch," he said, ruffling the lad's hair, aware with a sudden, odd power of a feeling for the boy that he realized could only be paternal love.

"I'M ROBIN, one of the seniors of the Midnites. You finished the food?"

Krysty looked up from the narrow bed where she'd spent the remainder of the night. They'd searched her with a brutal, indifferent efficiency, taking away her blaster and knife. Two of the women had locked a chain around her right ankle, the other end fixed to an iron ring set in concrete on the wall.

It had been obvious as soon as they neared the heart of the ville that their hideout had to be subterranean. Nothing else would have made any sort of sense. It also explained the peering, protruding eyes they all had, living in a world of perpetual semidarkness.

Everyone was female, and all wore black pants and woollen coats, with black leather boots. There was a range of ages and sizes, most of them seeming to be in their late twenties to midthirties.

Krysty noticed that the ones she'd heard speaking had masculine names, or ambiguous names that could be either male or female. Freddy, Sam, Frankie, Robin, Jo.

She wondered about their sexuality but didn't see any clues in the way the women behaved toward each other.

"Food was awful," she replied.

Robin was slender with a long, narrow face. A tiny silver stud sparkled in her nose, and she had a number of plain metal rings through both ears. She carried a cocked Navy Arms .22-caliber Luger, aimed steady on the chained woman.

"Food's always awful. Awful when you get born. Awful when you die."

"How do you get any babies when there's no men around here?"

"We bring men in when we need them. Not very often. Put them in the milking cellar and drain them until we've got the needful going."

"Then?"

Robin smiled, the boggling eyes widening so far that it seemed as if they might plop out onto her cheek and dangle there like painted eggs.

"Then's the best time."

Krysty didn't ask her to elaborate. When you guess the end result, the details of it aren't really that important.

We was goin to bring the others in as well, you know

"Others?" Krysty shifted her position, trying to get her leg comfortable with the ankle lock tight around it.

"Yeah. The black woman, then men, little kid. If you hadn't walked out for a piss and fallen straight into our hands, we'd have come in the store and taken all of you."

"Why didn't you go in after the others, anyway? There were enough of you."

"Course." She laughed and spit on the floor. "Easy as crushing a roach under your heel. But once we got you, the rest didn't matter."

"Why?"

Robin shook her head, waving the handgun threateningly at Krysty. "That's enough talking for now."

She took the metal soup plate with her, slamming the heavy iron door. There was a metallic thump of a bolt, then silence.

Krysty lay still, conscious of the great weight of stone hanging above her. As the women had driven her along endless corridors and narrow passages, she'd lost all sense of direction, only knowing that they were going ever deeper beneath street level. She wondered how long it would be before Ryan tracked her down and staged the rescue.

IT HAD BECOME increasingly dull and overcast. A penetrating drizzle came drifting in from the east, bringing the faint taste of salt.

Water misted the outlines of the scarred and twisted ruins, gathering in dull pools among the ash-smeared rubble.

From where they were concealed, Ryan and Dean could see the locations that Mildred and J.B. had chosen for their own hiding places.

"What if they don't come?"

"We think of something else, son. Try and pick up tracks nearer in."

"What do we do when they come?"

"Play it like it looks."

"Chill them?" Dean caught the look in his father's eye and tried a second thought. "No. Course not, Dad. Sorry. That's stupe. Chill them and it doesn't help us find Krysty, does it?"

"No. No, it doesn't. Now, cut the talk, son. Watch and wait."

Ryan lay back against a flat wall, resting, leaving it to Dean to watch for anyone moving through the ruins.

It was late morning before Dean touched him on the arm.

"Dad?"

There were four of them, moving in a spread skirmish line, showing a degree of military organization that gave Ryan a pang of concern. All wore black clothes and had handguns holstered at the waist. Oddly every one of the women had on dark glasses. Since the day wasn't exactly flooded with dazzling sunlight, it made Ryan wonder that they might have some kind of vision problem It wouldn't be the first time he'd come across muties like that, and it would tie in with his suspicion that their headquarters could be deep beneath the ravaged heart of the ville.

If there'd only been a couple of them it should have been possible to take them without any shooting. Double the number and you doubled the odds against success.

Ryan had long ago lost count of the times he'd been in this sort of situation. It wasn't possible to make a hard plan of what you'd do. There were far too many imponderables. All you had to do was agree what was the broad aim, then let everyone do what they thought best to achieve that aim.

Which meant that a lot of times things didn't go like you hoped.

The four women picked their way across the open space, occasionally glancing around.

Ryan pushed the barrel of the Steyr into the open, resting it on a shelf of concrete. The laser image enhancer brought the nearest of the muties into sharp focus.

She was hunchbacked, and her pale face was striped with black. Ryan recognized a powerful .357 Magnum on her hip.

He knew that Mildred and J.B. would also be watching the women over the sights of their own weapons, waiting for him to open fire first.

Ryan hesitated. The area was a maze of fallen brick and metal. Once he squeezed the trigger there would be no going back There might be other armed patrols in the vicinity who d come at the double as soon as they heard gunfire.

There was no doubt he could put the hunchback woman down with a single bullet, but a bolt-action rifle wasn't ideal for rapid, accurate fire. Mildred's target pistol would certainly take out a second mutie. J.B. would open up with the Uzi and probably chill a third target.

"Still leaves one to run," he whispered, his cheek pressed against the smooth walnut stock of the Steyr.

Dean was crouched at his side. "You goin' to do her?" he asked quietly.

"Trader used to say that if you wait long enough you wait too long."

He pulled the trigger, working the action, the spent case tinkling on the stone by his feet.

It meant taking his eyes off the scene below him for a moment, but he could hear and interpret what was happening: the snap of Mildred's ZKR 551; a scream; the sound of ripping silk as J.B. opened up with the machine pistol.

At his side Dean opened up with the Browning, though the range was likely much too far for him, and he lacked the physical strength to control the big blaster.

By the time he had the rifle leveled again the scene had totally changed.

His target was down, her skull blown apart, a puddle of blood and brains around what remained of her face. Her feet were still moving as though she were making a desperate effort to run away from her own death.

Mildred had used her great skill with the revolver to chill the woman who appeared to have been leading the patrol. The big .38 round had hit her in the side of the neck, ripping out her throat and taking half the cervical vertebrae with it. The mutie was lying on her back, completely still.

J.B.'s weapon wasn't much use for accurate single shots, and the Smith & Wesson scattergun was only really effective up to about fifty yards. But he'd hit the short woman with gray hair at least three times. She was down but not dead, and screamed shrilly.

The fourth hunter, slender and young, had set off like a startled hare, darting toward the building where Ryan and Dean were hiding. She'd had enough sense not to waste time drawing her own blaster. Her feet kicked up rainwater as she sprinted, head back, arms pumping, jinking as she ran to throw off the aim of her unseen attackers.

Ryan stood, trying to bring the Steyr down to a sharp enough angle, but the blond-haired mutie was already close beneath him. Her dark glasses had fallen off as she ran, and he could see her staring, goggling eyes.

The Czech target pistol snapped again, the bullet kicking sparks from the stone a few yards ahead of the woman.

J.B. was no more successful, trying another burst from the Uzi, but the bullets hissed wide of the dodging figure by several feet.

Ryan glanced sideways, wondering why Dean hadn't tried another shot from the Hi-Power. But his son was no longer there.

A handgun fired from the center of the plaza as the wounded woman struggled to her knees, drawing and shooting in his general direction, with an agonized slowness, still screaming raggedly at the top of her voice.

"Fireblast," Ryan said, putting a bullet through the center of her nose with the Steyr, killing her instantly.

By then the fourth of the patrol was out of sight, disappearing into the first floor of the ruin where he was standing.

"Dean!"

"Down here," came the muffled reply.

Ryan turned and ran for the wreckage of the stairs, picking his way carefully, the rifle slung across his shoulder. As he began to move he caught a glimpse of both J.B. and Mildred starting to come out of hiding.

"Dean!"

This time there was no answer.

When Ryan reached the street level he saw why.

His son was busy.

The last surviving mutie woman was in the doorway, holding a rebuilt automatic pistol, pointing at the center of the skinny chest of Dean Cawdor.

Chapter Thirty-Eight

Close up Ryan could see that the blond woman was only in her midteens. Her eyes were like pool balls, brimming out of the sockets of wind-washed bone. She was panting hard, but the old repaired automatic pistol was very steady in her right hand.

Dean's Browning was just as steady in his hands, centered on the woman's midriff.

They stood about twelve feet apart.

Ryan looked at them, locked in a gaudy-house standoff.

"One of you pulls the trigger, then you both get to be dead," he said in a casual, conversational voice.

"You chilled my three friends. Midnites'll have you by the balls for this."

J.B. and Mildred appeared in the other doorway, blasters ready. Ryan shook his head to warn them not to try anything hasty. The most important thing was to save the threatened life of the boy. But he wanted—needed—the woman kept alive to be questioned about Krysty.

It would have been absurdly easy for any of them, including Dean himself, to chill the black-clothed woman. But that brought the strong probability that she'd still get to fire her own gun, and blow a plate-size chunk out of the boy's spine.

"Let me go and I'll not shoot."

"Fuck you," Dean said. "Don't let her go, Dad, don't."

"Not a lot of choice, boy. Got the drop, hasn't she?"

"You better run from here," she said venomously "Because you'll get to shit yourself when we track you down."

It occurred to Ryan that, despite being outnumbered by four to one, the mutie wasn't at all frightened. Angry, but not frightened. And that was strange, because it spoke of unusual confidence.

"Talking of messing yourself," he said quietly. "Knew a Mex woman near the Grandee made a chili stew so hot that you shit blood for a couple of weeks after eating some."

"What?"

She turned a fraction toward him, the gun moving with her.

And Mildred immediately shot her through the right elbow, the bullet splitting the joint apart, exploding through cartilage and tendons.

The mutie's own blaster fired, by a reflex action, her round smashing into the concrete wall a yard from Dean, gouging out a chunk of weathered stone.

She screamed in pain and shock, staggering sideways, her left hand clawing toward a knife that dangled in a homemade, beaded sheath on her left hip. Ryan stepped in and kicked her hard, with a planned, brutal efficiency, feeling the impact of the steel toe cap as it pulped her right knee.

"Tie her," he ordered.

HIS FIRST SLAP landed across the mutie woman's left ear, a loud crack breaking the stillness as he connected.

She winced. "Fuck you," she said quietly.

"You tell me now or you tell me later. Sooner is easier and later is a whole lot harder."

"Christ, Ryan," Mildred muttered, unable to hide her distaste for what was happening. "You sound like someone in a cheap gangster novel."

Dean had been sent to wait outside and keep watch, though Ryan didn't think there was any danger of a search party coming out after the four women for some time yet.

Their prisoner was still clothed, her ankles bound with thin waxed twine, thumbs tied behind her back. Though with the shattered elbow and the broken knee, she wasn't going anywhere.

"You think I like beating up on a helpless woman, Mildred? I get off on it? Because if you think that, then you don't know me and ... and I don't fucking know you at all!"

His flaring anger came from nowhere, flooding over his mind like a tumbling veil of spilled crimson. Ryan could feel the scar across his cheek throbbing with his rage. His fist was clenched as he turned to face the black woman.

"You want to know where they've taken Krysty. So do we, Ryan. Let me ask her."

"She won't talk."

"I'm a doctor. I can help to ease pain. I know how to cause it. Not just a brutish and bloody beating, Ryan."

As the blinding fury slithered away from him, back into its hidden lair, Ryan calmed down.

"You got any drugs that'd make her tell us what we want?"

Mildred shook her head. "No."

The woman's eyes turned frantically from face to face. "You won't know. And if you fucking know it won't do you no good. We got her now, like we've always known we would."

"What do you mean, you've always known about her? How can you?" Ryan shook the mutie by the shoulder, making her wince with pain.

"Midnites' laws said we'd have a leader from beyond. And that she'd have a head of flaming, burning fire. And now we got her. And you can't do fuck about it, can you?"

He shrugged and turned away. "Mildred. Do what you have to. Just find out how to get into their base. Best is, she comes with us to show us, but that's difficult. Could easy make some kind of noise."

"What are we planning to do about her afterward, Ryan?"

He simply looked at her, his face like frosted granite, saying nothing.

IT TOOK LESS than ten minutes.

Ryan walked outside to keep watch with Dean, leaving J.B. inside with Mildred and their prisoner.

The boy hadn't said anything at first, then, as the noises began behind them, he looked up at his father. "She going to tell us where Krysty is?"

"Hope so."

"They're torturing the mutie?"

"Right."

"Hurting her badly?"

Ryan sucked at a hollow tooth that sometimes gave him a pang in the night. "I don't like this, Dean, but there isn't any other way."

"Sure, Dad, I understand about that." He hesitated. "Can I go watch?"

"No!"

THE MUTIE WAS barely conscious, head slumped on her chest. Her breathing was shallow, harsh and irregular.

Blood soaked her shirt, puddled in her lap. Mildred glanced up at Ryan. She was wiping the blade of a small scalpel on her own pant leg, before returning it carefully to its sheath.

Her cheeks were wet, and the tracks of tears showed in the dust on her face.

"Glad I don't get to do that too often," she said, her voice breaking.

J.B. moved to stand by her, and in an uncharacteristic gesture he put his arm around her, holding her tightly for a dozen heartbeats.

"Had to be done," he said.

"Not something that featured big when I took my oath," she muttered.

"Woman told you?"

"Yeah, Ryan, she told me."

The mutie mumbled something, coughing up a great clotted gobbet of thick blood. But she didn't move her head.

"Well?"

"Follow the main drag to the east. Keep going until you reach what used to be the El, then turn north a block. Lots of big offices. One has a mark in white paint on it. Go round back, to the left. Cellar entrance. In there."

"Good."

"Think she told the truth?" Dean asked, bending down to try to see into their prisoner's face.

J.B. answered the boy. "I'd have been telling the truth," he said. "I don't have any doubts about it."

"Now what?" Mildred asked, rubbing her sleeve across her eyes.

"Wait outside for me." Ryan motioned to them with his hands. "Won't take a minute."

He thought that the black woman was going to argue with him, but she turned on her heel and walked out into the daylight.

Dean followed her, but J.B. remained behind a moment longer.

"Ryan?"

"Yeah?"

"Hard," he said, his voice as flat and cold as a cemetery slab.

"I know it was, J.B., I know it. But you know that it had—"

The Armorer held his hand up. "Sure I know it. Mildred knows it, too. Why she did it. Did what she did here."

Ryan nodded. "Best get to it."

"Sure. See you outside."

He walked out, hat tipped back, leaving Ryan alone with the blond mutie.

"Kill me . . . please kill."

Despite being used to pain and death, the depth of suffering in the woman's voice sent a chill down Ryan's spine.

Bullets were gold in Deathlands, but he drew the SIG-Sauer, the narrow ridges on the trigger against the skin of his index finger. He pressed the gaping mouth of the barrel to the matted hair at the side of the mutie's skull, just behind her left ear.

The silencer muffled the explosion, but the power of the handgun kicked the head sideways, so that it rolled faceup.

He saw what Mildred had done with her small sharp scalpel to persuade the woman to talk.

It was an image of horror that remained with Ryan Cawdor all the rest of his life.

Chapter Thirty-Nine

It was nearly evening.

Michael had been sleeping, using his long experience of meditation techniques to slip easily into a dream-free rest.

Doc had also been dozing, but the pain from his badly sprained ankle kept tugging him back into a state of wakeful confusion.

His voice woke the young man. "Emily will have prepared a fine supper for us, I'm sure. We must try to return before the little ones have been sent to the nursery. Perhaps it will be poached salmon and minted potatoes. Sugared carrots and a sauce of parsley. That will not butter many parsnips, will it?" His voice rose. "Trample not upon my vines! The center will not hold!"

"Doc!"

"Greetings and salutations, dear boy. Went the day well?"

"Well enough. Dusk's closing in on us. Think we're safe here?"

The old man stretched, wincing, his hands reaching down to tenderly touch his injured ankle. "Still damnably painful. Are we safe here? Are we safe anywhere, Michael? Is no man an island, entire unto itself?''

The teenager smiled. "Ask not for whom the bell tolls, Doc. It tolls for thee." He clapped his hands together. "Brother Lewis taught us that."

But Doc wasn't listening, his eyes staring out into the gloaming beyond the broken windows. "Tomorrow, Emily," he whispered. "I swear it. The laws of time are at our command, and woe unto any man who stands against us."

IT WAS nearly evening.

Krysty's visitors had just left her.

They had arrived an hour or so earlier. With no chron and no glimpse of the outdoors, Krysty had no way of being sure of the passage of time.

There were five of them: the slender Robin, the torchlight dancing off the stud in her nose; Frankie, smelling even worse in the confined space; Laurie, whose face was badly pockmarked and who carried six little over-and-under derringer pistols stuck into a broad leather belt. The fourth of the women was called Jackie, and she stood several inches over six feet tall. She kept smiling, slack-lipped, for no particular reason. When she wasn't smiling, Jackie was constantly sucking at her left thumb as though it contained the elixir of life.

The fifth was the self-styled leader of the Midnites, and her name was Billy.

Apart from the grossly protruding eyes, she would have been stunningly beautiful. She was around Krysty's five feet eleven in height, with a long tumbling mane of rich chestnut hair. In normal company it would have been admired for its lustrous fire. In the same room as Krysty, it looked dull, more like smoldering embers than a full-hearted inferno of flame.

All of them wore the same black clothes and black leather boots, and all carried handguns. Billy had a beautiful chromed Ruger .44 Magnum Blackhawk, with a ten-inch barrel that seemed to go on forever, an enormously powerful 6-round single-action revolver that sat easily against her right thigh in a hand-tooled fast-draw rig made from dark blue leather.

Krysty knew enough about firearms to spot that a fast-draw rig was a pointless affectation with such a long-barreled blaster.

Billy introduced them all, herself last. They stood around Krysty in an uncomfortable semicircle. She noticed a curious hesitancy on their part to catch her eye.

"Midnites run Shytown. Have for years. Live in the underearth here."

"Why did you lift me like this? What's going on with you?"

"Old stories in the ville. We live okay here. Triple hard in snow time. Old stories. Told mother to daughter and on down. How one day we'll leave the dark and go out into sun. Won't hurt our eyes like it does now. Be led west way cross Sippi."

"By me?" Krysty said, unbelieving. "You think I'm some sort of messiah? Gaia! You're crazier than bombed-out stickies."

"You shut the fuck up about us!" Laurie shouted, drawing two of her derringers and flourishing them toward Krysty.

"Let it lie," Billy said. "Stories say a tall woman with norm eyes. And hair like the living fire."

"Amen," Jackie said, taking her thumb out of her mouth.

"Living fire," Robin breathed, the lids coming down over the swollen eyes like security blinds across blank windows.

"I'm not your savior. I'm just an ordinary woman, traveling through Deathlands with a group of friends. Just a few people, doing the best we can."

"No."

"Yes. Now, why not just let me go and there'll be no trouble?"

The women all laughed. "Trouble!" Frankie bellowed. "We won't have no fuckin' trouble."

Billy bent and touched Krysty on the shoulder. "Don't worry. We'll talk a lot more. Lots of time. We've waited here for many long years for you to come to us. Now you have."

They all went out, leaving her in the cellar, with the guttering torch stuck in a makeshift iron bracket on the wall.

She lay back, trying to avoid making the chain rattle. And wondered where Ryan was and what he was doing to save her.

IT WAS nearly evening. They'd left the cover of the building, walking eastward toward the lake, away from the sinking orange orb that flooded the western sky with a watery glow.

The stumps of the solid metal columns that had supported the elevated railway were soon visible, like massive blackened fists of iron.

"North a block."

They went in a strung-out skirmish line, pausing at every intersection or patch of open ground to come together again.

At the first stop J.B. beckoned to Ryan.

"Those four muties we chilled."

"Yeah."

"How long before they miss them?"

"I reckon another—" Ryan glanced at his chron "—say two more hours. Then they'll allow another hour. Be full dark before they get seriously worried about them being ambushed."

"Way it looks, they run a good force."

"Yeah. Like some flash baron's sec men. Apart from the dark-light eyes."

J.B. hesitated. "We find this entrance   we going to go in as soon as we get there?"

"Mebbe not. Could be they'll be on red watch, if they miss the four we took out. Get there. Take us a look. Then decide about going in."

THE OFFICE BLOCK had a streak of white paint daubed across its front, a great slash of brightness, twenty feet long and three feet high, startling set against the charcoal stone and melted, bubbled glass.

"That it?" Dean asked.

"How she described it," Mildred replied. Since they'd left the tomb of the tortured mutie, Mildred had hardly spoken a word, trudging on in silence, head down, barely bothering to keep proper watch.

"Sure about it?"

Ryan was too far away to intervene before the brief scuffle was over. The black woman had taken a dozen quick steps, grabbing Dean by the front of his denim jacket, hefting him off the ground in both hands. She pressed her angry face close to his.

"You brainless little shit! Am I sure about it? Do you think I'll be able to forget every word that poor damned soul said to me? Never, Dean, you stupe little bastard!" She dropped the boy, and his legs folded under him. He sat in the street, face paper white. "Never. Like etched in acid into my brain. Never."

THE BASEMENT ENTRANCE was just where they'd been told, a gaping chasm in the back of the building, with a dim light glowing somewhere inside.

"Bet they got dozens of ways in and out," J.B. whispered from where the four of them crouched behind the piled mountain of rubble the next block along.

"The way their eyes were," Mildred said, "means they're nocturnal."

"What's that?" Dean had quickly recovered from the shock of the woman's anger.

"Nocturnal. At night. Their eyes are bigger so they see better in darkness."

"They'll have a big edge over us in their cellars," Ryan said thoughtfully.

"No way around that. Unless they happen to bring Krysty outside." J.B. looked around them again. "Night's not that far off."

"And they'll see much better than us." Dean sniffed. "That's a real hot pipe for them. Cold one for us, though."

"Wait and watch," Ryan said. "We don't have any idea of their numbers or how they run things. Look out for guards."

Ryan, Mildred, J.B. and Dean waited for full dark.

Chapter Forty

Only a single woman stood watch at the entrance, but she carried a Colt Magnum drawn in her right hand and showed every sign of being alert and efficient.

She walked steadily up and down, across the dark mouth of the cavern, head turning constantly, her night-seeing eyes scanning the surrounding ruins. Then she would pause and sit for a few minutes, her back against the rough wall, before standing and resuming her guard.

It would be ridiculously easy to take her out, using the night sight on the Steyr rifle. The range was only about seventy yards. But the noise would bring every mutie for blocks around. They might have poor day vision, but there was no reason to think they were also deaf.

"Go in with a knife?" J.B. suggested.

"They'll mebbe know that their patrol was chilled. They won't just let a man walk up to them and stick a blade through their heart." Mildred shook her head. "Perhaps I could do it."

Ryan rubbed a finger across the stubble over his chin. "What we've seen, these muties are tough,

Mildred. Streetwise. She won't allow you in close. Blow your guts apart first."

"Me?" asked Dean in the sort of hesitant voice that made it obvious he expected everyone to laugh at his suggestion.

But nobody did laugh.

J.B. opened his mouth, then closed it again, looking intently at Ryan. Mildred said nothing, also staring at the silent one-eyed man.

"All right."

THE GUARD'S NAME was Ronnie, short for Ronalda. Every woman within the mutie commune had a feminine name that the rules demanded should be shortened into a masculine form: Francesca was Frankie, Samantha was Sam, Frederika was Freddy, Jackie had been Jacqueline and Billy had been Wilhelmina.

Ronnie was nearly forty years old and had been in Chicago all her life. She had given birth to six children in all, as well as having close to a dozen miscarriages. And every one had been male, suffering the fate of all boy children within the group.

Ronnie knew that a perpetual shortage of food, especially meat, meant that no opportunity should be wasted. But she had still found it difficult to partake in those six feasts.

Now she was on single patrol, with urgent orders direct from Robin to keep an extraspecial watch for outlanders.

"Two men and a black woman. Might be three men or might be a girl with them. Scouts weren't sure. Traveling with the fire-haired one. Think they could've burned four of ours. Out west. Haven't come back. So watch."

Ronnie worked out with weights and prided herself on her strength. The big Magnum was like a little toy pistol in her beefy fist.

Her protruding eyes gave her keen vision in the gloom, as well as wider peripheral sight than the average norm.

She caught the flicker of a movement among the deep shadows and spun quickly around, leveling the blaster, holding it in both hands. "Hey! Who the fuck are you?"

"Just me."

The voice was odd, halfway between a man and a boy, cracking as though with nerves.

"Come closer, slow and easy, hands out where I can see them proper Or I turn your head into gilded splinters."

Ronnie didn't know what that meant, but she'd once heard Billy say it and she'd liked the strange sound of it.

It was a boy, looking to be around ten or eleven years old. Be about the same age as her last baby, Ronnie thought. The same age he *would* have been. He was stocky, with thick unruly hair. Dark eyes, wearing blue pants and shirt. He was holding out empty hands like she'd told him to.

"Who are you?'

"Name's Will, ma'am I'm lost and cold and hungered."

"Where you come from? Get closer so's I can see you. And lift that fucking shirt up high to show me you aren't carrying a hideaway blaster Turn around."

"I come from way north, ma'am. My mother was a singer in gaudies. Got snakebit five days ago. Blood come from her eyes, and she just died. Buried her and come on alone here."

He stopped two paces from her. Ronnie was suddenly shaken with a mix of emotions. She should shoot him down Get praised for that. And then there'd be good tender meat. But he was only the age her last would've been. That was all.

"Fuck off, lad," she muttered, looking nervously over her shoulder to make sure nobody was coming from the cellars.

"Hungered."

"Fuck off, or you'll disagree with something that eats *you!* Go on. Just get out of this place, now!"

She thought she saw something moving in the direction the boy had come from. Ronnie started to turn and felt a jarring blow to the pit of her stomach, a fiery pain that reached between her ribs to pierce her heart.

There was a sudden weakness, and she heard the blaster fall to the dark stones beneath her boots. Someone sighed and there was a seeping wetness between her thighs, trickling down her legs.

The boy s hand was pushing against her body, twisting his wrist backward and forward as though he were trying to drill a hole in a piece of wood. Ronnie could see the glint of turquoise stone in his fist.

But she couldn't see as well as usual.

"Why?" she said, puzzled.

Ryan watched the boy step away from the mutie woman, a few drops of blood falling black from the razored edge of his slim knife.

He saw her slump to her knees as though she were about to take her final communion, hands clasped to the gaping wound to try to staunch the gushing flow that carried her life with it.

"He's done her," he said. "Come on." Ryan led the way at a crouching run toward the opening in the devastated building.

Dean sheathed his turquoise-hafted knife and reached his hand out for the Browning Hi-Power that the Armorer had been holding for him.

"She warned me to run away," he said. "Felt sorry for her."

Ryan patted him on the shoulder. "You did well. Good lad. Now let's go find where they're holding Krysty."

"WANT ME TO COME and suck and lick you?"

It was Robin, the nose stud gleaming in the torchlight. Her slender face was tight with a sexual hunger, eyes seeming to burst from their sockets toward Krysty.

"No."

"I'm good at it."

"So am I. But no thanks."

"You like men?"

"Most the time."

Robin pulled a face, miming puking on the floor. "All hard cocks and soft brains. Don't know how to give pleasing. Just take it. All they do. Take it. When we catch them, we teach the shit-for-brains real different."

"Yeah, I bet you do."

Robin smiled at her. "You'll have first go next time. On account of who you are. We strip them and tie them. Blind them, most times. Pull out any teeth they got left, so's they can't hurt us. Then they use their tongues like we tell them. Hurt them if they stop. Why, we use their greedy little mouths for just about *everything* "

Robin's fingers were straying down across her own stomach, inside her pants, moving faster.

"Then you kill them."

"Sure. Eat them."

"Eat them. Oh, Gaia!"

Robin giggled, a soft, obscene sound that made Krysty want to throw up. "They eat us first. Then we eat them. Only fair."

IT WAS EVERYTHING that Ryan had been fearing about the muties' lair.

Once he'd seen their eyes, he'd figured on subterranean life. And if there were enough of them, they must have excavated tunnels and caves from block to block.

Now they found precisely the gloomy maze that Ryan had suspected.

Tunnels opened in every direction, most sloping downward. There were smoky torches burning at intervals, filling the passages with the stench of kerosene, casting only limited pools of orange light, with chasms of blackness in between.

"Now where?" Mildred asked.

"No idea." Ryan shaded his eye with his hand, trying to peer past the row of flaming torches.

"Can't stay here, Dad."

"I know that. Anyone could come at any moment. Either from outside or inside."

J.B. spun around, looking into the night, then back again to stare at the row of tunnels. "Yeah, Ryan. Both at once."

"Run for it!"

Ryan was off to a flying start, heading into the extreme left passage. Behind him they all caught the sound of yelling and the crackle of gunfire. By sheer luck he hadn't picked the corridor already filled with muties running toward the entrance.

It was a maniacal labyrinth.

Dark tunnels yawned on both sides, some lighted, some in pitchy blackness. The shouting echoed and swelled, seeming to come from all around them. Above and below, to right and left.

Behind and in front.

Ryan sprinted for his life, aware of the clattering of boots as the others trailed at his heels.

When the main tunnel forked, he paused, doubled over, fighting for breath. J.B. and Mildred were at his side.

But not Dean.

The boy had disappeared.

Chapter Forty-One

"Oh, we all do the wibbly-wobbly walk, along the wibbly-wobbly road. Keep up, Emily, my sweetest treasure."

Even with the help of the cane, Doc was making painfully slow progress. His ankle had eased a little during the night, but began to swell again once they were moving across the uneven landscape of the ville.

There was a fresh breeze from the west at their backs, and a bright sun rising in the clear, cloudless sky.

Michael considered leaving the mad old man alone. He had learned enough during his scant few days in Deathlands to know that this was a terrifying place of pitfalls and traps. Of mutated creatures on two legs, four legs and no legs.

Of smiling murder in the pitch of night and in the heat of the noon sun. A world where sense and logic seemed to have no home.

He knew that you walked carefully in the shadows, as though eggshells and glass crystals lay beneath your feet.

What you didn't do was hobble along in the center of the rubble-strewn suburban highway, shouting and singing at the top of your voice, calling out to your wife, who had been dead for the better part of two centuries.

But Doc Tanner was so far over the brink of sanity that he was way out of sight.

And out of reach.

The breeze lifted the rich silver locks off Doc's shoulders. His knee joints cracked and creaked as he dodged around patches of mud.

"Berry dung with crow," he called out. Michael was in front and ignored him. "I said there was a merry lung with dough."

The young man turned. "Doc, just what in the name of my sweet Lord are you babbling on about? Please stop it."

"A wherry clung with blow."

Doc was grinning, as though he'd just thought of a most cunning ruse.

Michael closed his eyes and stood still for a moment, trying to hang on to his own control.

Doc cackled. "A cherry hung with snow is what I meant. Of course."

FRANKIE BROUGHT THE NEWS to Krysty along with her breakfast.

There were some grits, and strips of unidentifiable gray meat that Krysty resolved not to risk touching at all.

"Trouble in the night."

Krysty was spooning up the greasy grits, mopping at the thick gravy with a hunk of stale bread. The juices from the meat had a vague flavor of pork, which did nothing for her digestion.

"Trouble?"

"Fuckin' A, trouble. Billy reckons it could be your friends done it."

"Done what? I mean, did what?"

Frankie sniffed and wiped her nose with her sleeve, leaving a slimy trail on the black material as though a large snail had just passed by. "Lost four sisters. Chilled yesterday, late on. Patrol found their bodies. Then Ronnie was stabbed."

"Who?"

"Oh, yeah, Ronnie. I couldn't stand the bitch. We called her Six-cocks, on account of her having only boy babies. Useless slag. On watch at one of the main entrances to Midnites' home."

"She got killed?"

"Sure. Thin steel ripped her up. Then, the patrol comin' back in saw them. Ronnie was only just about gone."

"Saw who?"

"Black slut with braided hair. Little bastard with a hat and glasses. Smaller one, we reckon's a young male. And a big fucker with only one eye. They sound familiar to you? Like you might mebbe recognize who they are?"

Krysty nodded. "Course. You know that. They were with me when you lifted me a day ago. My own true friends."

Frankie smiled, showing yellowed stumps of rotting teeth. "Well, looks like they come in to try and lift you back again. Reckon they know how important you are, don't they? Any road, Red, they're someplace inside the burrows now. Won't take us long to track them all down."

"Mebbe," Krysty said. If the fat woman stepped in a little closer she could probably grab her, get her handgun.

But, if Frankie didn't have the key to unlock the chain, it would be futile. And if Ryan and the others were already in the underworld ville, then the light was a little brighter.

DOC AND MICHAEL were limping slowly toward the lake, some way farther north than when they'd ridden in the opposite direction in the armored malfunctioning wag. The ill-matched pair was now only a mile or so away from the concealed entrance to the redoubt and from the chron unit within.

But Doc's ankle was becoming more painful, and he finally collapsed.

"Rest awhile," he said slowly. "Emily and my dear children must wait for us. Must wait just awhile longer."

"Sure," the young man agreed, looking around the desolate wilderness. "Doesn't seem to be any danger, does there, Doc?"

"Much darkness, my old, old friend."

Michael stretched. His feet, hardened though they were, had become tender from walking across the ruins of the city. "Wonder where Ryan and the others are, Doc?"

"I know not about them. Their names are a small memory, not worth forgetting. My heart yearns for rest and light. For me, and for you, Emily."

"Can rest some, Doc."

"Requiem aeternam dona eis, Domine. Et lux perpetua luceat eis."

The teenager backed away as the old man babbled gibberish at him. "What in the name of the Lord is that, Doc? You really lost it, haven't you?"

Doc laughed. "Oh, my boy. In the name of the Lord, did you say? That was the meaning of that pattering of half-remembered Latin. And small Greek, I had."

"What's it mean? Brother Thelonius used to say he knew some of that old Latin."

"It is a plea. 'Oh Lord, pray give them rest eternal and let thy perpetual light shine upon them.' I pray for my wife and children, the lost ones. For you and I, who are nearly found. And for light and rest for Ryan Cawdor and the others." He paused. "Wherever they be."

THE LOSS OF HIS SON was profoundly upsetting. But
Ryan had seen enough of Dean's survival abilities not
to feel desperately pessimistic. If any boy of eleven
could escape from the dank underground maze, and
the bloodthirsty female muties that inhabited it, then
that boy was Dean Cawdor.

"Go back and look?" Mildred panted. "Can't be
far."

"Far enough. He'll hide up and then try and make
his way out to the surface." Ryan sucked in several long
breaths.

"This dark-nighted labyrinth carries echoes all over
the place. I think we've shaken them, but they could be
ahead of us." J.B. took off his fedora, brushing dust
off the brim.

"If they put out the torches we'd be in the deepest
shit. They can see good in the dark." Ryan eased the
long rifle across his shoulder.

"How do we track Krysty down in this . . . this damnable place?"

"Don't know, Mildred." Ryan sighed. "These passages could easy run for miles in all directions."

"Figures they're keeping Krysty reasonably close to
that main entrance. Otherwise they wouldn't have used
it."

Ryan nodded. "Yeah. I'll take that one. Means we
got to work our way back up again."

"Or find an exit. And come in again from the same
entrance. They wouldn't expect that, would they?"
Mildred said.

"Best plan I've heard yet. We'll head upward whenever there's a choice at a junction. I'll go first, then you, Mildred, and J.B. bringing up the rear. Let's do it."

But the tunnels were more intricate and complicated than Ryan had guessed. Over the years, the basements of most of the buildings in that part of Chicago had been tunneled and joined, cellars tying in with main drains and sewers. The larger blocks had once had as many as a dozen floors below the earth, linked by stairs and ramps.

Ryan glanced at his wrist chron, unable to believe that they'd only been trudging through the low-roofed passages for an hour and a half. Despite having the compass, it wasn't possible to set a course and hold it. The pipes and ancient electrical conduits all combined to form a weaving pattern of magnetic interference, making the tiny needle spin like a jolt-head dervish.

Every place seemed the same, with piping and wires running near the rounded ceilings, with only the occasional torch to show them any light. It was like being in a scaled-down version of some of the older redoubts.

But infinitely more confusing.

"We lost?" Mildred asked.

"No, course not."

"No?"

Ryan whistled between his teeth. "Before you get lost, you have to know where you are. We don't. So we aren't lost."

LAURIE AND FRANKIE had been sent down to the sub-basement where Krysty was held prisoner after the threat of outlanders running loose throughout the Midnites' underground ville.

They both squatted on the floor on either side of the door, in the deep shadow. Laurie's pocked face showed a mixture of superstitious awe and anger. She was playing with the derringers in her belt, taking them out one at a time, cocking them and pointing them toward Krysty.

But not directly at her.

None of them spoke.

It was obvious to Krysty that things had gone wrong. If Ryan and the others had been captured, then the mutie women would have been unable to conceal their delighted gloating.

Nobody heard feet outside in the main corridor. But the door was suddenly shoved open and Dean Cawdor jumped into the room.

"Hi, Krysty." He grinned, then saw the movement behind him. "Oh, shit." The smile disappeared.

"Hi, Dean," Krysty said. "Welcome to the pleasure dome."

Chapter Forty-Two

By the reckoning of the local people, it was around ten in the morning. The early sun had vanished to be replaced by a cover of purple-gray clouds. Over to the east, hanging across the sullen expanse of the old lake, was a belt of heavy rain, its edges dark against the lighter gray of the rest of the sky. The air tasted colder and bitter, like setting your tongue to the frosted blade of a sword.

The water was close ahead of Doc and Michael, salt bitter in the nostrils, its surface rippled by white-topped wavelets.

"White horses. Ride a white horse. A white swan. Wild horses. Wild duck. Wild cherry." Doc looked sideways at the younger man. "Cherry," he said experimentally. "Hear that?"

"Sure, Doc, and I bet anything that it's hung with snow. Oh, creeping, weeping Mother Mary! Can't you snap out of it?"

"Out of what, old friend? Snap. Crackle. Pop. Whiz and whir. Rattle and hum."

Michael shook his head sorrowfully. His shoulders drooped, and he shuffled his bare feet in the dirt of the street.

"Like Brother Frederick used to say, Doc, your elevator doesn't go all the way to the top floor, does it?"

But the old-timer wasn't listening, leaning on his sword stick to take the weight off his sprained ankle.

"Another hour, Emily, my queen of all hearts. And we shall reach the redoubt. After that it will be all haste toward the chronological transfer unit. A little, little while to prepare the consoles and then...then it will be farewell forever to this dank and dangerous future world!"

"I CAME TO HELP."

The boy's voice was trembling on the edge of tears as he lay chained next to Krysty.

"Hush. Keep your voice quiet, Dean. Lie still and rest a little."

"We fucked up. I fucked up worst."

It had been easy for the two mutie guards to take the boy. Laurie had clubbed him to the dirt, using the butt of one of her range of small pistols. The blow had been hard enough to knock him out for a good half minute. Dean came to flat on his back, with the heel of one of Frankie's boots crushing his windpipe, pinning him in the dirt, nearly strangling him, while the other woman snapped the brass lock onto a chain around his ankle.

He was as helpless as Krysty, on the opposite side of the cellar.

Now the members of the Midnites had gone out and left them alone in the basement.

"The fat bitch mean what she said?" This time there was ragged terror skating under the surface of the boy's voice.

"Probably trying to scare you, Dean. Just cheap mutie talk."

But she knew that he knew that she knew it was a lie. And that they'd be back with their leader, Billy.

Frankie had done the talking, uttered the threats that sounded convincingly like promises, laughing down at the boy, with his big Browning Hi-Power stuck into her belt.

"Red Lady here is going to be our chosen one. Lead us from this dark life to the lands of the west. And you, little malekind, will be the sacrifice to seal our bond."

She'd been explicit on what they would do to the boy's naked body, with sharp knives and with needles. With heat and with liquids. Fire and water. Blood. Steel scraping along the marrow of living bone. White iron probing at the back of an eye socket. The parts of Dean's body that would be removed in front of all the tribe by cutting and tearing.

"And after it, you shall have the fuckin' honor of being a dish fit for a queen, sonny."

He'd spit at her, making the woman laugh even more.

But now Krysty and Dean were once more on their own. And time was racing by.

RYAN HAD FOUND two different exits from the complex, but each was heavily guarded and barred. The handful of mutie women wouldn't have been an insoluble problem, but the steel doors were likely to be solidly locked.

With every heartbeat he knew that the situation was slipping away from him. For the first time in years, Ryan found himself doubting his own ability to lead. From their first night in the abandoned house in the suburbs of old Chicago, things had begun to go sorely wrong: Abe's departure, then Doc running off, taking their newest recruit with him. Then Krysty being lifted by muties, almost under his nose, and whisked away into their stinking underground lair.

The last cut was the deepest of all.

To lose his only child in the raven heart of that same stygian maze.

Now he couldn't even get J.B. and Mildred, last of the band, out of the Midnites' den into the clean air.

"Fireblast!"

"Must be some other routes out," Mildred said. "Why not look for small side passages? Then there could be a way into the streets."

THE IRON DRAIN COVER hadn't been moved for a hundred years. It had rusted solidly into the metal ring that surrounded it and resisted all of Ryan and J.B.'s efforts to shift it. They were balanced on a crumbling ladder, and it was difficult to put any real pressure on the cover.

There was a pattern of tiny holes drilled through the center and Ryan was able to see chinks of daylight through them.

He realized that he was becoming seriously disoriented, wandering through the dangerous corridors, expecting to be attacked at any moment. Ryan was losing track of the passage of time.

He punched at the manhole cover with the flat of his hand, jarring his wrist, making the metal sing. A great cloud of rust flakes fell into his face, drifting over J.B. and Mildred.

"Dark night, Ryan! Be careful." J.B. paused a second. "No, do it again. Around the edges."

"Hurt my hand."

"Use the butt of the Steyr. Short, hard, repeated blows. Could loosen it."

Ryan tried what the Armorer had suggested.

The noise rang and echoed, as though it were finding a resonance within the arch of skull bones that enveloped his brain. Every blow seemed to be so much louder than the one before, threatening to draw the muties.

Mildred and J.B. had gone back down the ladder, to where the drain opened into a wider tunnel. Both crouched with blasters drawn, watching for a patrol.

The rifle was awkward to handle on the cramping ladder, but Ryan persisted. The longer he tried, the greater the risk of their being trapped by the nocturnal women.

"Yes," he said, feeling the exultant rush as the cover shifted an inch.

"Someone coming," Mildred hissed. "Hear boots on the stone."

"It's moving."

"Coming fast." This was J.B., back at the bottom of the ladder.

"Get out in the daylight and we got an advantage over those blind sluts." Ryan set his shoulders against the center of the iron circle and pressed with all his strength. It crossed his mind to wish that Krysty was there, with her fearsome reserves of power from the Earth Mother, though Ryan also knew from experience what a dreadful toll was taken from his beloved by using that secret power.

There was a grinding noise and the disk lifted in a flurry of rust, rolling out into the sunlit street above him.

"Go!" J.B. called from beneath him, with an intense urgency.

Ryan was out in a moment, his eye raking the street for signs of danger. There were the usual piles of blackened rubble and a surprised mutie rat only a dozen yards away. It twitched its long whiskers and loped casually off into the distance.

Mildred was on Ryan's heels, following him at a crouch to take shelter behind the rotting hulk of a burned-out transit-authority bus, J.B. only seconds behind them.

They watched the shadowed circle, but nobody emerged from it for a full minute. Ryan had the cross hairs of the laser sight pinned to the open manhole, finger light on the trigger, butt set solidly to his right shoulder.

Finally a head appeared, a long, narrow face, with something glistening in the nose like a jeweled stud. The protuberant eyes were concealed behind dark glasses, against the daylight. The gloved hand was holding a blaster.

"Twenty-two Luger, Navy Arms," J.B. whispered from Ryan's side.

The mutie woman vanished for a moment, as though she were reporting back to someone else on the ladder. Then her head reappeared.

Ryan didn't hesitate.

The Midnites knew that they were there, had tracked them through the tunnels and were still on their trail. Silence would gain them nothing.

He squeezed the trigger.

The Steyr kicked against his shoulder.

"Jesus," Mildred breathed.

The big 7.62 mm full-metal-jacket round hit the woman through the center of the forehead. The impact knocked off the dark glasses, sending them tumbling into the road. Horrifically the bullet angled downward behind the eyes, forcing them clear out of their sockets, so that for a frozen moment they dangled across the pale cheeks. They were suspended there by threads of pink gristle, like pieces of bizarre jewelry.

The distorted round exited through the back of the head in a sucking whoosh of blood and brains, emptying the cranial cavity.

Both the mutie's arms jerked upward in a spasmodic reaction, hurling the blaster impossibly high into the air.

By the time it struck the highway in a fountain of sparks, the woman's corpse had disappeared into the manhole.

"Slow them down some." Ryan slipped on the safety.

It had all happened so fast that the ejected cartridge case still rolled at his feet.

"Best get a move on. There must be other bolt holes around here." J.B. stood, looking up at the sky. "They got such bad sun sight, we can probably dodge them."

"Then what?" Mildred asked.

Neither of them answered her.

Chapter Forty-Three

'You sure it's going to work for both of us at once, Doc?"

The old man didn't answer Michael at first. He was bent over a huge computer console, his gnarled fingers tapping at the complicated keyboard. The screen above was constantly changing in a swirl of green and yellow information. Letters and numbers and unguessable symbols flowed and vanished. Graphs were erected and destroyed in the wink of an eye.

"Doc?"

"Later, Emily."

"Doc!"

The face swung away from the consoles, tinted by the dancing screen and shadowed, so that it looked like a badly made-up corpse.

"What?"

"Can you be certain we can both get jumped back to our own times—"

"Of course."

"No, I hadn't finished. Both jump at the same time, Doc?"

"There is a time delay built in, Emily. I set the chronological parameters, which is damnably time-consuming." He broke into a burst of cackling laughter that made the young man's hands drop instinctively to the hilts of his twin daggers. "Time-consuming! Did you hear that, dear heart? I made an inadvertent jest about time. It is all time-consuming, is it not? All time is present and past and no future for us."

"And we go together?"

"We all go together when we go, Emily. I set the time-delay controls and we take our places, you in your small capsule and I in mine. It is a slow process, for a mistake could cast us into a placeless timeless limbo forever and a day. It will still take me some hours to complete the computations. Then the relays are thrown, and off we both go. I to my old life and..." He hesitated, struggling to come to terms with who the young man was and why he was asking him questions. "And you, Michael, for that's your name, is it not? You back to your own world."

"At least you know who I am, Doc."

"But of course, dear boy. Why should I not know who you are?"

"You keep calling me Emily."

"Do I?" Doc seemed genuinely puzzled. "I confess that my mind over the dusty years has become a mite scrambled, but to call you after my wife.. Still, time's a'wasting and there are fields to mow and there is likewise a wind on the heath, brother."

Michael smiled. "I know that as well, Doc. A wind on the heath, brother. Life is very sweet."

"Who would wish to die?"

"GO IN WITH blasters firing?"

Ryan looked at J.B. They'd moved down the street three blocks, watching for an ambush from every sewer cover they passed. But there was neither sight nor sound of pursuit. Now, at the corner of a devastated office building, they spotted another of the entrances to the Midnites' underworld.

"Beginning to think it's mebbe the only way," Ryan replied.

Mildred sat on the melted stump of a streetlight, smoothing dirt off the legs of her reinforced military jeans. "This place is like living inside a locomotive's firebox. Look at my shirt." Once white, it was now a gritty gray. The toes of her leather boots were dulled by the ash that lay all around Chicago like black snow.

The Armorer coughed, muffling the sound with the palm of his hand. "We do it, then we might as well do it now. Won't get easier."

Ryan nodded. "You're right. Go in. Chill anything. Keep going till we find Krysty and Dean. Or we run out of ammo."

Mildred grinned. "That's what I like about you guys. Your plans. Sophisticated and subtle. Kick in the doors and shoot the shit out of everyone. Real subtle. Yeah, gang, let's do it."

KRYSTY HAD RARELY FELT so hemmed in by the choking spirit of evil. The powers that she had been born with had been developed by her training as a young girl. Long hours with wise Mother Sonja had taught her how to utilize her mutie skills to "see" and to "feel" things locked away from norms.

Now, in the semidarkness, with only Dean for company, Krysty's spirits were sunk to their lowest ebb. Billy, the leader of the Midnites, had paid a brief visit to them, her sneering arrogance only confirming what they already knew.

That the young male was to be ritually tortured and then sacrificed.

"When?"

"When the hurtful Father Sun has left the earth to his sister, the gentle Moon."

"If you think I'm a sort of chosen one for you, why won't you listen when I say the boy should be spared and set free?"

"Because that's not what the fuckin' old ones said. Just that you lead us out of here to the far, far west. And that's all."

The mutie leader had laughed again, stooping and deliberately spitting into the boy's upturned face, her saliva hanging in a string of sticky pearls from his cheek. Krysty decided at that moment that she would chill Billy the first chance she got, and the Ruger Magnum Blackhawk revolver would do nothing to prevent her.

Now they were alone again.

"Dean, shuffle over as close as you can to me, this side."

"Why?"

"So's we can talk without one of these blood-eyed bitches hearing us from out there in the corridor. All right?"

"Sure."

"I don't think Ryan's coming."

"He is!"

"Quiet."

He lowered his voice, the anger still riding bare-toothed through it. "Dad won't let me die here. He'll come and get me."

Krysty could hardly make out the small pale face in the gloom, the face that was so heartrendingly like Ryan's. "Listen to me. Ryan Cawdor is the finest man I ever met. Or will meet. I love him with all of my soul, Dean. If he's dead, then the rest of my life will be spent in shadows. But he isn't a god. He can't really do the impossible."

"I know that. But Krysty. . ."

"Hush, boy. I've been here long enough for me to know that something is wrong. Wrong in a way that stops the breath and turns my heart to ice. We know there's been fighting. Some muties dead. But this place is a warren. This is the country of the blind. Uncle Tyas McCann used to say that in such a place as this the one-eyed man would be king. It's not true. These bitches are queens here. They know every blind alley and black turning."

"There's J.B. and Mildred as well. Three of them coming."

Krysty hated the way she was forced to shatter all the boy's hopes. But until he realized the odds, he might still want to sit back and hope.

"Three against a hundred? I don't know how many of the vermin are scurrying through these holes. Could be more. Triple sickies, Dean."

"So, what do we do?"

"Ryan ever tell you about the power?"

"No. What sort of power?"

"Long story. I'll keep it short as I can. Way of getting out of this room. But it'll need a shit lot of help from you."

"COMING ALONG SPLENDIDLY, Emily. As fine as a silk parasol on a May morning."

The voice tugged Michael back from a dream. He'd been running through an old house. Behind him, he had a dreadful awareness that the whole building was rapidly turning into a malevolent entity. Stairs became cracking, brass-edged teeth and doorways converted to rheumy, spiderwebbed eyes.

Ahead of him he had seen the end of the darkened passageway begin to yawn, revealing a shining, moist gullet, waiting to suck him into its crushing, rippling heart.

Considering the horror of the nightmare, Michael was surprised to find that he'd awakened with a diamond cutter of a hard-on.

"Rachel, my child of the angels. Jolyon, my brave warrior. Your father is coming back to you. Back to

hold you safe in his arms and never, never leave you
again.''

"Doc, you all right?''

The old man turned from the keyboard, face sag-
ging with weariness. But his eyes flamed with a ferocious purpose.

"I'm as chipper as can be expected. Thank you for
your courtesy. The agony has finally somewhat abated,
Mother.''

"How much longer?''

"It is a famous question among natural philoso-
phers, Emily. How long is a piece of string? What is the
sound of one hand clapping? What is a circle, turned
in on itself? A Möbius strip? Occam's razor? Mor-
ton's fork? The answer, my dear heart, is not long. We
have been parted for so many many years that an hour
or so, more or less, will really make only scant difference.''

"An hour or so?'' Michael echoed. "Then I'm home
again, Doc?''

"Home again, home again, jiggety jig, my little
ones.''

"An hour?''

Doc turned and looked at him. "Eagerness killed the
bunnies. I think it will be more than one hour, but no
more than three. It is going well, my friend. Very well.''

"Then we go?''

"We go. By the three Kennedys, we go!''

DEAN LOOKED at Krysty, his eyes wide. "You sure about this?"

"You got a better idea, kid?"

"But if you can't . . . If someone comes in?"

She managed a confident smile. "If we fail, then we're both definitely dead. But if we don't bother to try at all, then I figure we're both probably dead anyway."

"So, when do we go?"

"Now, Dean. Gaia! Why not?"

RYAN LOOKED all around. There was still no sign of any pursuing muties.

"I reckon we might as well get going. Can't see any point in delaying."

J.B. nodded, cocking the Uzi. "Might as well," he said.

Mildred sighed. "Daddy always said I'd come to a bad end, and here I go."

They emerged from cover and started to sprint toward the entrance to the Midnites' warren.

Chapter Forty-Four

"Earth Mother, aid me now in this my hour of darkest need. Give me the power of Gaia that I might free this child and myself from the toils of these wicked and murderous people."

Her voice was quiet, her lips barely moving. Dean was almost close enough to touch her, but he could hardly hear what Krysty was saying. He sat very still, his ears straining for the sounds of anyone approaching along one of the underground passages.

Krysty knew from her previous experiences that she could draw on the mysterious power within her. With it she could certainly snap the chain that bound her to the wall. But it would weaken her, and she would need to use that same power to break Dean free. It would be useless to only sever her own bonds.

But by the time she'd liberated both of them, she was likely to be so weak that even to stand would be a major undertaking.

"Give me strength to challenge and strength to win. Earth Mother, I, daughter of Sonja, pray for your assistance."

She had her emerald eyes closed tight, her hands clasped together like a marble saint. Her mouth was pressed shut, and a thin trickle of blood was inching from the corner of her lips.

Dean also had his eyes closed. He could half remember a prayer that Rona, his mother, used to say, when things got tough. Which was most of the time.

"Dear Lord, I'm standing here in the middle of emptiness and if you can't help me, then they can bring down the curtain."

Krysty didn't hear him.

She was slipping into the trancelike state that she knew was essential for her to do what had to be done.

"Gaia, Gaia, help me now. Power of the Earth Mother fill my body. Through my heart and lungs and woman's blood... Now."

She took the heavy chain in both hands, breathing slow and deep, and tightened her fingers around the cold, rusting links.

And pulled.

Metal squealed softly, like a hungry rat cowering behind the arras. The muscles in Krysty's wrists and arms stood out like whipcord, as taut as bowstrings.

She was pushing her legs out ahead of her for extra purchase, her teeth grinding together with the massive effort.

Dean was watching, gaping at how the woman had become unrecognizable. Her eyes were slits, the tendons creaking in her jaw as every fiber of her being went into the struggle. There was a brittle snapping sound, and she was free.

"Oh, hot pipe, Krysty," he whispered. "Real triple jolter."

The woman's breath was coming faster, her nipples like the stones of a cherry, pressing painfully against her shirt.

She hadn't opened her eyes, crawling toward Dean, hands out like claws, straining at the still, damp darkness.

"Don't hurt me," he whimpered, suddenly terrified by this demonic harpy from the farther side of nightmare. Dean clamped his thighs together, so that the hooked fingers couldn't grab at his genitals and tear them from his body.

"Gaia, one more time, I pray you!"

Now she was scrabbling at the boy's feet, reaching for the brass lock on the tight chain around his skinny ankle.

"Don't hurt me," he whispered, so softly that he couldn't even hear himself.

It was an impossibility.

The torch in the iron sconce on the stained wall didn't give much of a light. But its smoky red glow was just enough for Dean to watch Krysty.

She took the brass lock and twisted it between her fingers as though it were made of tin, the metal flowing and distorting, shearing in a jagged crack that broke the bolt in half.

Dean reached down and pulled the long chain free of his leg, then stood shakily, his hand on the stone for support.

"You done it," he breathed.

"Did it," Krysty said, with a torn rictus of pain that was the closest she could manage to a sort of a smile.

"Yeah. Let's go." He took a few hesitant steps toward the open door.

"Wait."

She was still lying on the floor, her body trembling. As the boy looked down at her, she doubled up and vomited, a copious flood splattering from her open mouth, bringing the bitter stench of bile.

And still she didn't move.

"Krysty?"

DOC CLAPPED HIS HANDS and leaned back. "Ready for final testing." He pressed the Go function control on his keyboard.

In the corner behind Michael one of the ancient block consoles of comp equipment found the strain too much and imploded in a burst of azure flame and silver sparks.

But most of the units in the chron section were working well. Needles jumped from zero, balancing themselves toward the top end of the green dials. The brilliant dot-matrix numerals and symbols danced across screens while the patient data banks gaped to suck in the eruptions from a nearly infinite number of microchips.

"Looking good and feeling fine," chanted the old man. "This works and we're gone within the hour."

A bewildered Michael stood behind him, looking at the dazzling memory displays that shimmered across the main screen.

Then it all went blank, leaving the single line: Computation error detected. Check on integer calculus for reapplication of negative data.

"Shit," Doc said with surprising mildness. "Oh, shit and shit again." He grinned at Michael. "Back to the drawing board, dear friend, once more. And close the error with our number crunchers. In math there's nothing so becomes a scientist as languid care and accuracy."

"This a disaster, Doc?"

"No. A tiny setback. I know what went amiss. I shall correct it. Punch it back in. Take another couple of hours is all. No problem."

ONLY TWO WOMEN GUARDED the entrance to the cellar world of the Midnites. The attack was so swift and ruthless that neither had a chance to fire a single shot in her own defence. Their blasters were still holstered as they went down in the dirt.

Ryan shot one woman with two bullets through the chest and throat while Mildred picked off the second with a single round from her ZKR 551.

"Which way now?" Mildred asked, breathing fast, looking into the gloom.

Five or six tunnels opened off the entrance cavern, without the least clue to where any of them went.

"Just have to go for it, friends. Follow close and chill anything that moves." Ryan wiped sweat from his forehead.

"Unless it's Dean or Krysty," J.B. added with a tight, mirthless grin.

THE BOY HAD finally managed to get Krysty to her feet, where she sagged against him like a gaudy drunk.

"Told you be bad," she whispered. "Be better but takes time."

Dean glanced into the corridor, leaning a hand against the wall to help hold Krysty upright. He could hear the sound of voices, shouting, screaming. The maze of basements and culverts distorted and amplified the noises, making it impossible to work out where they were coming from.

And how far away they were.

"Don't have much time," he panted.

"Leave me if you have to, Dean."

"Fuck that!"

The yelling was louder and undeniably closer. And now Dean heard the crackle of gunfire.

It had to be . . .

"Ryan's coming, Krysty!" he said. "Come on, let's find a place to hide up. Come on!"

"Can't. Too weak. Drained…power. You go, Dean. Let me rest."

"No."

THE TWO MUTIES FOUND Krysty lying in the corridor, huddled up like a child, unconscious. One of them drew Dean's Browning Hi-Power from her belt while the other was gripping the red-haired woman's captured Smith & Wesson.

"Where's the little cock puller?" one of them said.

There was no reply.

Chapter Forty-Five

Michael was sleeping in a corner of the chron unit. His bare feet, the soles layered in white cement dust, were resting on a pile of brittle comp paper while his head was pillowed on the broken seat of one of the swivel chairs.

Doc was still leaning intently over the main control panel, head on one side, lips moving silently as he pecked in more and more information.

"The cherry's hung with snow, Emily. It's the waiting that's so hard, the dying that's so easy. We shall lock our hands together and run through the meadows, silvered with the dew of early morning. Last chance. Last chance. Last chance. Listen, Emily, my dear. Time passes. Listen, time passes."

There was a faint pale froth crusted around his cracked lips, trickling down over the gray stubble across his chin.

It didn't matter what measure was used for normal behavior.

Doc Tanner was over the brink and sliding helplessly into total insanity.

Michael slept on.

ONE FACTOR WAS on the side of the trio of attackers. The lair of the Midnites was so vast that it wasn't possible for the defenders to get together in serious strength to try to locate and check the fast-moving raiders.

In the first eight minutes Ryan, J.B. and Mildred were involved in three brief, sporadic and bloody firefights.

One of the goggle-eyed muties had tried to ambush them from the top of an iron ladder. J.B. had spotted her and raked the narrow drain with the Uzi, ripping her apart. Her body fell head-down, trapped by the legs, blood cascading over her face, pouring noisily into the culvert.

Ryan shot another of the women as she ran around a corner, straight into them. She was actually holding the SIG-Sauer as he squeezed the trigger twice, the muzzle rammed beneath her breastbone. The double impact of the 9 mm bullets sent her staggering away, blood jetting black from her screaming mouth.

The third of the firefights was the most hazardous to Ryan and the others.

Half a dozen muties had started to throw up a barricade of tumbled bricks. But the rapid arrival of the three invaders took them by surprise. They managed no more than nine or ten ill-aimed, desperate rounds before the hail of lead from the Uzi, the SIG-Sauer and the Czech target revolver cut them down in the sewers.

Two at least were only wounded, but there was no time now to worry about chilling them. Speed was the

essential element in Ryan's plan. Lose that and all was
lost.

THE TWO MUTIES STOOD side by side, uncertain how
their star prisoner had freed herself from the strong
chain, and the mewling boy as well. They'd heard the
warning bells going and had just caught the sound of
shooting. There was obviously a rescue bid under way.

But where and who?

"Better chain the bitch-god again," said one of
them, moving to lean over Krysty.

"Yeah. I'll—"

Her words died in an explosion of staggering pain in
her lower back, a ferocious blow that knocked her to
her knees, the gun dropping from her fingers to clatter
on—

It didn't clatter.

"Why?" she gasped.

Dean had catfooted behind her and struck her with
all of his wiry strength, a brutal double-fisted, club-
bing blow, aimed at the woman's kidneys. The boy
twisted around like an eel to snatch up the dropping
Browning.

"Why the fuck not?" he gritted, shooting her
through the side of the head.

The other guard, bending over Krysty, started to
turn.

But the unconscious figure at her feet had grabbed
at her ankles, a weak, feeble effort that she was easily
able to break free from.

But the half second's delay was enough for Dean to shoot her through the side of the neck.

The powerful handgun's booming explosion filled the basement, making Krysty wince from its violence. It threw the second mutie guard across the room, stumbling over the flailing corpse of her colleague.

Dean hesitated, waiting until he was sure that both the women were dead or dying. He holstered his own blaster, also collecting his favored turquoise-hilted knife from the waistband of one of the fallen women. The short-barreled Smith & Wesson 640 that they'd stolen from Krysty was also retrieved and stuck into his leather belt.

"Well done," she breathed. "Ryan'll be real proud of... of you."

"You helped," he said.

"Sure."

"Can you stand?"

"Try me, Dean. Give me your hand and... and I'll see."

"HELLFIRE AND BLOODY sodding bastard slumgul-ion! Rat's piss and llama crap!"

"Something wrong, Doc?" Michael blinked awake, wondering for a moment where on the good earth he was, then recognizing the chron-control suite.

"Wrong? Wrong? Something wrong? I sometimes wonder, Emily, whether the Lord contrived to over-ook you when it came to the handing out of the supply of brains. Of course something is wrong, woman! Something is always wrong.''

Michael stood, rubbing at his eyes. ''What's the time?''

''What's the time, Mr. Wolf? How little Rachel liked to play that game. The time is late. The cock hath crowed thrice. And I can find no way around this wretched time delay.''

''What's that do?''

Doc still wouldn't look directly at the young man, speaking, instead, to the far side of the big room. ''I had hoped to set up all the temporal and spatial coordinates by now, then utilize a short delay before the system becomes operational and the jumps begin.''

''Short?''

''Fifteen minutes. No more. Simply enough for me—'' he paused ''—for *us* to climb into the capsules and ready ourselves.''

''So, why doesn't that work? You can still get us home, can't you?''

Though Michael was aware in his heart that it didn't somehow seem quite so important now. Nil-Vanity was no longer the attractive fortress it had been all his life. In the past couple of days he'd seen new sights and experienced a dazzling, stupefying range of new experiences.

Not all pleasant, by any means.

But all challenging.

''We can still get home. It's the place, Emily, where they always have to take you in, is it not? But there is ;

persnickety glitch in the system. I can set it to make the chron procedure, but I can't reduce the countdown below two and a half hours. I can set it for ten seconds, but that's really nowhere near long enough. Then the numerals leap up to one hundred and fifty minutes.''

"That's all right, isn't it? We can wait and watch the clock ticking on down. Then get ready when it gets to the last ten minutes."

"Yes, we can, can, can. Can you do the cancan, can you?"

"So, why not do that, Doc?"

The note of exasperation still rode high in the old man's voice. "That's what I'm doing, for Christ's sake!"

"So, it'll be two and a half hours and then we're history."

"No. Look at the countdown clock on the wall. It's already running."

Michael glanced up. The clock was rectangular, nearly three feet long by eighteen inches high. It showed days, hours, minutes, seconds, tenths of seconds and hundredths of seconds, the latter section a blur of movement.

But it was currently at two hours and twenty-three minutes.

And some seconds.

DEAN LED KRYSTY through the basements and cellars of old Chicago. As they moved cautiously and slowly along, they passed through the jagged holes, feet wide, where passages had been knocked from building to building, constructing the Midnites' maze.

The boy was following the noise. Once or twice there was gunfire, but mostly it was the flow of movement from the chalk-faced muties. Running past in ones and twos, all of them were heading in roughly the same direction.

They made sufficient noise for him to lead Krysty, unresisting, into side culverts and ancient drains, waiting in the dank, trembling stillness until they'd gone by.

"Feeling stronger," she said.

"Can you walk some on your own, Krysty? Want to try it?"

"Soon."

There was the sound of a firefight, with the unmistakable rippling of the Uzi on full-auto.

"Getting closer," Dean said, trying to encourage Krysty as well as himself. "Soon be back with the others."

DEAN'S RUN OF GOOD LUCK evaporated three or four minutes later.

He had stopped at a multiple junction, trying to ease Krysty's weight a little, when he heard the cold voice from his right, emerging from one of the black caverns.

"Rats are running right up to us, sisters."

It was Billy, her Ruger Blackhawk steady on him. The hugely tall Jackie smiled vaguely at him at her side, holding an indeterminate little .22, a chromed Saturday-night special, in her hamlike fist. Completing the trio of leering harpies was the pockmarked Laurie, two of her array of derringers drawn and cocked.

"Let us go," Dean said.

"No way, cockling."

"Let him go and I'll come back with you," Krysty offered weakly.

"Reckon you've blown your chance, sweetheart." Billy grinned. "Blown it right out of your fucking fat ass."

"We got friends coming," Dean protested, trying to calculate his chances of a clear shot.

"Too late," Laurie said. "Way too late."

And the shooting started.

Chapter Forty-Six

The first shot punched Laurie between the shoulder blades, exiting through the center of her left breast.

To Dean it looked as though some horrifically powerful demon had come to malign life within the mutie's chest and decided it was time to get out, erupting from her body in a sudden welter of blood and pulped flesh.

The spent, blood-slick bullet pinged off the concrete wall only a scant yard from the boy's left arm, narrowly missing Krysty.

Billy reacted with lightning reflexes, while the giant-like Jackie didn't react at all. She stood still, swaying a little on her flat feet, the smile slowly being replaced by a look of bewilderment as Laurie's body slumped in the dirt.

Billy dived forward, rolling out of shot, coming up in a crouch. Dean tried to get the Browning, but Krysty was still leaning on his arm, hampering him. But comprehension dawned, and she managed to draw her own blaster from the boy's belt.

Krysty leveled it shakily at the tall mutie's protruding eyes and fired, nearly missing in her weakness. The

.38 slug clipped Billy's shoulder, making her drop her Blackhawk.

"Bitch! You could've been—"

Ryan appeared in the tunnel and shot the kneeling woman once through the heart.

Mildred was at his elbow, J.B. right at her side. "A contender," she said. "You could've been a contender."

"Who are you?" Jackie asked slowly, stooping to peer at the newcomers. "Outlanders, aren't you?"

"Want me to chill Lady Goliath?" Mildred asked, drawing a bead on the mutie's throat.

"No," Krysty said softly. "Been enough chilling for a while." She turned to Jackie. "Go on, that way." She waved a hand to point back into the torchlit gloom.

"No. Gotta save you...."

Ryan gunned her down with a 9 mm bullet in the head.

"Let's get the quickest way out of here," he said, "then head for the redoubt. I got a seriously bad feeling."

"ONE HOUR and eleven minutes. I think we should begin to make ready for our departure when the clock has run down to fifteen minutes or so."

"Sure. How you feeling, Doc? Excited? Looking forward to it?"

"I am an exhilarating mixture of bubbling emotions, Emily. As who would not be?"

Michael sat again, drawing his knees up to his chin. And waited.

One hour and ten minutes and nineteen seconds.

Another thought struck the young man. "Will it be sort of instant, Doc?"

"I do not feel able to reply to that question, Professor Barrell."

"But you've done this before."

"Ah, that is correct, my dear. Twice. Once trawled from the far past to a closer past. Then placed within the projectile and hurtled to this nameless place of slouching monsters."

"So? So, Doc, when you make the chron jump, is it instant?"

"Was it instant for you, Michael?"

"Can't remember. Dizzy... then sick. Like falling, but not falling downward. Falling in every direction at once."

Doc clapped his hands. "Good. Out of the mouths of babes! Falling in... how did it go? In every direction at once. Precisely. Project Cerberus, being a part of Overproject Whisper that was, in its own turn, a small cog within the madly spinning wheels of the Totality Concept. And Operation Chronos itself."

Michael leaned against the wall. "When we make the jump, we'll never meet again, will we? It won't be possible, will it?"

"I had not considered that. No, we will not. I shall live out my life and, if actuarial tables are to be believed, I should shuffle off this mortal coil some time in the 1920s or 1930s. A good half century before you are born, Michael. And more than a hundred years before Ryan, John and Krysty are born. Even that argumentative black woman won't be born until many years after my demise. She would like that, would Mildred.''

"You'll miss them, Doc?"

But the old man wouldn't answer him.

Just under one hour and seven minutes remained on the clock.

THE DAY WAS PASSING.

Ryan led the way, using his instinct to find the route toward the surface and fresh air. The others took turns to help Krysty along. She had been desperately weakened by the enormous effort of using the power of the Earth Mother, but she was recovering all the time.

The surviving members of the Midnites seemed to be keeping to their own dark recesses, out of the way of the blood-eyed invaders. Ryan spotted a small figure, like a crippled child, stumbling ahead of him at one point. But by the time he reached the place the mutie had vanished.

The relief when they emerged from the smoky gloom was palpable. All of them took in deep breaths, and Mildred dropped to hands and knees, plucking a tiny white-and-yellow flower that she found growing among the blackened ruins.

"How far from the redoubt?" Krysty asked.

"Water's ahead of us, easterly," J.B. replied. "Step it out and we should be there in around half to three-quarters of an hour."

THEY WERE safely inside the heavy sec doors in forty-one minutes.

J.B. spotted the trail, pointing at the dusty floor. "Doc and Michael are back. Boot marks and some-one with bare, dirty feet."

"Chron section." Ryan glanced around at the oth-ers. "Just pray we aren't too late."

They headed out at double time, pausing at the air lock doors a short time later.

"Blaster's ready?" Ryan asked.

"For Doc?" Mildred half smiled, then saw the taut expression on Ryan's face. "You think the old bas-tard's freaked?"

"Mebbe."

"Better go find out."

Air hissed softly as they pushed through into the time-jump section of the complex. The main clock had repeaters all around and they saw one, directly in front of them. It was running down, and showed seventeen minutes and a couple of seconds.

There was also a red flashing sign above the next pair of doors: Caution! Experiment in Progress. Do Not Enter.

"He's started!" Krysty exclaimed.

They burst in, all stopping at what they saw in the heart of the chron unit.

Doc sat in one of the capsules, gripping his big Le Mat, the railroad-tunnel muzzle pointing toward Ryan.

Michael stood near a second capsule, and he turned to look at them.

"Stop them, Emily!" Doc screamed in a high, thin voice. "They'll ruin it! Slaughter them!"

Chapter Forty-Seven

Ryan's eye was caught by the main control screen at the heart of the rows of desks and consoles. It was showing a number of crimson warning lights, and the repeated word: Malfunction.

"Doc," he shouted, "it's all going wrong. Get out of there."

"No. Emily, take them."

Michael began to advance toward the armed group, hands empty, feet sliding over the smooth floor. "Going to do what Doc wants," he said. "Not for me. Just for him."

"Get out of the way." Ryan was almost overwhelmed with the desire to squeeze the trigger on the SIG-Sauer and blow the young man out of his path, but he managed to hold back.

"No. You have to make me."

"I'll chill him," J.B. offered, but Ryan waved a warning hand at the Armorer. He holstered his own blaster, watching Doc out of the corner of his eye.

"The equipment is failing, Michael," he said, aware of the speed at which the master clock was ticking on down.

"Liar!" Doc yelled. "They're all scientist murderers, dear heart. They intend to stop us returning home safe and snug."

"The odds are thousands to one if everything went well. They had hundreds of top men and women working on this blighted project for years. You and Doc are about the only two successes they ever had. You try and jump back to your own times, and you'll both finish up horribly dead." Ryan looked over at Doc, staring into the barrel of the Le Mat. "You got no chance, Doc. No fucking chance."

"Still got to try," Michael said.

And he came in at Ryan, using the terrifying speed he'd learned through his Oriental martial skills.

The whirling feet and clenched fists were only a blur, and Ryan ducked three steps back, knowing that the teenager was the fastest he'd ever seen, knowing that Michael could take him out, permanently, if he wasn't very, very careful.

He watched, seeing that his opponent was building up a rhythm as he spun closer. Ryan took a clumsy half step in, stumbling and slipping on the floor. Michael's eyes opened wide, and he kicked out at Ryan's shoulder.

But Ryan had lifted his right leg, with its steel-tipped combat boot, allowing it to take the jarring impact. Michael's bare foot was toughened, but it couldn't stand against the steel.

He staggered, yelping with pain, trying to get his balance, legs spread.

The one-eyed man was on his feet in a microsecond and kicked Michael in the groin, trying to temper the force so that he didn't kill him. The toe crushed into the soft genitals, ramming them upward against the pubic bone. Michael gave a pathetic, strangled scream, and fell backward, unconscious.

The clock was showing twelve minutes and eighteen seconds.

"You've done it for him, Beelzebub!" Doc shouted, "and I'll do it for you before leaving this midnight place forever."

"Don't, Theo!" Mildred was at Ryan's side, staring down the old man, ignoring the trembling hand that held the Civil War blaster.

"Don't call me that!"

"Theo, we're your friends. We love you and we'll do anything to save you a ghastly passing. Get out and talk to us."

"Never."

"The place is folding up around us. Look!" She gestured to where sparks were exploding from several of the comp screens, many of them already gone to black. Only the clock clicked remorselessly on. "You'll die, Doc."

He laughed, the hand with the Le Mat sticking out from under the rim of the chron pod. "Oh, queen of air and darkness, yes, darkness. I'm sure it's truth you say. And I will die tomorrow, but you will die... today!"

The last word a terrible cry of torn emotion as he tightened his finger on the scattergun trigger of the blaster.

The boom was preceded by the light crack of Mildred's own target revolver. Firing from the hip, she'd managed to hit the overhead catch, allowing the heavy top of the capsule to drop onto Doc's arm, the impact knocking the Le Mat from his fingers.

The old man was left lying helplessly inside, weeping.

"Best get him out before the clock runs out," J.B. advised.

"That was one of the best shots I ever saw, Mildred." Ryan went to help J.B. release Doc from the imprisoning capsule.

"Yeah. I'm real proud of it," she said bitterly. "Good way of slamming the door on someone's last best hope."

MICHAEL CAME AROUND a few minutes later, standing doubled over, hands pressed in between his thighs, his face as white as parchment.

"You don't fight fair, Ryan," he said quietly.

"Not about fighting fair. Not in Deathlands. Learn from it, Michael."

"How about the lesson you've taught Doc?"

"You can't go home anymore." Ryan watched as Mildred knelt by the old-timer, her arm around his shoulders, trying to comfort him in his heart-torn grief. "He'd have died, Michael."

"And me, too."

"Yeah. You, too."

"Clock's into its last thirty seconds, Dad."

Ryan looked, seeing where his son was pointing. "Twenty seconds. Doc, sit up and take some notice. See what's happening   what would've happened if you'd tried this time jump."

At least half of the comp screens had aborted, memory banks spilling their blind matrices into the void.

At the moment that the main control clock reached zero, there was a jagged flash of light from one of the overhead power conduits.

The capsule that Doc had been sitting in vanished in a purple lake of rolling flames. The top began to crack and then melt, and the fire spilled over the side, turning from purple to gold, then down to a dark cherry red, tipped with silver.

"Would have been me," Doc whispered. "And I tried to kill you for wanting to save me. By the three Kennedys, but there's no fool like an old fool. I am so sorry, my friends. So deeply sorry."

"You wouldn't really have killed Dad, would you, Doc?" Dean asked.

"I don't know... No, I don't believe that I would, on."

Ryan remembered the blast of lead that missed him by a scant couple of feet when Doc fired the Le Mat. and he wondered.

"Flames are spreading," J.B. warned. "Looks like me to get out of here."

"One thing," Krysty said. "Nobody'll ever make any chron jumps from this place again."

THEY REACHED the mat-trans unit without any problems, and Doc seemed contented to walk with them. The armaglass walls were a rich, deep crimson.

"In you go," Ryan said, waiting by the heavy door to trigger the jump mechanism.

Dean skipped in and sat facing the entrance, knees under his chin, the Browning laid carefully at his side on the floor. Krysty sat next to him, her face still pale from using the power.

Mildred and J.B. picked their places around from Dean, keeping close together.

"Wonder where old Abe's gotten to?" the Armorer said. "Think he'll find the Trader?"

Ryan shook his head. "I figure he's likely dead. But you never know. Can't be certain of anything, can you?"

Michael sat next to J.B., tucking his robe around his ankles. "I am not looking forward to this at all."

Doc was last to take his place, moving carefully as though his bones had turned to strands of fine crystal. "You get used to it, dear boy," he said quietly. "It is a great truth about the human condition that you can get used to absolutely anything. Eventually."

"Ready?" Ryan asked, joining the others and firmly closing the door, sitting between Doc and Krysty.

There was the familiar humming sound, and the mist began to appear around the glowing disks in the crimson ceiling.

"It looks like a cherry hung with snow," Doc mused.

"How's that?" Ryan asked, not sure he'd heard him correctly.

"A cherry hung with snow."

"Yeah. I guess so."

"Hung with snow."

The mist was thickening, and Ryan could feel himself losing his hold on reality.

"With snow," Doc whispered.

Ryan tried to repeat it, but their jump was already under way.

"Snow..."

WELCOME TO

JAMES AXLER

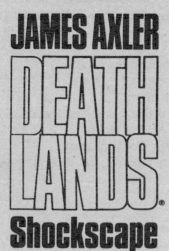

DEATHLANDS®

Shockscape

A shockscape with a view—
and the danger is free.

Ryan and his band of warrior survivalists chart a perilous journey
across the desolate Rocky Mountains. Their mission: Deliver the hired
killers of a small boy to his avenging father.

In the Deathlands, survival is a gamble. Death is the only sure bet.

In the 21st century, a new breed of cop
brings home the law in the latest
installment of the future law-enforcement
miniseries . . .

CADE

MIKE LINAKER

In the 21st-century nightmare, marshals like Thomas
Jefferson Cade carry a badge, a gun and a burning
sense of justice.

In Book 3: FIRESTREAK, Cade and his cyborg partner,
Janek, follow the bloody trail of a renegade drug
dealer to the electronic wonderland of Los Angeles and
enter the killzone . . . guns loaded, targets in sight.

Available in January at your favorite retail outlet.

Back to the beginning . . .

PILGRIMAGE TO HELL $4.99
Out of the ruins of worldwide nuclear devastation emerged Deathlands, a world that conspired against survival. Ryan Cawdor and his roving band of post-holocaust survivors begin their quest for survival in a world gone mad.

RED HOLOCAUST $4.99
Ryan and his warriors must battle against roaming bands of survivors from Russia who are using Alaska as a staging ground for an impending invasion of America.

NEUTRON SOLSTICE $4.99
Deep in the heart of Dixie, Ryan and his companions come upon a small group of survivors who are striving to recreate life as it was once known.

CRATER LAKE $4.99
Near what was once the Pacific Northwest, Ryan's band discovers a beautiful valley untouched by the nuclear blast that changed the world forever

HOMEWARD BOUND $4.99
Emerging from a gateway in the ruins of New York City, Ryan decides it is time to face his power-mad brother—and avenge the deaths of his father and older brother

Here's your chance to find out how it all began!
